Pretty Girls Do Nasty Things

Lock Down Publications and Ca$h
Presents
Pretty Girls Do Nasty Things
A Novel by
Nicole Goosby

Lock Down Publications
Po Box 944
Stockbridge, Ga 30281

Visit our website @
www.lockdownpublications.com

Lock Down Publications
Like our page on Facebook: Lock Down Publications @
www.facebook.com/lockdownpublications.ldp
Book interior design by: **Shawn Walker**
Edited by: **Mia Rucker**

Stay Connected with Us!

Text **LOCKDOWN** to 22828 to stay up-to-date with new releases, sneak peaks, contests and more…
Thank you.

Submission Guideline.

Submit the first three chapters of your completed manuscript to ldpsubmissions@gmail.com, subject line: Your book's title. The manuscript must be in a .doc file and sent as an attachment. Document should be in Times New Roman, double spaced and in size 12 font. Also, provide your synopsis and full contact information. If sending multiple submissions, they must each be in a separate email.

Have a story but no way to send it electronically? You can still submit to LDP/Ca$h Presents. Send in the first three chapters, written or typed, of your completed manuscript to:

LDP: Submissions Dept
Po Box 944
Stockbridge, Ga 30281

DO NOT send original manuscript. Must be a duplicate.

Provide your synopsis and a cover letter containing your full contact information.

Thanks for considering LDP and Ca$h Presents.

Prologue

"We're going to throw you a party, Casci. That's all there is to it," Coffee concluded after hearing her cousin protest the event.

"Yeah, Casci, let us do this. Hell, you just spent five years in prison. I know you can use a good time, and some dick. I don't give a damn about all that other shit, 'cause right now, we 'bout to kick it," Reniya added.

Casci looked from one girl to the next and shook her head. "See, that's what's wrong with y'all now. Dick the reason y'all still living in these run-down ass apartments, struggling." She stood, stretched her five foot two frame, and yawned. "I got business to take care of."

"Aww, there she go with that shit." Ariel sighed. "Girl, dick is the reason I keep the hair and nails done, a fat ass, and a ride outside. My nigga and dick take care of me."

"Yeah, you and every other bitch willing to fuck his ass," Casci said to her, referring to her no good boyfriend, Stacy.

"Dick or no dick, we're going to throw you a welcome home party. And afterward, we're taking you shopping. It's time to get you fancy, bitch," Reniya told her, and slapped her on the ass.

Casci walked over to the bay window, parted the curtains, and peered out over the courtyard. "Wait until these niggas realize it ain't same game they been playing anymore," she said to herself.

Her thoughts took her back. Back to the day she and her partner, Marcus, carried out the plan he'd been plotting for a while. It was one that would allow them to become players amongst players—as well as her way out of the Gardens.

"You're sure about this, Marcus?" she asked, after being told the lick promised over $20,000.

"Man, you know I'm not going to lie to you about no shit like this, Casci. This is going to be like taking candy from a fat ass baby," he assured her.

Casci weighted out her options. Either she'd hit the lick with Marcus and split the money, or she'd go back to complaining about not having any. She wasn't like most of the girls in the Gardens, who sucked, fucked, and allowed niggas to run through her for the sake of a dollar. She was the go-getter, who damn near all the hoes wanted to be, and the girl most guys wanted to fuck. Her short but thick frame, bronze-colored complexion, and gray eyes had even the prettiest women who came through the Gardens envious. And her tomboy persona had some of the guys looking at her as one of their own.

For those who knew Casci, hustling was her M-O, and popping pistols was something she did without hesitation. For those who questioned her potential, it was a lesson well-learned.

"And you say it's one guy in there?" she asked, the excitement of the win boosting her adrenaline.

Chapter One

As soon as the girls were seated in the VIP section of the club, several bottles of liquor arrived, courtesy of the club's owner. Women and guys filled the spot from wall to wall, and they were dressed to impress. Casci sat in the middle of the booth, surrounded by her girls, her Cloe shades covering her eyes. Instead of the Chanel mini dress Ariel wanted her to wear, Casci slid into a pair of ragged jeans, a T-shirt, and some Retro shoes. She could've cared less about the designer clothes her friends spent thousands of dollars on.

While she sat, taking everything in, she noticed the changes around her. Guys she knew from back in the day, who were small-time hustlers, were now arriving with their own cliques, draped in expensive jewelry, and stepping around in thousand-dollar shoes. Some of the girls she recognized were up on game, but most of them were still doing the same shit they were over five years ago.

She scoffed and twisted her lips when witnessing a group of guys groping a young girl at the far end of the bar. By the way she was smiling, laughing, and accepting every drink they gave her, Casci knew she would end up in some motel room with those same niggas standing over her with their dicks out. And they would most likely leave her there, once they were done fucking her dry.

She looked around from one scene to the other, saw the different players, but the same games being played. She was *not* going to become prey amongst predators.

"Casci, you hear me talking to you?" Reniya asked with the snap of her finger.

"Bitch, I'm in my own little world." Casci readjusted herself, reached for one of the GTV bottles, and sat back.

"Guess who's here?" Reniya asked, now that she had her attention.

Casci had her mind set on one person in particular, Marcus. He'd done the unthinkable as far as she was concerned, but she did have more than a bone to pick with him.

"Who?"

"Shun and Trish." Reniya nodded toward the bar at the two women in the sheer body suits.

They were the center of attention. Guys were trying their hands, and even girls were trying to get in where they fit in.

"Them hoes still stripping, or what?" Casci asked, not impressed.

She stole glances at the women in the see through cat suits, but tried not to be too obvious. Casci admired both women from afar. With nothing left to the imagination when looking at them, Casci knew exactly what she wanted to do with them, and how she'd do it.

"Nah, them hoes getting paid to be in magazines and shit now. Shun just bought a new Range Rover, and Trish pushing a Lexus. Them hoes get paid out the ass just to walk through clubs and different events and shit."

Casci looked over at Reniya and smiled. "I'm surprised you ain't got one of them see through suits on. You're just as fine as them hoes."

"Hell, they might as well wear the shit. Everybody done seen them with they ass out in them magazines."

"I'll fuck the shit out of that bitch, Trish."

"Don't start that shit, Casci. It's too many niggas in here for you to be sizing up some bitch," Reniya told her, before handing her the honey blunt she'd just rolled.

"I bet that hoe pussy pink as hell. You know y'all dark-skinned bitches be having them colorful pussies."

Reniya pointed toward the DJ booth, ignoring Casci's comment. They were used to hearing her say some of anything, when it came to her preference.

"Here we are trying to get you some dick, and you thinking about some pussy." Ariel laughed. "You just make sure you don't pass me that blunt you're smoking," she added.

"That's Delvin right there," Reniya told her, still pointing toward the DJ's booth. "That nigga pay for the pussy like you wouldn't believe. He gave me three hundred just to finger fuck me last week."

"Nasty bitch, Reniya. You a nasty bitch," Ariel said, shaking her head, but still making a mental note of the guy.

"Fuck 'em. Niggas gon' do what they got to do for the pussy," Casci agreed.

"Especially mines. I'm a bad bitch, and I know it." Reniya shifted in her seat, patted her lap, and took a sip of the drink she held.

"And don't let them see my shit from the back," Ariel chimed in.

Reniya was the tallest of the clique, she was the sexiest also. Her chocolate complexion, five foot seven inch height, slim-thick physique, and slightly bowed legs only added to her appeal. Her dark brown eyes, thin lips, and high-cheek bones made people question her gene pool.

Ariel was the heaviest out of the group, but she was definitely the freakiest. Her five-foot four-inch height, fat ass, and thick thighs got noticed just as much as her pudgy stomach. Her brown eyes, full lips, and pouty cheeks got her paid just the same. She prided herself in her ability to fuck. She even went out and got a tattoo of a leprechaun on her right thigh with the words 'Gold Mine' above it. She loved for her man to fuck her doggy style, just so he could repeat the chant while he stroked her. At twenty-three years old, she made more sex tapes than Cherokee D's ass made in a whole year.

"Where is this bitch at?" Reniya asked them. She checked her watch because Coffee should've been there by now.

"Probably somewhere sucking some dick. You know she can't begin or end her day without a dick down her throat." Ariel smirked.

Just as the words came out, Coffee walked through the crowd. After checking in with the security guy, she walked in their direction—her chinky eyes looking as if they were closed. She applied a coat of lip gloss to her full lips.

"What's up, bitches? I know y'all over here talking about a bitch," she greeted them, and slid into the booth beside Ariel.

"Girl, what the fuck you got on?" Reniya asked.

"This that outfit Derick bought me the other day. You like?"

Coffee stood, modeled the hip-hugging shirt and held her leg up, showing off the Gucci boots she wore. Her naturally long lashes batted themselves. Although she and Casci were first cousins, her dark complexion was a result of both Black and Creole parents. Casci, however, looked more Puerto Rican than anything. They were both Black women and proud of it.

"Where you been, bitch? You were supposed to have been here," Reniya told her.

"Nigga acted like he wasn't going to ever nut," she told them with a smile.

"Told y'all." Ariel bounced.

"Y'all sad," Casci told them, before taking another swig from the bottle she had. "All y'all think about is some dick."

"And money," Coffee added.

The four of them sat and laughed at the memories they shared. They joked about the many times they went to see Casci, while she was on lock, and even made her promise to chill out. They all knew about the plans she had for Marcus, but still tried to talk her out of doing something foolish, not wanting to see her locked back up. That was a depressing time for all of them, but they got through it together.

***

Stacy pulled into the lot of the club at a slow clip. He recently had his Denali detailed and took every precaution when it came to keeping its appearance up to par. He, Black, and Doom had thrown numerous parties at the club themselves, but after hearing that the bad girl was back on the streets, he wanted to extend his generosity personally. He and Casci went back a long way, and he knew what she was capable of. He needed her on his team.

"Yo, Stacy. Ain't that J-Rod parked over there?" Black pointed.

Stacy had been on the lookout for J-Rod for over three weeks because of the $5,000 he owed him. J-Rod had taken a front and swore to pay his debt as soon as he could. For Stacy to see that J-Rod chose to buy a new BMW instead of paying his money, he wasn't about to let that nigga make it. He needed his money.

"Look out, Black. You strapped?" Stacy asked after pulling into the lot and heading to where the silver BMW sedan was parked.

"I stay strapped, nigga," Black shot back. He pulled his Desert Eagle from his waist and filled the chamber.

Stacy parked, climbed out of his truck, and walked to the driver's side of the Sedan. J-Rod was leaning against the new car with his back facing him, surrounded by niggas who wanted cheaper prices on the work, and girls who wanted an even cheaper thrill. Everyone knew J-Rod paid to play. If you caught him in front of a crowd, his ego would get the best of him. He'd take on whatever bet wagered against him and flashed whatever cash he had on him at the time.

"Playboy, Playboy," Stacy yelled, while banging on the hood of J-Rod's BMW sedan.

J-Rod frowned hearing the loud bang behind him.

"Motherfucker, don't—" he began, before seeing the huge pistol pointed at his face. Stacy walked up on the other side of the car. He froze.

"It's about time you paid that debt, ain't it, J-Rod?" Stacy walked directly up to him.

J-Rod threw his hands up. He wasn't gonna try Black, who was still holding the gun to his face.

"Chill, y'all. Chill out, man," he pleaded.

Several of the girls standing around began making their way inside the club, and the guys, who were there, only looked on to see what would happen next.

"Pat his ass down, Doom. He's got to be sitting on something. He pulling up in a brand new BMW," Stacy instructed him.

"I was going to pay you, nigga. You tripping now, Stacy." J-Rod watched helplessly as Doom pulled the wad of cash from his pockets.

"Then you shouldn't have a problem with me taking this," Stacy told him.

"Do you, nigga," J-Rod responded.

Stacy counted the cash. Seeing that he was a few grand short of the $5,000 he owed, he lifted one of the diamond-embedded medallions hanging from J-Rod's neck.

"Come on, Stacy, man. You ain't have to clown me out here. This shit ain't gon' play out like you think," J-Rod told him.

"This should do it, huh?" Stacy lifted the necklace from around J-Rod's neck and put it on his own.

Weighing 300 pounds, the head of security for the club was known for bringing order to the worst situations in and outside of the club.

"Look, Stacy. Y'all take that shit somewhere else," the head guy told him. "And go put that shit back in the ride," he added, seeing the gun Black held.

"Alright, alright. We cool, we cool," Stacy told them, before nodding for Black to comply with the security guys' instructions.

"You straight, J-Rod?" one of the other guys asked him.

"Yeah, it ain't shit." J-Rod lowered his hands and straightened himself. He eyed Stacy contemptuously, then looked over at Black and tilted his head.

"We're here to have a good time, fellas," the head security guy began. "The club is filled with hoes, and I'm more than sure y'all would rather fuck something than be out here tripping over nothing."

"Yeah, you're right, you're right." Stacy rubbed the medallion on his neck and nodded at J-Rod.

They would take this up another time. His silence said as much.

***

Marcus was sitting in his theater room, making calls, when his line beeped. He was expecting to hear from Detrick, but not so soon. The money he and Detrick had been making was continual, and he always answered when he called.

"Hey, what's up, fam?" He smiled, knowing the call had to be about money.

"Man, you ain't going to believe who I'm looking at right now."

"Where you at, Detrick? Who you talking about?"

"Casci."

"Who?"

"Casci, nigga. She's sitting in a booth with Coffee, Reniya, and Ariel."

"You shitting me?" Marcus stood, looked around the room, and scratched the back of his head. He had to have heard him wrong. There was no way Casci was out.

"Looks like she put on a little weight, but she's still pretty as hell. That's a pretty bitch, Marcus."

Marcus smiled at the memory of his partner in crime. That smile faded, remembering the things he did to her in order to clear his name. He owed her. He thought about the many days he and Casci sat and shared the dreams they had, the plans they made, and the things they'd have to do to make them a reality.

They were close. Matter of fact, they were a lot closer than some would believe. Casci was that girl he would've done anything for. That was until his life was on the line. For the longest, he regretted what he'd done to her and wanted nothing more than to patch things up, but he knew he went too far. He knew they'd never be the friends they once were.

"Marcus! You still there?"

"Yeah, yeah. I'm still here. What she doing at the club? Casci don't fuck around like that."

"Coffee threw her a coming home party. You want me to put her on the phone or what?"

"Nah, nah. I'm going to catch up with her later," Marcus told him.

It was said that Marcus did some foul shit back in the day, but since Casci never confirmed it, he was given a pass in the streets. Despite the rumors, Marcus went on to do business with some of the heaviest players in the game and never once requested the action of selling neither of them out. For years, he was able to spend money, flip money, and live out that dream he and Casci wanted for each other. It was because of her, he was now living in a $150,000 home, owning a couple of foreign cars, and opening up a smoke shop.

"Well, I'm going to get at you later, bro. I'm out."

"Um, hey, Detrick," Marcus yelled before his friend could end the call.

"Yeah, what's up?"

"You got some change on you?" Marcus asked, thinking of something generous for his old friend.

"Yeah. I'm sitting on a little something. I'll just take it out of the next re-up."

Marcus rubbed his chin in thought.

"Bet. I'm going to give her five-thousand, then. That should help her out a little."

"Yeah, thanks, fam. Let me get back to this shit." Marcus walked out of his theater room and headed toward his kitchen. He had a few stops to make, and a few debts to collect.

"You want me to tell her it's from you?"

"Um, nah. I'm going to get at her later."

Marcus ended the call and threw the phone across the room. Things had been going good for him. Money had been made, and there was no drama. He was a game player now, and Casci could shatter the image he'd made for himself. If word got out that he was a snitch, he was good as dead. Not only would the guys he dealt with cut him off, but street niggas would come for him as well.

"Fuck!" he yelled. He grabbed the keys to his $320,000 Benz and hit the door.

***

Detrick had been standing at the bar, talking to the barkeep, when he made the call to Marcus. He smiled to himself after hearing the surprise in his friend's voice. Not only did Marcus's request mean he would be able to score the half a kilo for $5,000 or less, but him giving Casci money allowed him to get close to the pretty girl.

After downing the last of the shot he was drinking, Detrick promised Trish that he'd buy the latest publication she was featured in and made his way toward the booth where the pretty girls sat.

"Casci, is that you?" he asked, feigning surprise. He looked from Ariel, to Reniya and nodded. He then looked at Coffee and shook his head.

"What's good, D?"

"You. When did you get out?"

Before Casci could say anything, Reniya spoke for her stead. "Nigga, she out. Fuck all that other shit. Break bread, that's what you do."

"Damn, Reniya. Why you snapping at me?" He threw his hands up.

"Cause, nigga. She ain't trying to hear all that shit. My girl trying to have a good time. She ain't trying to answer all them damn questions," Reniya told him with a frown.

"He good, Ren. I'm not tripping," Casci told her.

"Matter fact." Detrick pulled a stack of cash from his pocket, unfolded the bills, and sat them on the table in front of Casci. "Hopefully, this will help you out a bit."

"That's what I'm talking about," Reniya told the group before reaching for a couple of the $100 bills.

"It's good to see you out, Casci. Let me know if you need anything," he told her, turning to Coffee a second time and winking.

Ariel waited until he was gone before telling them, "I don't trust that nigga."

"And you see the way he was looking at Coffee?" Reniya added.

"That nigga trying to get his dick sucked or something."

"Hell, he ain't got to try too hard, if he shitting out cash like this," Coffee told them, grabbing a couple of the bills he left.

"Y'all bitches trifling. That money is for Casci," Ariel told them, before peeling off a couple bills herself.

Before any of them knew it, people were walking up, dropping money on the table. Detrick had started something.

"Hello, ladies," said a tall, dark brother with a Bugs Bunny shirt on.

Reniya smiled, Ariel frowned, and Coffee rolled her eyes.

"What, Chris?" Coffee asked him, knowing he didn't want much other than to simply talk.

"I'm just paying my respects to a boss bitch, a bad bitch, and a bad ass boss bitch." He looked from Casci, to the bills scattered on the table.

"Thank you, Chris. Much love, bro." Casci offered him some of the blunt she was rolling.

Seeing the offer, Chris sat beside Coffee and scooted her over.

"Um, damn, Chris. Take that shit and go, nigga," she told him, moving closer to Reniya.

Reniya cut him off. "How much you need, Chris? Your black ass worse than some of these hoes, nigga."

"Y'all, let me hold about three hundred dollars. I'll pay y'all back when I get my check."

Chris was one of the guys who hooked the girls up when they came to eat at the Sonic he worked at. His stint at hustling ended after he was arrested and sentenced to eight months in County. He wasn't like the many guys who tried to impress them with the money they made, or the cars they drove, Chris was always the one knocking on their door, asking for money until he got paid. Chris was the tall, dark brother next door who should've been a runway model.

"Get what you need, Chris. You good," Casci told him.

"Ariel, when you gonna let me take you out?" he asked.

"Nigga, please. Sitting in a Sonic parking lot ain't some shit I look forward to doing," she told him.

"Come on, ugly ass girl. We can go skating or some shit."

"Bye, Chris."

Casci and Reniya laughed. As always, he tried to fuck with Ariel, and as always, she shot him down.

Ariel waved Chris off, looked toward her girls, and told them, "That nigga got to be crazy, thinking I'm the bitch to take skating."

"To be honest with you, y'all do make a pretty couple, Ariel," Coffee told her.

"Bitch, I don't do broke. That don't look good on me at all," she told them.

"Well, he ain't going to stop until he get some of that pussy," Casci said to her.

"Umph." Ariel lit up, seeing Stacy walk in. She took a sip of her drink and looked in the other direction. She didn't want to be the first to acknowledge him.

"Speak of the devil, and he shows up." Reniya scoffed.

"Don't hate, bitch. Don't hate."

Coffee tapped the table in front of Ariel. "Looks like y'all man need to know you're here," she told her, seeing him pushing up on Trish.

He palmed her ass.

Ariel reached across the table and grabbed a half-empty bottle by the neck.

"Don't start no shit, Ariel. Fuck that nigga," Coffee told her, before taking the bottle.

"I know this bitch ain't trying to fuck with my man. Stacy! Stacy," Ariel yelled, giving into the unspoken rule.

"Girl, don't call that nigga over here," Reniya said to her. "Hoe ass nigga ain't about shit anyway."

Hearing his name being called, Stacy turned, saw his girl, and whispered to Trish, "I'm going to catch up with you later."

Stacy and Ariel had been doing the relationship thing on and off for two years. It wasn't until they saw the other with someone else that they displayed their feelings.

Stacy was a mixed breed, pretty boy, who hustled in the streets. He spoiled his woman, and was no stranger to giving expensive gifts to women he wanted to fuck. His six-foot two-inch frame towered over Ariel. He was something she couldn't live without, and he knew it.

"Hey, babe. What are you doing here?" he asked, before acknowledging the rest of the girls. His eyes popped open, seeing Casci sitting in the middle of the booth, causing him to frown.

"The question is, why you over there feeling all on that bitch?"

"Casci?" he asked, ignoring Ariel.

"What it was, nigga?" Casci nodded.

"Damn, bitch. When you get out?" Stacy turned to where his boys Black and Doom were.

"You hear me, nigga?"

"Ariel, chill. That wasn't shit." He saw the money on the table and smiled. "All this yours, Casci?"

"You dropping something off or what?" Reniya asked him.

Stacy pulled out the cash he'd taken off J-Rod and threw it onto the pile of bills. He then nodded his head. "Real niggas do real things," he said to them.

"Yeah, right," Reniya mumbled.

For the longest, she and the other girls had been telling Ariel how fake her man was, but she wasn't trying to see it. He came on to both Coffee and Reniya, more than once, and it'd reached the point where they no longer said anything to her. She would have to see him for the trick he was herself.

As long as he spoiled Ariel and fucked her like he'd been for the longest, it would be something she looked past. Ariel was out there behind Stacy, and they all knew it.

Chapter Two

While Casci sized up most of the women in the club, Reniya and Coffee were sizing up the guys, who were known to be big spenders, especially when it came to impressing the most sought out women in the city. They laughed at Ariel, who was pretending as if Stacy was the only guy in the club. Due to their off and on relationship, she wasn't able to enjoy the setting or entertain any of the men who approached her. She had her eyes on Stacy alone.

"I'm going to ride with Stacy when he leaves, y'all," Ariel said to them.

"I thought we were going out to eat breakfast afterward?" Reniya asked.

"She only doing that shit because she know that nigga will most likely be with some other bitch," Coffee added.

"Girl, fuck that nigga."

"That ain't got shit to do with it. I had already told him I was going to give him some pussy tonight. He's not going to leave without me anyway."

"Let her go be with her man, y'all. If she thinks she can cuff that nigga, then that's on her." Casci spoke for the first time in minutes.

"Ariel just cock-blocking and hate to see the next bitch get some of that money her nigga giving away," Reniya mumbled over the rim of the glass she was holding.

"Whatever, bitch." Ariel looked around the club for Stacy.

Casci smiled at the woman who walked by their section, wearing a leopard print cat suit and black heels. "Let me out right quick," she told Ariel.

"For what?" Reniya asked, noticing the way Casci and the woman eyed each other.

"I've got to use the restroom, Reniya. Is that all right with you?" Casci rolled her eyes at her and scoffed.

"Come on. I'm going with you, with your nasty ass," she told her.

"Who's cock-blocking now?" Ariel questioned her friend.

Coffee stood, hearing one of the City Girls' jams play over the sound system. "Ouuuu, bitch, that's my song!"

"Girl, sit your nasty ass down." Reniya laughed.

"Rich nigga, eight figure, that's my type. Eight-inch, big dick, that's my type, that's my type," she yelled along with the chorus of women.

Ariel closed her eyes, seeing Chris approach the table for the second time. She didn't need Stacy tripping with her over a nigga who wasn't even worth her time.

"Ariel." Chris stopped where she sat. His look of concern was evident.

"What, nigga?" she asked, still looking through the crowd for her man.

"You know that nigga Stacy just robbed J-Rod outside, don't you?"

"What?" Coffee leaned forward.

"Yeah. The nigga J-Rod apparently owed the nigga some bread, and Stacy, Doom, and Black just hit the nigga up right before they walked in the club," he told the group.

"And how you know all this when you've been right here trucking with us all night?" Ariel asked, ready to defend her man's actions.

"Because I heard the security dudes talking about the shit. That's how."

"Well, it ain't got shit to do with us, so we good," Ariel told him, redirecting her attention to looking for Stacy.

"Thanks, Chris. Appreciate the heads up, homie," Casci told him. She offered him another blunt.

"Your ugly ass gonna get fucked off messing with that nigga," Chris told Ariel. He looked down at her with a disbelieving look. *He* even knew Stacy didn't give a damn about her.

"Ugly, black ass nigga, you need to back up," she said to him as he approached where she stood.

"Is there a problem here, babe?" Stacy asked Ariel, while his eyes silently addressed Chris.

Back in the day, they had a few words, and even fought a few times, over Ariel. Chris had gone back and told Ariel that Stacy was seen pulling out a motel parking lot early one morning with a known stripper. Word got back to Stacy, since Ariel couldn't keep her mouth closed. After he threatened to break up with her, she gave Chris up, placing Stacy in a position to get the best of Chris on more than a couple occasions. Ariel couldn't see herself going against her man.

"Nah, everything good, Stacy." Casci subtly nodded her head at Ariel, not wanting any drama to unfold between them.

"Yeah, nigga, don't come over here starting no shit," Ariel told him, seeing the stares he and his boys were giving Chris.

"Okay, well, we about to roll. I'm going to call you later on, though," he told her, still watching Chris.

"I thought you said we were going to hang out, Stacy?" Ariel looked over at him with pouty lips.

Reniya elbowed Casci and stood up.

"I got some shit I need to take care of, babe. I'm going to make it up to you tomorrow."

"Oh, you got some other bitch waiting for you outside, or something?" Ariel went off.

Stacy smiled and tried to silence her with an extended hand. "Girl, you tripping."

"I saw you over there feeling all on that bitch's ass earlier, nigga."

Reniya and Coffee knew Ariel was drunk and high. They also knew she would make a scene for the entire club to enjoy.

"Let the nigga go, Ariel, damn. You see he ain't trying to fuck with your loud ass tonight," Reniya told her.

"Fuck that! I'm leaving, too." Ariel grabbed her phone and drink, leaned over to kiss Casci's cheek, and stood. "Welcome home, baby."

"I got her, y'all. She ain't gonna do shit but fall asleep on a nigga anyway," Stacy said to them.

He might not have planned on fucking her tonight, but he wasn't going to leave her with Chris either. He knew he had feelings for her, and he also knew how gullible she got when she was drunk.

"You're damn right, you got me, 'cause you ain't fucking no other bitch tonight." Ariel walked off, leading Stacy and his boys off as well.

"See you later, Casci."

Doom and Stacy threw her deuces.

"Bet."

"Maybe I can take you out one day soon, Casci," Black said, before leaving. He didn't wait for her response.

Reniya checked the time on her watch. They'd been there four hours already. "Wait, let me make a round so these niggas can place they bids for tonight," she told them, before sitting her glass down. Before she could turn to face the crowd, she was approached by a very familiar face.

It was Jingles himself, the club owner.

Jingles was a thirty-year-old gangster, who fronted dope to guys who worked for him. He was as ruthless as they got. And no one dared to short him on money owed or favors that needed to be re-paid.

"Leaving so soon?" he asked her with raised brows.

"I was just about to come holla at you," Reniya lied with a smile. "You hungry?"

Reniya turned toward Casci and Coffee and questioned them with her eyes. She'd yet to tell them that it was because of a favor she promised Jingles that they got VIP treatment for Casci's welcome home party.

"Y'all hungry?"

"Hell yeah," Coffee said to her.

Jingles looked toward Casci. He smile, Casci shrugged.

"Let me close up my office right quick. Meet me out by the Phantom," he requested. Jingles was a sucker for pretty girls, and being in the presence of Reniya, Coffee, and Casci was something he didn't mind paying for.

***

Several stops later, Marcus pulled up at one of his main spots off Wintergreen Rd. He had already collected several thousand dollars from the other spots and was looking forward to the payment he was sure to get here. He walked straight to the rear of the game room, entered his office, and closed the door behind him.

He crossed the room, opened the safe he had under the wall shelf, and pulled out the four kilos he had there. That, along with the $8,000 he collected, was way less than what he owed Casci, but it would have to do for now. He'd put most of his money into the renovations and debut of the smoke shop he was about to open.

He picked up his phone to call Detrick, but thought better of it. It was already later in the night, and since he knew Casci really didn't do the club scene, she most likely would be gone anyway. He placed his phone onto his desk and took a seat in the recliner behind it. He looked toward the door, saw the all-black Mack-90 standing behind it, and smiled. He then walked backed to his safe and retrieved the chrome .380. He planned on throwing it in with the $8,000 and four kilos of cocaine.

He rubbed his chin in thought. The smoke house would be a perfect place for her to hustle out of. The thought of him delivering the car, along with everything else, brought a smile to his face. There was no way she wouldn't accept his peace offerings. It was better than getting nothing. As soon as he got the car detailed, he would have it delivered to her, and once he got word that she accepted the gifts, he would then make plans to see her himself.

***

Stacy handed Black the keys to the Denali and stood on the stand of the club with Ariel and Doom. It was already agreed that he would let Doom and Black drop him and Ariel off at the hotel, and come back to pick them up once he called later.

He winked at the scantily clad Trish.

She winked back at him.

"What the fuck she winking at you for, Stacy?" Ariel went off after seeing the disrespectful gesture.

"Man, that woman ain't even looking at me," he lied. He then laughed, liking her jealousy.

"Let me catch you with one of those hoes, Stacy. I'm going to cut that bitch up. I told you before."

"You know you the only one for me." Stacy turned her body to where the side of her face was against his chest. He then hugged her.

They stood and watched car after car pull to the bottom of the stairs. Guys were pulling up, and girls were either jumping in various cars or getting pulled into them. They were either headed to the after party or some motel. Stacy watched as Trish climbed into the car with a couple of her friends. He nodded when he noticed her saddened expression. He understood her disappointment. He'd promised to fuck her all kind of ways. He even promised to take her shopping afterward. Seeing Black pull to the curb, he and Ariel began descending the stairs.

Just as they were about to clear the second step, a series of shots rang out, sending guys to the ground and causing women to scream for their boyfriends and husbands. The sounds were deafening, and seemed to be closer than they should've been. Stacy pulled Ariel down beside him because the pretty girl froze with fear, while Doom ran toward the nearest car and took cover there, along with several women.

For what seemed like forever, the shots rang out in a repetitious fashion. Whoever was shooting had a fully automatic rifle with a huge magazine. The night sky lit up just across the lot from where they were. From between the trunks, Stacy could see a figure standing, holding the rifle. Then, as soon as the gun fire stopped, the figure was gone.

"You straight, Stacy," Doom yelled from where he and the women kneeled.

"Yeah, I'm good," he replied. He checked on Ariel. "You alright, babe?"

Ariel didn't respond. She only looked up at him with wide eyes. She'd never been that close to gun fire, and the sound alone spooked the hell out of her. She simply nodded her head, instead of responding to Stacy.

"Yo, Stacy." Doom pointed toward the Denali.

It had ran up on the curb and was stopped by one of the security barricades. The windshield was riddled with holes, and the driver's side of the truck was shredded to shit.

"Shit," Stacy yelled, running toward his truck.

He stopped short of it when he noticed Black lying against the steering wheel. His lifeless eyes were positioned skyward.

"Bitch," Doom yelled, seeing his childhood friend slumped in the truck.

Stacy pulled Ariel toward his body to shield her from the sight of the carnage. Her sobs could be felt on his chest.

"Sssh. It's alright, babe."

Despite people still running way from the scene, some of the bystanders were walking toward the sight to get a look at what took place. Among them were Reniya and Coffee.

"Ariel! Ariel," they yelled when they noticed Stacy holding her.

"She alright. She alright," Stacy tried to assure them.

Reniya pulled her from his grasp and pushed him. She looked from his truck to him. He was the reason his friend was dead, but he wouldn't be the reason hers died.

"What the fuck you do, nigga?"

"Bitch, I didn't do a mothafucking thing!" Stacy went off. When he noticed Jingles descend the stairs with Casci at his side, he took a step backward.

"Who you calling a bitch? Punk ass nigga!" Reniya took a step forward, but was stopped when Jingles grabbed her arm.

"Let it go, Reniya. Let it go," he told her.

"Yo, Stacy, look." Doom pointed out toward the club's entrance.

J-Rod's silver BMW was creeping out the lot.

Sirens could be heard and were getting closer by the seconds. Women and guys were beginning to leave the scene, not wanting to be asked questions about the murder.

"Goddammit," Jingles mumbled under his breath.

This was the third shooting at his club, and he was warned about what could possibly happen to his establishment if another fatal incident occurred.

He looked across the lot, spotting a few of his security detail directing traffic away from the scene, and told Reniya, "I'm going to have to catch up with you later. I've got to get a handle on this shit." He pulled a couple hundred-dollar bills from his pocket and handed them to her. "This should get you ladies something to eat."

Reniya took the money and handed it to Casci, since she had pockets. She turned her attention back to Stacy, who was still looking toward the entrance of the lot.

"Let's go, y'all," Casci said to her girls. "Y'all know I'm on papers, and I don't need to be questioned about no shit like this." She began walking toward Reniya's Charger.

The girls followed. Before they could all climb into the car, Chris pulled alongside them in his late modeled Accord.

"Y'all alright?"

"Yeah, Chris, we good," Reniya told him.

"Where y'all headed now?" he asked them.

"To get something to eat, nigga," Coffee yelled from her side of the car.

"Um, is there a Taco Bell still open?"

"Cheap ass nigga. Break bread. Let's go to IHOP. Follow us," Reniya countered, before pulling off.

The ride to the eatery was a one-sided conversation with Reniya going off on Ariel about the things her man did and the trouble he was always in. It was a good thing she saw that someone was apparently trying to get at his ass.

"That shit was meant for that nigga. I know that much," Reniya told them.

"Chris did say something about him, Black, and Doom robbing that nigga J-Rod earlier."

"Yeah, well. I didn't see shit, and I don't know shit," Casci told them.

"And stop all that damn crying. Niggas get stepped on every day, Ariel." Reniya shook her head.

She and Casci had seen a *couple* dead guys before.

"Leave her alone, Ren. You see the girl is shook up," Casci defended her.

"If she keep fucking with that nigga, she gon' see her ass lying across the front seat or on the ground beside that nigga."

Ariel groaned and shook her head.

"But I will leave her ass alone," Reniya added.

"Thank you!" Ariel joked, and added, "But I hear you."

"Your ass *better* hear me," Reniya retorted.

"Aye, y'all ready or what?" Chris appeared once Reniya brought the vehicle to a halt.

"Hell yeah, nigga, with your cheap ass," Reniya shouted out, causing all three ladies to bust out laughing.

Ariel smiled and Casci laughed, while Coffee simply nodded.

Chris was one of the brokest niggas they knew.

"Just wait until I come up. I'm going to show y'all, especially your fat ass, Ariel," he said to her.

"Fuck you, nigga. My man like it."

"Yeah, 'cause all your fat ass wants to do is eat. Nigga can't even fuck without buying you a bucket of chicken or a basket of fish or something."

"Oh, is that why the pussy fat?" she asked him, knowing he wouldn't know.

"Yeah, ya pussy, legs, neck, and that fat ass head you got. A nigga get you naked, he ain't going to know whether to punch your ass or boil you."

"A nigga know exactly what to do when I get naked, nigga. You better ask about me."

Coffee pointed toward a table once they entered the restaurant and were greeted by a host.

Once they were seated, they each placed their order with the waitress.

Casci smiled at herself in that moment. Chris hadn't changed a bit. He was still in love with Ariel, and she was sure she wasn't the only one seeing it. She also thought about what Chris said when speaking about his come up. It was then that she decided that would be something they did together.

Chapter Three
Two Days Later

With Reniya and Coffee in the streets and Ariel at work, Casci had time to sit and think about her next moves. She'd been given over $7,000 since she'd been back on the scene, and it was time for her to make a play. The girls were calling her every thirty minutes to see what she was doing, and it was getting to her. It made her think about the many counts she'd endured in prison.

Hoping the fresh air would do her some good, Casci stepped into a pair of baggy shorts, slipped on a white wife-beater, socks, and her blue fuzzy house shoes. Ariel had hooked up her shoulder-length hair, put it in four cornrows, and arched her eyebrows.

Casci stepped out of the apartment, leaving the phone they left her behind. All she wanted to do was take a little walk around the apartments. With her freshly-rolled blunt hanging loosely from her mouth, Casci waved at some of the people she knew, and nodded at the ones she didn't. She chuckled when seeing some youngsters posted on the corner hustling. She used to be one of them.

Her thoughts took her back to the days when she corner hustled. She couldn't help but to think of her partner in crime, Marcus. They'd done so much around the Gardens. They got their names and reps because of the shit they did in the Gardens.

She shook the thoughts and returned her attention to a couple of the youngsters posted up. She wondered if they were hustling for Marcus. She'd already been told that Marcus was on and had niggas pushing the work he was buying and getting fronted. Casci knew Marcus, and sitting in some trap waiting on customers wasn't something he'd do. He *would* have a few spots where people worked out of, though.

Casci was walking past the bus stop when she saw Chris pull into the apartments. She smiled when seeing the Sonic hat he wore.

"What's up, Casci? Where you headed?" Chris yelled. He pulled into a parking spot where she stood and climbed out. He'd just finished his shift at the fast food place.

"Just mobbing, trying to get my head right." She offered him the blunt, her gray eyes bloodshot red.

"Yeah, let me hit that shit," he told her. Before he put it up to his lips, he looked over at her and frowned. "You ain't been sucking no dick, have you?"

Casci laughed, looked toward the street, and nodded. "Yeah. A nigga just got through shoving a dick down my throat."

"You know I got to ask nowadays. Hoes be sucking dick just because in 2019."

"Nigga, give me my shit back, then."

"I didn't say I wasn't going to hit it. I just wanted to know how to hit this bitch." Chris pulled on the blunt deeply. He coughed, shook his head, and hit it again.

Casci watched him. She smiled.

"What?" he asked her, seeing the mischievous grin she had.

"You don't taste that?"

"Taste what, Casci?" Chris looked down at the blunt. He smacked his lips. "Taste like some honey or something in here."

"I had to stick it in my ass when the cops rolled up earlier. You smoking my shit, nigga."

"Bullshit! If your ass taste like this, then as soon as I cash my check, I'm coming to find your ass."

They both laughed until she had to snatch the blunt back.

She looked over at Chris and had to step back. "Nigga, why you looking at me like that?" she asked, knowing he was about to say something stupid.

"You a pretty motherfucker, Casci. You're supposed to be on TV somewhere."

"Oh, yeah?"

"Hell yeah. You look good, fine as hell, and you real. It shouldn't be shit for you to get on."

Casci climbed onto the hood of Chris's car and pulled her feet up on the bumper.

He did the same.

"I'm putting some shit together now right now. What you talking about doing?" she asked him, her demeanor now serious.

"Like what?" Chris watched his friend.

"It's time to eat, Chris, and a bitch hungry."

"I got a couple cheeseburgers and some fries in the car."

"Shut your dumb ass up, nigga. You know what I'm talking about." Casci playfully elbowed him. "I'm talking about getting this bread."

"I can get you on at my job. I know my freaky ass supervisor will hire a bitch like you."

Casci didn't answer. She only looked over at him then back to the scene before her. Hustlers were hustling and hoes were, too. "I need some heat, Chris," she said barely above a whisper.

"Casci, you ain't got to do none of that shit. You too pret—"

She cut him off. "I'm too what, nigga? Pretty? Is that what you gonna say?"

"I mean, yeah. You can be doing something else besides hustling out here in these streets."

Casci scoffed and told him, "I can go get a bullshit job like you, and still end up begging motherfuckers for some bread until I get my check because the shit I'm making ain't enough to keep a roof over my head or my bills paid."

"Damn, I be doing that shit?"

"Every week, nigga. That ain't no life. That ain't about shit. I'd rather play my hand out here than wind up on that shit you on, Chris. I'm just being real." She rested her elbows on her knees and put her chin in her palm.

"I'm a hoe ass nigga, huh?"

"Nah, it ain't that. It's just that you have to do something to make something happen. You let a few months in jail scare the hell out of you. Fuck that shit, nigga. You grind that shit out, get up, and go get it."

Chris sat and listened to her. He liked hearing her spit game. Even if he wasn't gon' do any of the shit she talked about, he liked listening to Casci.

"I don't know, Casci. Niggas out here getting killed and everything, but I don't have to tell you that."

"If dying is the reason you scared to live, then you already dead. A walking zombie. That's what the fuck you become," she told him.

"I ain't scared of living. I just don't want to lose my life 'cause another motherfucker don't give a damn about losing his life," he argued.

"Then you know what you got to do. The only way to solve a problem is to solve it. A nigga get in your lane with that bullshit, you slump his ass and push on."

"What you gonna do with some heat, Casci?"

"*We*, nigga. It's what *we* gonna do with some heat." Casci pulled a couple grand from her pocket and handed the cash to him. "Get a couple of Glocks, two AR's, and extra magazines for us both. We're gonna need some firepower for this shit I'm talking about doing."

"Damn, Casci. You serious, huh?"

"Prey and predators, nigga. It's time for some of these motherfuckers to step into the waters."

Casci watched him for a response. Once he stuffed the bills into his pocket, she knew he'd just found the answer to his question. It was time for the rules to the game being played around them to change.

***

Marcus was standing in the entrance of the detail shop when Detrick pulled into the lot. They'd talked earlier, and Detrick was insisting on his re-up before Marcus could renege on the deal they'd already come up with. On top of that, Marcus was wanting him to do another favor regarding Casci.

He smiled, seeing Detrick climb out if his truck with the small duffle. He was ready to do business.

"Come on in here, Detrick. I need to holla at you."

Marcus led Detrick into the back room and closed the door behind him. He'd always paid the owner to have meetings at this establishment, and did most of his dealings in this same room.

"I brought sixteen thousand with me. I'll have the—"

Marcus waved him off. "I need you to do something for me, homie," he told him, and walked over to the huge window, facing the service center.

"Yeah, what's up?" Detrick asked, seeing his friend's mind was elsewhere.

"I need you to drop the Chrysler off to Casci. I have four kilos and a pistol inside, and I need it to get to her."

"Why you giving that hoe all of that?" Detrick frowned.

He already knew it was more to what Marcus was doing. Years ago, it was said that Marcus fucked over Casci, but with nothing and no one to confirm it, it was something he pushed to the back of his mind. Now that she was back, he was seeing Marcus break bread with her more than he'd done with anyone he knew. Him being the front man wasn't without notice.

"She just touched down, and I know how it is when you have to start this shit from the bottom. I'd do the same for you." Marcus smiled, turned to face him, and tossed him the keys to the 300.

"Looks as if you trying to lock her in. Or fuck," Detrick told him, knowing otherwise.

"Nah, you know me and Casci past that shit. That's my little sister."

"Oh, okay. So what's up on that other issue we talked about?" Detrick set the small duffle on the desk and opened it.

"Um, we'll take care of that when you get back. Have her drop you off here. I'll swing through later so we can do that."

Marcus walked Detrick back toward the front without as much as a word about the matter that should've been discussed. As soon as Detrick pulled off in the 300, Marcus climbed into his Benz and made a few blocks. He dialed a number, placed the phone to his ear, and once the line was answered, he told the person, "We need to talk."

"Name the place," said the guy.

Marcus thought for a second before saying, "I'm on my way to your home now." He hung up, checked his rearview mirror, and allowed the butter-soft leather to engulf him.

***

Coffee and Reniya pulled into the lot and parked alongside Chris's Accord. They'd been out on their grind early this morning—the heavy bassline from Reniya's speakers setting off a couple alarms.

"That's my type, that's my type," Coffee sang aloud.

Both she and Reniya climbed out of the Charger and began pulling bags from the rear of the car. Coffee wore a black pin-striped pants suit with a pair of open-toe heels, a pair of oversized shades covering her eyes. The blonde wig she wore cascaded over her shoulders.

Reniya, on the other hand, was wearing a mini-dress with multiple colored flowers, a cropped blouse, and a pair of thigh high boots that laced in the front. The pink and black wig she wore was cut into a shoulder-length bob. Some designer frames with clear lenses covered her eyes.

Chris pushed himself off the hood of his car. He looked back toward Casci and shook his head when seeing all the bags in the rear of the car.

"Looks like you two had a nice morning," Casci told them from where she sat.

"You know how this shit goes, Casci," Coffee responded, still gathering bags.

"We got you some more shit, too," Reniya yelled from the passenger's side.

She and Coffee had cashed several huge checks, boosted some high-end clothes from a couple boutiques they'd been casing, and did a walk-away at a jewelry store. They had a wonderful morning.

"All y'all bitches do is steal shit and fuck over niggas," Chris told them with a frown on his face.

Coffee pushed her shades atop her head and twisted her lips. "Really?" she asked, not believing he'd have a complaint with what they did. "And all your black ass do is beg for the shit we get," Reniya told him.

"Here it is a week before Halloween, and y'all already wearing costumes," he cracked off.

"Um, Casci, why you out here with this hating ass dude for?" Coffee walked past them and headed toward the stairs.

"Knowing her, she up to no good," Reniya said, following Coffee.

"All y'all need is some red roses and some balloons, with y'all clown asses." Chris rolled his eyes at the duo and leaned up against his car again.

"They out there getting it, Chris. Can't knock them for that," Casci told him.

"Yeah, I know. I just be fucking with them." He reached for the piece of the blunt she offered him, inhaled, the smoke, and said, "I do be begging, huh?"

"Like a motherfucker." Casci laughed, nodded her head, and laughed some more.

There was humor in his assessment of himself.

***

Ariel was on her second head of the morning when she heard her co-workers begin talking about the shooting that happened at the club just two days ago. They always talked and gossiped about the things that happened in the streets and the people who did them, and Ariel, being the person she was, only listened. The last thing she wanted any of them to know was that she was just a few feet away from the incident and knew more than some, when it came to what really transpired. For two days, the gossip was just that. No one really knew the "who" or "what" about it, but when hearing about the shooting from the mouths of the women who walked in this morning, she knew it would be something she could use.

"That wasn't nobody but J-Rod's crazy ass cousin, Peanut," one of the girls said, as if it was public knowledge.

"Peanut? You talking about skinny ass Peanut?" another of her co-workers asked.

Ariel knew exactly who Peanut was. He'd been out of prison for several months himself, and when thinking about it, she could see him doing something like that. Peanut was known to play with the heat, just as Casci was. She continued to listen.

"My nigga said J-Rod stopped scoring from Stacy and he was mad because of that. That's why he and his boys jacked J-Rod up outside of the club. I was standing right there when they did that," she lied.

"So, J-Rod had Peanut shoot Stacy, but he shot Black instead?" her co-worker, Mildred, asked.

Mildred was the oldest in the shop, but she was also the nosiest. She spoke about people as if she knew them personally, despite not knowing who the hell was being talked about.

"That's what they say. Peanut known to do some stupid shit like that. It's only a matter of time before someone get at his ass."

Ariel thought about the conversation she and Stacy had. Him telling her that he was taking care of everything had her questioning the way he was doing it. He hadn't been home since the shooting. At first, she thought it was done so he wouldn't be questioned by the cops. But now that she'd heard about Peanut, she figured he was hiding out until he found out who was trying to get at him for sure. He even told her that J-Rod wasn't the triggerman. He was seen climbing in the car with a young girl just before the shots rang out.

All she knew was that she had to tell her man what she'd heard. She was hoping she could do that before any harm found him. She was going to go by the motel herself, as soon as she got off work.

"Just ask Ariel. She would know what's up," one of the girls said, snapping her out of the thoughts she was having.

"Ask me what?" Ariel asked, acting as if she hadn't been paying any attention.

"She wants to know if that nigga, Doom, still fuck with that fat bitch, Melissa."

"The last I heard, he was, but you know how them niggas is," she responded.

Those words resounded in her head, and she couldn't help but hear the same thing being said about her man, Stacy. She knew exactly how them niggas were.

***

Casci and Chris were laughing about the old days and tripping on the couple arguing across the parking lot when a cream-colored Chrysler 300 pulled into the Gardens and slowly headed their way.

Chris pointed.

"Ouu, that bitch nasty," he told her. Huge chrome wheels were sparkling under the big body sedan.

"See, that's how you supposed to be rolling, Chris. That's you all day long," Casci told him.

"You've got to have a couple dollars to throw away, driving something like that, Casci."

"Then get off the porch, nigga."

Casci could only watch as the show-stopper slowly approached them. If it was a hit, she and Chris were slipping in the worst way because she wasn't strapped and knew Chris most likely didn't have shit to defend them with. Once the car pulled past them, it stopped, backed up, and the passenger's window lowered.

Casci smiled.

"Look out, Casci. Come bend a few corners with me," Detrick told her.

Casci climbed off the car, looked over at Chris, and said, "Take care of that for me."

"What you want me to tell Coffee and Reniya's thieving asses?"

"Tell them I'll be right back."

Casci climbed in, closed the door, and sat back. Detrick had shown her nothing but love, but even she knew it came with a price. She was sure he came to name his.

"You spend any of that money yet?" he asked, once they were pulling out the complex.

"Yeah, a little. A bitch got needs."

Detrick laughed, fingered the volume selection knob on the steering wheel, and hit his right blinker. "I've got something else for you, Casci. You ain't one of these hoes out here that's gonna let niggas do any and everything, so I figured you could use a little something to help you plant your feet."

Casci listened while taking in the passing scene as he drove. They were leaving the hood, instead of bending a few corners, but she said nothing.

"Look in the compartment and get that package," he told her.

Casci frowned at the bulk of it. "Damn."

"That's four kilos, a .380, and a scale." He nodded.

"Man, you ain't got to give me all this shit. I'm good, nigga."

"Well, it ain't from me."

"Who—" She stopped herself. It was obvious.

"He's even giving you this car. That's why I'm driving back to mines now." Detrick shrugged.

"Where the nigga at?" Casci looked over the contents of the package and placed it back in the glove compartment.

"Hiding, I guess. But, hey. I'm not going to get in y'all business. He told me you're his sister, and he's doing what he'd do for me if I was the one touching down."

Casci watched the uncertainty in his expression. She knew Marcus, and she knew differently. "So you hustling with him now?" she asked.

"We do good business, Casci. And now that you're out, I can tell he's a little distracted." Detrick smiled, chuckled, and told her, "It's obvious something happened between y'all."

"So, the money you gave me at the club was from him also?"

"You can say that, but I wasn't the one who told you. I'm just cashing in on a few favors, that's all."

While they rode, he put Casci up on game when it came to who was doing what and who they were doing it for. He was able to fill in the many gaps in her thoughts when it came to Marcus. She nodded, hearing a few things, and frowned at most of the rest.

Coffee and the girls had told her that he'd just stopped coming around after she got locked up, but Detrick had a much different version as to what took place. He and the girls had words, and they promised to have him stepped on if he even showed his face again. Where Marcus used to be that nigga who spent plenty of nights with the girls, he was now the one they demanded stay the hell away from them.

Casci smiled to herself, hearing that her girls were the ones who kept her name alive in the streets. She laughed, hearing that niggas were out selling dope just so they could come up with the $1,000 price tag what came with fucking Coffee. Just a few days ago, there was no way Coffee would've fixed her mouth to say something like she'd let niggas fuck for a thousand dollars. And Reniya was just a department store booster. Things had definitely changed. Everything and everyone, except Chris.

"Now that you're out, I know you want to get money, and I can help you with that," he told her.

"I'll think about it, Detrick. But for right now, I just want to walk around with my shoes off. If you know what I mean," she lied.

She wasn't about to work for Detrick, and she damn sure wasn't going to let him know of her plans. Like the pretty girl she was, she only smiled, gave terse answers when being asked shit she didn't know about, and made him feel as if there was nothing to be concerned about when it came to her.

"And if you can't move them bricks, get at me. I'll take 'em off your hands for thirteen thousand apiece."

The numbers flipped in her head. It was a good lick, but she'd be chumping herself. She remembered the youngsters hustling outside the Gardens. She'd just have to shut down whatever shop niggas was running in her complex. If nothing else, she'd have Reniya, Chris, Coffee, and Ariel making calls. Either way, she was going to accept the things Marcus sent her.

"Let me see what I can do first, Detrick. I'll make sure to get at you, though."

"Maybe we can hit a few spots together or something. You know I ain't against taking a bitch on a shopping spree," he stated with a smile.

"And I ain't against going."

Detrick pulled up beside his truck and stopped. He threw the car in park and opened his door.

"Well, I'll leave you to it, Casci. Don't forget what I said, though."

On the way back to the Gardens, Casci's mind turned from this idea to that possibility, from one scenario to another, and to the reasons Marcus would try to regain her trust. She thought of him playing position to where he could get under her, one that allowed him the advantage when it came to having the upper hand and leverage. Or maybe he was genuinely being sincere and was really wanting to make things right with her. Casci weighed her options, searched her mind for reason, and came to the conclusion that she'd never be played with again.

As soon as she pulled into the parking lot, she grabbed the package she was given and headed inside.

It was time.

Nicole Goosby

Chapter Four

The minute Ariel pulled into Southern Motel's parking lot and headed toward the black F-150 at the rear of the building, her phone chimed. It was Reniya. She'd left work a little early so she could get at Stacy and let him know what she'd heard personally—as well as to see what all he had going on at the spot.

"Hey, Reniya, what's up?" she asked before backing in the parking spot behind Stacy's truck.

"Bitch, where you at? I thought you were coming straight home?"

"Um, I'm up here at the room with Stacy. I'll be through there later on."

"Alright."

"Where's Casci?"

"That bitch jumped in the car with Detrick's trick ass and disappeared."

Ariel frowned. "Whaaat?" she asked her.

"Yeah. Chris said she said she'll be right back, though."

"And where that broke ass nigga at?" Ariel said, looking at the room door open.

"He standing right here listening to you." Renita laughed.

"Broke? Your fat ass ain't fixed neither," he yelled through the receiver.

Ariel's mouth fell open when she saw a dark-skinned Trish exit the room. "Um, bye y'all. I got to go," she said before ending the call and reaching into her glove box for the box cutter she kept there. Ariel fought with the door handle until the door pushed it open. "Is Stacy in there?" she asked the woman, while walking across the lot toward her.

Stacy and Doom filed out the room with smiles on their faces. It wasn't until Ariel was walking up on Trish that Stacy realized his girl was there, and she held a box cutter in her hand.

"Ariel, what the fuck?" he yelled, before running in between the two women.

"You fucking this bitch, nigga?" Ariel raised the box cutter above her head.

Stacy managed to grab her wrist before she could do any harm.

"You tripping, girl. What the fuck's wrong with you? She here with Doom. She was here with him."

"Move, Stacy! Let me go! I know this nasty bitch probably fucked both of y'all! Move, nigga!"

"Ariel, stop!"

Stacy picked her up off her feet and walked her back toward the room he, Doom, and Trish came out of.

"It's whenever I see you, bitch," she yelled over his shoulder.

Once the door was closed, Stacy sat her on the bed and gave her a stern look. He stood to where she couldn't stand. "What the fuck's wrong with you, Ariel, drawing all this heat and shit?"

"I know that bitch was in here throwing pussy everywhere." Ariel began looking around the room for tell-tell signs that would've been visible had they just finished fucking the woman.

"Girl, we hustling up in here. She just came by to score some weed from Doom. We smoked some just to show her the quality, and she left. That's it."

Ariel closed her eyes, threw her head back, and said, "You don't know hoes like I do, Stacy. That bitch been wanting to fuck with you, and if buying some weed gets her closer to the dick, that's what she's going to do. That nasty bitch ain't no different."

Stacy smiled, grabbed the box cutter from her hand, and held it up. "You were really going to cut her, wasn't you?"

"*You* and that bitch had it coming, Stacy. You know I don't play that shit. You know I don't."

Stacy set the blade on the table behind him and pushed her back onto the bed. He pulled her heels off one at a time, climbed on the bed, and began kissing her neck and lips.

"Move, boy. You ain't even lock the door."

"Ain't nobody coming in here. Doom got us." He pulled at the waistband to her pants and tugged at them until she raised her middle.

"Oh, now you want to fuck on me?" Ariel let him pull her pants off, and she slid off her panties.

She then pulled the shirt she wore over her head and turned around so he could undo her bra. They hadn't fucked in three days, and she was needing some sex.

"What if you would've cut that woman, Ariel?" he asked before unbuckling his pants and stepping out of them. He unclasped her bra and pushed her onto the bed. He slapped her ass cheek.

"Fuck that bitch. She lucky you came out when you did," she told him, while raising her ass and putting her face onto the bed pillow. She yelped, feeling the sting of the slap, looked back at him, and spread her legs.

She loved the way Stacy freaked her. He was one of the few men she knew didn't mind pleasuring her the way she needed to be.

"This all you wanted in the first place, huh?" He kissed both her ass cheeks and licked the tattoo she had on the back of her thigh. "*My* Gold Mine. That's what you should've put on here." Stacy turned his head and gently licked across her asshole. He held her hips to keep her from running, then licked it again and blew on it. "I'm about to fuck the shit out of you, girl."

"Do what you need to do, nigga."

Stacy looked behind him toward the table, made sure his phone was still positioned the way he'd set it, and entered her from the back. He pulled his belt from his pants and wrapped it around her waist. With one hand pushing her face down on the bed, he used to other to grip the belt and pulled her ass up to meet his thrust.

"Throw that ass back, babe! Open that Gold Mine," he coached her.

"Don't pull my hair, Stacy. Just don't pull my hair," she told him, before grinding back into him.

Ariel loved the fact that Stacy's dick was the perfect size for her. He could go balls deep without causing her too much pain, and he stretched her just right. With him not being too big, she could clown him when she wanted to. And she knew he loved the way she gripped the dick like a glove.

***

Marcus pulled to the curb and parked. Three of the biggest Rottweilers he'd ever seen sat obediently in the same front yard. He thought back to the day he and Casci jacked one of the same guy's old spots and how they silenced the Pitbull's he used to protect the premises. A half-smile creased his lips. He climbed out and was greeted by Alex Minez himself.

"Come on in, Marcus. It's been a while."

Marcus climbed the stairs two at a time until he was on the same landing as his plug. He gave him dap and followed him inside.

"Them dogs look like monsters sitting out there, man," he told him, once they were in the foyer area of the home.

"Yeah, they got to be. You and ya girl, Casci, made me upgrade that shit," he said jokingly.

"Aw, man. There you go with that shit."

"I'm just pulling your balls, Marcus. That's old shit."

Marcus took a seat at the island counter in the huge kitchen, tapped his fingers on the granite counter top, and said, "Speaking of Casci, you know she's back out, right?"

"Casci out? Bullshit." Alex retrieved two Coronas from his ice box and walked back over to where Marcus sat. He handed him one and popped the top on the other.

"Real talk. I got a call the other day. They say she's looking good, too."

"Oh, you haven't seen her yourself?"

"Nah, not yet." Marcus looked down in thought.

"Hmm. This can be bad for you, homes."

"Yeah, tell me about it?" Marcus agreed.

"Why come here instead of going to see her?" Alex asked, before taking a sip of his beer. "I'd be more worried about the shit she'd do, Marcus. Casci isn't the type to go around doing a bunch of talking. You know this, *hombre*."

Marcus looked to his left, saw a woman in a wheelchair wheeling herself toward them, and nodded. She only rolled her eyes and continued past them.

Marcus's heart skipped a beat when seeing her.

"I'm stuck in the middle of my thoughts. My mind is telling me one thing, and my heart is screaming something totally different."

"Don't trust that bitch, Marcus. You took too much from her," Alex advised him.

"I sent her some cash, gave her four kilos of soft, and even threw in the Chrysler 300. She has to know that I'm trying to make the shit right," Marcus vented.

"You know her better than anyone, Marcus, and you know what you have to do."

Marcus slowly nodded, downed the rest of the Corona he was given, and sighed. He knew exactly what he needed to do.

***

"Don't trust that nigga, Casci. That nigga don't give nobody shit unless he's getting something in return," Reniya went off after seeing all that Marcus gave her.

"And we don't need that nigga coming around here thinking everything cool, so don't even start that shit with him," Coffee told her.

Casci nodded. She understood exactly what they were saying. But they were thinking and speaking from the hate they had for him, instead of with the power of the mind.

"He know he fucked over a good bitch, and now the nigga want you to think he breaking himself just to make the shit right. Fuck that nigga, Casci." Reniya went on.

Knowing there was money to be made, Casci handed Chris one of the kilos and emptied half of another inside of a glassware dish.

"What's this for?" Chris asked her.

"That's you, nigga. Make something happen, or I can sell the shit back to Detrick. He said he'll pay thirteen thousand dollars for it."

"Thirteen thousand dollars?"

"It's up to you," she told him, really wanting to see if he'd take the easy way out.

"That nigga had to have been smoking something. Motherfuckers making sixty thousand off these bricks, and he talking about thirteen thousand. Fuck that."

"I'm about to put some of these niggas in the Gardens to work. What I need you hoes to do is make some calls and let my spenders know y'all trying to get off some work for cheap."

Casci had thought of a way to spread word that she was hustling without too many people knowing. There was an image she was trying to establish, because her next move required just that. The streets talked, and those who didn't know what was going on, only guessed about it. For the ones who did, they were able to spin whatever story they wanted to. And Casci had a story to tell.

"Speaking of cheap. Has anybody heard from Ariel?" Reniya looked from Casci to Coffee.

"Not since we last spoke with her. Knowing that freaky ass bitch, she got her ass in the air," Coffee replied.

Casci watched Chris shift. She laughed. "Don't forget that business we got to take care of, nigga."

"While you was riding around sucking dick, I was making a few calls, and I'm going to scope things out tomorrow," he retorted.

Nicole Goosby

"Well, good for you, Chris. You finally decided to step off the porch, huh?"

"Yep. It's time for me to get my dick sucked."

"You get on your feet, you're going to get more than that," Casci assured him.

"I'm telling y'all now. If I go to jail, y'all better hold me down." He looked from one to the other.

"Nigga, ain't nobody going to jail." Casci adjusted the fire under the glassware and got a fork from the drawer.

"I'm just saying."

"Long as you don't start doing no dumb shit, drawing heat to yourself, and get caught up behind these hoes out here, you'll do good."

"Hell, I'm already caught up with some of the most scandalous hoes it is," he quipped and spun around with his arms outstretched.

Reniya leaned back in the seat she was sitting in and crossed her legs at the knee. She said, "And don't forget it. Your ass get to tripping, I'm going to be the first to remind you."

Chapter Five

For an entire week, Casci and Chris hustled together. She'd fronted dope to a handful of the youngsters around the Gardens, and to her and Chris's surprise, they were returning for more.

One of the guys from the Northside was coming through, chumping the youngsters for drugs they pushed for him, and Casci had to change that. For the longest, guys and girls from different hoods came through the Gardens because of the money that was sure to be made, but they didn't give a damn about looking out for the residents who lived there.

Casci, at first, thought Marcus would've been the one to employ some of the youngsters, but after learning of the threat her girls issued him, she understood. Reniya and Coffee might've been known for boosting, cashing checks, and gold digging, but they weren't strangers to assaults and murder. Ariel was the good girl amongst them, but even she'd spill a little blood if it came down to it.

The threat they issued to Marcus was not to be taken lightly. They knew people and knew how to get things done.

"So, have you figured out who we're going to start scoring from, once we get rid of this drop?" Chris asked Casci.

"Hopefully, we'll be through with this shit. I'm not trying to sell this shit forever, nigga. I want to open up a boutique in the Galleria or something."

"Hell, the way you was talking, I thought this was some long-term shit."

"Nah, I'm on some more shit, Chris. That's what I'm trying to get these crazy ass girls to see."

Casci handed him the freshly-rolled blunt and began rolling another. He'd come over early to make sure everything was right, as far as the money went, and to deliver the order she wanted.

"So, why all the guns and...?"

"That's our hunting material. Can't rob no bank without no gun, Chris."

"Rob a bank, are you crazy?"

"Shut up, Chris. That's a quote from *Jason's Lyric*, clown." Casci laughed.

"Oh, 'cause I thought you lost your damn mind, bitch."

"What you in here laughing about?" Reniya asked. She walked from her room wearing a sports bra, matching boy shorts, and a purple and gray scarf wrapped around her head—her toned thighs flexing with each step.

Chris watched her pass. He frowned when seeing her ass jiggle.

"Chris's dumb ass," Casci answered.

"What the hell you over there frowning for, nigga?" Reniya turned, put her back to the counter, and gave him a frown of her own.

"Bitch, I thought you were bowlegged? All this time your ass been walking around here like you just super fine, and your ass ain't even bowlegged." He scoffed.

"What the hell y'all in her smoking, Casci, because this nigga is too stupid right now?" Reniya went back to what she came to do.

"And the camel toe don't even look as fat as it do when you be wearing the cat-suits." He walked around to where he could see her pussy better and shook his head.

"Dumb ass nigga, that's what the cat-suit is designed for. And for your information, my pussy is fat as hell." Reniya pat herself with her left hand.

Chris looked from Reniya to Casci and scrunched his nose. "Y'all smell that?"

"Don't start, broke ass nigga. It's too early in the morning for your shit, Chris." Reniya poured herself a glass of apple juice and pushed past him.

"You smell like a pot of boiled eggs, girl," he yelled after her. He smiled, hearing her bedroom door slam.

"You stupid, for real, man. You ain't got no sense," Casci told him.

"I was just fucking with her. Keep her on her toes and shit." Chris walked to the window overlooking the parking lot and asked, "Did Ariel ever come home last night? I still don't see her car."

"I doubt it. That bitch been chasing Stacy everywhere." Casci walked into the living room and flopped down on the couch, the blunt dangling from her lips and stack of fifty-dollar bills in her hand.

"I don't know why she be running behind that nigga like that, Casci. I mean, she know that nigga be fucking some of everybody. Hell, he tried to fuck Reniya and Coffee. And the only reason he ain't tried you is because you been locked up."

"Well, for one, the nigga spoil her ass, and for two, he's a damn freak."

"I'm a freak!" he told her angrily.

"You heard when I said he spoil the shit out of her?" Casci set the blunt in the ashtray and picked up one of the Glocks he brought with him.

"Yellow ass nigga ain't fucking that girl right." Chris walked from the widow and took a seat across from her. He shook his head.

"Stop paying her any attention for a while."

"Huh?"

"Just stop sweating her, Chris. Bitches hate that shit," Casci schooled him.

"I don't be sweating her. I just be—"

"Sweating her," Casci finished his statement.

"Showing concern and constantly hounding a bitch is two different things, Casci." Chris rested his head on the couch pillow behind him.

"Well, stop being so concerned, then." Casci began filling one of the clips they had.

"You know what? That's what I'm going to do. Fuck Ariel," he told himself. "Fuck that fat ass bitch."

Casci laughed. "Bet one-fifty you can't do it?"

"Do what?"

"Ignore her. Don't say shit to her." Casci watched him.

"I'll bet you a thousand. Fuck that bitch. I mean that shit," he declared with his hand pushed toward her.

Casci smiled, set the clip down, and dapped him up. "Bet that, nigga."

"You got me fucked up. I'm not out there like that behind that girl."

***

Ariel had spent the weekend with Stacy. He'd taken her to Houston's Galleria mall so she could get a couple pairs of Gucci boots and a few outfits she was sure no one had yet. He also wanted to get out the city for a few days to get his head straight. After losing his best friend, Black, he wasn't thinking straight when it came to what he was going to do and how he was going to handle the situation. Ariel was a much welcomed distraction.

She pulled several bags from her passenger seat and headed upstairs. It was still early, and she knew the girls were most likely still asleep. Since Casci was sleeping on the couch, she would be the first she awoke. She was dying to tell someone what a good time she had in Houston.

The second she closed the door behind her, she was looking at two sets of eyes. Casci was sitting on the couch, smoking a blunt, and Chris was sitting across from her.

She smiled at her friend. "Hey, y'all. What y'all doing up so early?" She watched Chris stand and walk toward her.

"Where in the hell you been, fat ass woman?"

"Um, excuse me?" Ariel looked at him with wide eyes. She pushed past him and went to hug Casci.

"Ya man talking to you." Casci nodded toward Chris and smiled.

"Anyway. Bitch, we got to go to Houston," she told her, totally ignoring both Chris and Casci's statements.

"Why? What's in Houston?"

"Girl, them niggas balling down there. Money everywhere, and the boutiques got some nice shit." Ariel began pulling clothes out of the bags she had.

"You can't call and let motherfuckers know you alright?" Chris now stood over her.

She pushed his middle and shoved him with her hands. That was when she noticed the guns laying on the table, along with clips and boxes of bullets. She looked from Casci back to him.

"She asked me to, so that's what I did."

"You know she just got out the pen, Chris. What the fuck's wrong with you, nigga?" Ariel stood and looked up at him—her expression serious.

"*She* asked me to do the shit, so don't be going off on me," Chris defended himself.

"She asked you? If she asked you to suck a nigga dick, you gonna do that, too?"

Chris raised his hands but stopped himself. He suddenly glared at her. "Bitch, I almost slapped the shit out of you."

Reniya stepped out of her room just as Chris raised his hand, the .380 Casci gave her a week ago in her grasp. She pat the side of her thigh with it. "Chris, don't make us spread no plastic on this floor."

Casci looked on in amazement. She'd never seen Chris so upset that he'd threaten to hit a woman. She loaded the clip into the Glock she'd set on the table and cocked it. They all looked at him with various expressions.

The room went silent.

Chris threw his hands up and closed his eyes. "My bad, y'all. I'm tripping."

"Yes, you are," Reniya agreed.

Seeing things not about to work out in his favor, Chris headed for the door.

"Hey, hey!"

He turned to face Casci.

"Don't you owe me something?" she asked with a smile on her face.

For the first time in years, Chris was able to reach down in his pocket and pull out a wad of cash. He peeled off $1,000 and handed it to her.

"Really?" Reniya asked, seeing the amount he'd just given Casci. "Break bread, nigga."

"Um, don't you owe me like a hundred dollars?" Ariel asked also.

He looked at them incredulously.

"Y'all was just about to kill me, and now y'all taking all my money," he complained.

"Before or after, it's the same shit," Reniya said.

Once he'd handed them the cash he owed, he walked out and closed the door behind him.

Ariel went to lock it. She faced Casci and said, "Did that just happen?"

"Damn near," Reniya added.

"I'm talking about him checking me when I walked through this door?"

"You know that nigga love you, Ariel," Casci chimed.

"That wasn't love," was her response.

"Damn sure ain't," Reniya told them before walking back into her room.

Once Ariel was alone with Casci, she told her, "It was that nigga Peanut who killed Black."

"How you know?"

"I heard Stacy and some niggas talking. They even told him where Peanut was hiding out."

Ariel told Casci all she'd heard and everything Stacy had told her concerning the matter. She intentionally stayed at the motel with Stacy to see if he and Doom were really hustling, and to her surprise, she'd witnessed them count the most money she'd seen in her life. They'd pulled money from the spots they hustled out of, fearing that J-Rod and Peanut would have them robbed.

49

"And the nigga J-Rod done started scoring work from somebody other than Stacy. They said he outgrew them. So whoever J-rod scoring from got to have some major bread," she told her, knowing how Casci got down.

Casci nodded her understanding with a totally different insight. Ariel was giving her all she needed when it came to the play she and Chris had been thinking about running. Casci wanted their first lick to be enough for Chris to want to do the shit again. Once the pistols were pulled, there was no turning back.

"So J-Rod sitting on a grip, huh?" Casci asked, thinking he'd be the first nigga they robbed.

"That's what they said."

***

Stacy and Doom were at the Big T Blazer, waiting for one of their regulars, when they spotted J-Rod's silver BMW in the service center. Stacy looked around to see if he could find him. They'd already gotten word that his cousin, Peanut, was the shooter behind Black's death, and they were looking for him. While in Houston with Ariel, he met with another connect that promised a cheaper price for the drugs he wanted to purchase. The quality of the drug was the reason they made the three-hour drive.

He and Doom stood by the jewelry counter. They didn't want to be seen before they saw J-Rod or his cousin.

"You think that nigga Peanut here with him?"

"I doubt it. J-Rod gonna play it like he didn't know what his cousin was going to do," Stacy responded.

"Let's follow that nigga and see where he going." Doom wanted to kill J-Rod wherever he crossed him.

"Let's see how this shit unfolds first. We might be able to grab a little paper in the process."

"Man, fuck that money. I want to smoke both of they asses."

Stacy didn't respond. He only nodded toward the guy they were waiting for. "Let's roll."

"That nigga J-rod mines, homie. I promise you that."

While walking toward the exit of the building, the trio passed a pizzeria, which was when Stacy saw why J-Rod no longer bought drugs from hm. Alex was his new supplier. Being that this wasn't the first time either of them had crossed him, the thought of killing two birds with one bullet seemed a little bit better than killing one with no less than fifty rounds.

"Let's make this quick. I have some more shit to do," he told the guy he was about to sell two and a half kilos to.

***

Detrick stopped when he saw Chris sitting on the hood of his car and lowered the widow. "Look out, Chris. Is Casci around?"

Chris looked up toward the door he'd just walked out of and nodded. "Yeah, she's up there."

He watched Detrick park and climb out. He wanted to question him about Marcus, but Casci had already told him that niggas saw him as an outsider, and that was the way she wanted to keep it.

"Them other hoes up there, too?" Detrick asked, just before he hit the stairs.

"Yep. The only one I didn't see was Coffee."

"Damn, I was hoping to see her this morning." He continued up the steps.

Detrick stopped just short of their door. He hadn't been there in forever, and memories of the last time he'd knocked on their door found him. Casci was on lock, and he was trying to get at Coffee.

It was after Reniya opened the door that he saw his old friend inside, sitting in the living room, laughing with Coffee. Not only did his old friend know he liked her, he always acted as if he couldn't stand her.

"Gold digging ass bitch ain't got shit coming, fucking with me," his friend used to say when speaking of her.

He inhaled, closed his eyes, and brushed his clothes off. He opened his eyes and knocked three times. He always liked seeing Coffee.

Instead of hearing the usual greeting voices from behind the door, it swung open, and Ariel was standing there, looking at him with one hand on her hip and the other on the door.

"Oh, I thought you was Chris," she expressed before giving him a warm smile.

"Glad I'm not him then, huh?"

"Yeah, it ain't a good time to be Chris right now. Come on in." She stepped aside.

Detrick nodded, seeing Casci sitting in the living room. He looked around for Coffee.

"What brings you to the Gardens?" Ariel asked, after looking to make sure no one else was coming up the stairs.

"I'm just doing a few favors, is all," he responded, before sitting across from Casci. He looked around the apartment in awe.

Their low-income apartment looked like a display straight out of an IKEA catalog. The leather and suede couch and love seat, the huge throw rug in the center of the room, the smoked glass tables, the African art, the wall to wall entertainment center, and the 110-inch smart TV impressed the hell out of him.

"Well, you tell him to keep it because she don't need it, and she don't want it," Ariel went on.

"That nigga don't give shit away for free," Coffee said from the hallway.

Detrick turned, saw the T-shirt she wore, and smiled. "There you are."

"Marcus is a roach ass, snitch ass nigga," Reniya spat.

Casci stood, stretched, and told him, "Come on, Detrick. You know how bitches get when they wake and it ain't no dick to suck."

"Hell, I'm sure we can fix that," he said, looking dead a Coffee.

"Give me a thousand dollars. My room right back there," she retorted, with a smile of her own.

Detrick went into his pocket and pulled out the $3,500 he had on him. He held it up.

"For all of that, we'll both suck that motherfucker," Reniya added.

Casci grabbed his arms and pulled him toward the door. "Maybe next time, bitches. He came to see me today."

"Next time, Coffee. Next time," he managed to say before Casci closed the door behind them.

Chris only nodded at Casci when she climbed into the car with Detrick.

She nodded back.

"I don't see how you do it, Casci, waking up to all that pussy." Detrick stared out through the windshield in thought.

"Them my sisters. Now if it was some other bitches, I might feel some type of way."

Detrick smiled to himself. He shook his head and told her, "They damn near got all my money."

Casci laughed. "It's free money, right?"

Nicole Goosby

Chapter Six

After leaving Alex Minez's home, Marcus headed to the smoke shop to oversee the renovation. They were behind schedule as it was, and for him to pull up and see that nothing had been done, he went off on the contractor.

"My shit supposed to have been ready by now. What the fuck am I paying you for?" Marcus walked from the rear office to where the ceiling-to-wall glass enclosure should've been erected.

"The materials you ordered were all wrong, and we had to send them back," the contractor explained.

"The longer this motherfucker stay closed, the more money I'm missing out on."

Marcus stood by the wall in thought. The contractor was explaining something, but his mind was on Casci. He wanted to go by the Gardens but remembered the girls' threats to ruin him. With Detrick being short with the answers to the questions he asked about Casci and the rest of the girls, he didn't know if it was a good idea or not. Regardless of what happened in the past, he wanted to see her.

"Um, what were you saying now?" Marcus asked, seeing the guy's mouth still moving.

"I said, we should be ready to roll by the end of the week."

"Okay, well, make the shit happen as soon as possible."

Marcus climbed into his car and sat there. Just a week ago, he had everything mapped out to the *T*. He knew what needed to be done the moment he woke up, and nothing and no one kept him from his grind. Now that Casci was out, he'd given away more money than he'd spent in a month, missed more than a couple big licks, and was confiding in Detrick to do what he should've been able to do. There had to be a way to get Casci to see that he was sorry for the mistakes he made and the pains he caused her.

***

Despite telling Marcus that he was giving Casci too much, Detrick took her to the mall and dropped an additional $2,200 on her. He was no stranger to taking broads on shopping sprees, but with Casci, it was something he was a part of instead of just standing at the counter, waiting for the girl to complete her spree.

"Those look good on you, Casci," he complimented, pointing at the cork-soled booties she tried on.

"Nigga, I have enough of them as it."

"Well, then, get those lace-up boots you just had."

Casci had heard Coffee talk so much about the trick Detrick was that she had to try him. She had to see what he'd do if tested.

"How many times am I going to have to give you the pussy now?" Detrick laughed.

"You buying me all this shit, spending the day with me, and feeding me. I know I owe you something," she continued.

"Tell me what's up with you and that nigga. That's what you can do."

Casci thought for a second, shook her head, and said, "He was supposed to help the girls with a lawyer. That nigga reneged."

"Reniya and Coffee make it sound like it's some more shit that happened between y'all."

"Yeah, they're not so forgiving, and they damn sure ain't gonna forget." Casci walked through the boutique with Detrick following close behind.

"That nigga making some moves, Casci, and I really think he wants you to be a part of it. He's even putting my money aside, trying to make sure he sends you something."

Detrick grabbed her hand, causing Casci to turn and face him.

"I respect what you're doing, but I know it's more, and you're right, it ain't my business. But don't leave me in the dark if it's something salty about that nigga, Casci. Yeah, we've done good business in the past, but I don't want to put too much trust in a situation that's liable turn on me at any time."

"Oh, you don't have to worry about no shit like that. You good." The thought did cross Casci's mind, but she knew Marcus wouldn't make the same mistake twice. That wasn't something he was known for.

"How about we swing through that nigga's spot after we're done here?" Detrick checked the time on his watch.

Casci tried reading him as best as she could. Them wanting to get her all the way out of pocket so they could kill or have her killed was something *she* would've done. She and Detrick weren't the best of friends, but here he was doing what besties did. There was no way she was going to Marcus' without a strap. They weren't going to get her like that.

"Nah, I'm going to get myself together first. Give me a week or so. We'll make a day of it then." She smiled.

Detrick understood.

"You know I haven't fucked nothing since I've been out, right?" Casci gave him a mischievous grin. She wanted to see just how far he'd go to continue his front. That was, if it was one.

"I'm pretty sure we can find you something to play with. Let me take you to the strip club tonight. I know just the place."

"Sounds like a date." Casci nodded. She was hoping the girls had something to do other than babysit her tonight.

***

Ariel was telling Reniya and Coffee about her time spent in Houston and all the possibilities she ran across; the many new boutiques, shoe shops, and jewelry stores she and Stacy visited. There was plenty of money to be made and plenty of ways to make it.

"We can use a lick like that," Coffee stated, when hearing about the room filled with ballers.

"We get a couple of them niggas on that syrup and burn they ass," Reniya added.

"And all them niggas had some heavy ass jewelry," Ariel said, knowing she was wiring them all the way up.

"We got to get rid of some of the shit we got here so we'll have a couple dollars to throw away when we get there." Coffee stood, hearing the knocking on the door.

Reniya thought about the fact that Stacy had pulled money from his other spots in fear that J-Rod would have his spot hit and robbed. She thought about the money she knew he had to have, and after hearing Ariel brag about seeing them with a shit load of money, she knew that was also a nice lick. All she needed now was to get Stacy and Doom away from the motel.

"Who is it?" Coffee yelled from the kitchen.

She swung the door open, saw Chris standing there, and looked at him sideways.

"What y'all in here doing?" He pushed past Coffee, walked into the kitchen, and opened the refrigerator's door.

"Stray ass nigga, ain't you supposed to be at work or something?" Coffee asked, after shutting the door behind him and snatching the pitcher of Kool-Aid from his hand.

"I want y'all to know, I called the cops and told them I just got robbed."

"Black ass nigga, you probably did," Reniya spat.

"Nah, I'm just bull shitting. I owe y'all an apology." He looked from Coffee to Reniya and walked over to where Ariel sat. He got down on one knee.

"Nigga, don't come in her with no shit you seen on one of them weak ass movies," Ariel stated.

"You do something to me, Ariel. You got a nigga fighting niggas behind you, over you, and for you. All I do is for you, and you know that."

"Serve that hoe, Chris." Coffee walked around to where she could see them better.

"I'm serious, y'all. I did some foul shit earlier, and that ain't me at all. Y'all know me." Chris reached for Ariel's hand and held it in his.

"Boy, get your black ass up. I'm broke, so this little performance you got going on ain't gonna get you paid." Ariel smiled.

"You know you're perfect from your head to your heels, don't you?" Chris questioned with as much sincerity as he could muster.

"Nigga, that's Bruno Mars." Reniya and Coffee began singing the song in unison.

"Can I do this, y'all? Damn."

"I wish a nigga would sing to me." Reniya snapped her fingers and reached for the remote. "Hold on. Let me find that song right quick."

"Gone ahead and give that nigga a chance, Ariel. He deserve it." Coffee smiled at the two of them.

"Chris, take your ass home before Stacy pull up and see you over here." Ariel crossed her legs at the knees and folded her arms across her chest. She swung her feet back and forth.

"Fuck that nigga. If that nigga pull up, he'll—"

"Kick your ass. Like he do all the time," Reniya said, cutting him off.

"I kicked his ass the last time, though." Chris sat beside Ariel and leaned into her.

"Move, boy!"

"Give me a kiss, and I'll leave you alone."

"One of those shoes gonna kiss your ass, Chris. Now move." Ariel laughed at his antics.

"One kiss. I'm not going to tell that nigga."

Coffee shook her head. "Don't do it, girl. One kiss gonna lead to another. And before you know it, ya ass in the air, and he gonna be slapping that motherfucker while you bucking on his shit."

"Shut up, Coffee, with your freaky ass." Chris frowned.

"One kiss, and you take your ass home?" Ariel asked.

"One kiss, and I take my ass home," Chris agreed.

Ariel smiled, closed her eyes, and puckered up her lips. She waited.

"What the hell is that?" Chris asked.

"You said one kiss, nigga."

"I'm talking about a real kiss. I want some tongue, a couple moans, and I gotta squeeze that ass."

"Nigga, get out! Get your black ass out!" Ariel stood up, pulling him by the arm. Once he stood, she pushed him toward the door.

"You gotta crawl before you walk, Chris," Reniya told him just before Ariel closed the door behind him.

"A nigga will fuck up a wet dream, wake up, and fuck up his chances with the pussy next to him." Coffee laughed.

Ariel walked back to where she was sitting. She told them, "If only that nigga had some money. I would've been gave that nigga some pussy."

"Hell, if he had some money, *I* would've been let him fuck, too," Coffee added.

They both laughed.

Chapter Seven

Later that night, Casci, Detrick, and Coffee pulled into the parking lot of the Butterflies Strip Club in the Chrysler she was given, and Ariel and Reniya followed in her Charger. It was a nonnegotiable agreement. Casci would accompany Detrick to the new strip club, and the girls would make sure she didn't get caught up in the bullshit that came with it.

Reniya wore a form-fitting shirt that tied low on the left side, some black leggings, and a pair of platform heels. Ariel slid into a pair of jeans that complemented her every curve, a sleeveless blouse, and sandals. Casci opted for a pair of loose-fitting sweat pants, a cropped shirt to show off her stomach, and a pair of Air Max tennis shoes. Coffee brought up the rear in a tan dress that hugged her curves, brown booties, and donned a blonde and black shoulder length wig. The half-inch lashes she wore made her already chink eyes look closed.

Detrick complimented her with each look, and made it known that he was the reason she looked so good. He'd spent so much money on her that he felt entitled when it came to who she'd entertained at the end of the night.

"Don't go in here starting no shit, y'all," Reniya told the group, once they'd exited the cars and were walking toward the doors of the club.

"We ain't tripping on no shit like that. We're just here to make sure Casci don't get into anything," Ariel replied. She threw her arm around Casci and kissed her cheek.

"I'm coming to see what these hoes got going, and to make sure Detrick don't spend too much of my money," Coffee stated, while applying a coat of glitter-n-gloss to her full lips.

Casci slapped Reniya's ass and said, "We here to see some pussy, squeeze some ass, and maybe get my pussy ate."

"Nasty ass!" Coffee laughed. "Prison fucked you all the way up, girl."

The inside of the club offered dimly lit sections, booths, and a lounge. The private entertainment rooms were on the second floor—several elevated platforms had both single dancers and couples doing the wind and grind. Two stages were in the center of the room, and the music blasted from huge well-mounted speakers strategically placed around the club.

Coffee nodded her approval with the set up. Once again, they chose a booth not too far from the second stage. "I like this here," she told them as she slid to the center of the booth.

"How'd you know about this spot, Detrick?" Reniya asked.

"Some girls I knew was talking about it," he answered. Detrick sat on the end and waved over a dark-complected waitress wearing a skirt so short her ass cheeks could be seen.

Coffee watched him with twisted lips and rolled her eyes.

"I'm serious. I heard some girls talking about it while I was at one of the spots," he defended himself.

"Let me find out you tricking with some of these nasty ass hoes, nigga. I promise you I ain't sucking your dick no more," Coffee replied.

"Look, y'all. Look." Reniya pointed to a tall light-complected chick in a net body suit. "That bitch is bad."

"Call her, Detrick. Call her over here." Coffee bounced when seeing the goddess of a woman walk past their section. "I'll bet y'all she from the islands or something."

Casci bit her bottom lip, seeing the stallion of a woman with a long, braided pony.

"Um, bring us three bottles of that Ace of Spades, two bottles of that GTV, and a bottle of Cîroc. And let ole girl in the fishnets know we trying to spend some money," Detrick told the waitress. He turned back to Coffee and added, "She bad, but she ain't got nothing on you."

"Nigga, please." Ariel shook her head and said, "Look how long and thick that bitch's legs are. Umph."

Casci smiled, seeing the woman walk in their direction. She sized her up with her eyes, and nodded. She definitely approved. All that mattered now was if she kept good hygiene.

"Eh, mon. How you do tonight?" the woman greeted with a Jamaican accent.

"I told y'all, bitch," Coffee said excitedly.

"How about you give my girl a lap dance later?" Detrick nodded toward Casci. "How much?"

"Sixty dollar," she said with a smile of her own. She looked at Casci with raised brows.

"Nigga, I want a lap dance, too," Coffee chimed.

"Fuck all that. How much for some of that island head? My girl wants to feel some of that Jamaican fire," Reniya went off.

"Don't pay her no mind," Ariel told her with the wave of her hand.

"No worry. I give your friend fire for fifty."

"Ouu, and the head cheap." Reniya beamed. She pulled a fifty-dollar bill from her clutch and handed it to her.

Once it was agreed that she'd take Casci to a private room later, the bottles arrived, and Ariel was the first to de-cork the black one. Casci had already fired up a blunt of Mango Kush, and they were all feeling themselves.

As soon as the tunes of the City Girls number one hit came over the speakers, Reniya threw her hands in the air and began singing along with the lyrics.

"Eight inch, big dick. That's my type. That's my type…"

Ariel poured herself a glass of the liquor and passed the bottle to Casci. She nodded. "And look at this ashy ass bitch in the green thongs. That don't make no sense."

"She might've just got out of the shower, Ariel."

"Her broke ass might not have no lotion or baby oil," Ariel responded.

Casci laughed, seeing Detrick act as if the scantily clad women weren't fazing him. He subtly eyed them when they passed and only looked their way when he was sure Coffee was looking elsewhere. He was supposed to be her escort, not Coffee's prisoner.

"Relax, nigga. That bitch ain't going to trip with you. You here with me," Casci told him.

"I'm good, Casci. I just want you to have a good time." He looked over at Coffee.

Ariel set her drink down and shook her head, seeing a short, slim chick drop into a split on stage. "She know she wrong. That bitch's toes hanging all over her heels, and them stockings she got on got all them holes in them. These some low-budget hoes in here."

"Ariel, these hoes at work," Casci countered. "They know niggas don't give a damn about the shit they got on."

"Well, they should. Niggas ain't going to spend no money on no raggedy ass woman," she shot back.

Reniya huffed. "You must don't know a nigga named Stacy, then. Because all that nigga do is fuck with them stanky hoes."

"Whatever."

"Now that don't make no damn sense right there." Coffee pointed to a plus-sized woman with saggy titties. Gold and black pasties covered her nipples.

"Big girls need love, too. And if you don't change the shit you be eating, your ass is going to hanging a little lower than it is now, too," Casci declared.

"I'll do cosmetic surgery first. I'll spend that eight thousand dollars."

Ariel was looking toward the DJ booth when she saw the dark, handsome brother smile and nod at her. She waved back. "Who is that?" she asked the girls. "I ain't never seen him before."

"Must be a new DJ or something because I ain't never seen him either," Coffee told her.

Reniya was the one who caught the stares of the women from three tables over. They were talking amongst themselves, and by the way they were mean-mugging, they were either dykes or haters. Either way, she put her girls up on game.

"By the way, them hoes over there looking at us. He might belong to one of them, or they want him, too."

"Who?" Coffee looked to where Reniya nodded.

"Reniya, don't pay them hoes no attention." Casci shook her head.

"As long as they talk that shit over there, we good." Reniya reached for the blunt Ariel fired up and continued bobbing to the beat blasting around them.

Casci looked toward the stage for the amazon she anticipated being entertained by later. She couldn't wait to taste her.

"Look at you, with your nasty ass," Coffee said, following Casci's eyes.

***

Reniya and Casci had taken seats in the lounge area for the lap dances they had coming.

Reniya held $200 in $1 bills in one hand and a bottle of Cîroc in the other. She pointed at the short, thick stripper. "Take that shit off, bitch!"

"Turn around so we can see that ass," Casci told her. With the ass so close to her face, Casci spanked the woman, grabbed her ass with both hands, and started pulling her down into her lap.

Detrick stood over the woman and showered her with bills. He smiled, seeing the girls enjoying themselves. Marcus had told him bits and pieces about the girls, but it was nothing like he was witnessing now. Detrick had seen all of them in and outside the clubs, parties, and different events, but he'd never seen them in this light. They were some freaks for real, and they knew how to have a good time. He looked back to where Coffee sat, and she was knocking back drink after drink. He was more than sure she'd be the one he left with, when the time came.

"Shake that ass, bitch! Shake that ass, hoe," Reniya sang along with the song playing.

Casci slid a handful of bills into the thong the chick was wearing and kissed her ass cheek. "Where'd that tall Jamaican chick go?" she asked her.

"You talking about Melody?" the stripper asked her.

"Yeah. The tall, yellow bitch, who was walking through here earlier."

As soon as the thick chick went to find the stallion of a woman called Melody, Ariel walked up and sat on Casci's lap, the drink she was holding was damn near empty. She was drunk as hell.

"How do you fuck a bitch, Casci? I want to fuck one of these hoes." Her words slurred.

"Girl, sit your drunk ass down somewhere," Reniya told her, and pushed her out of Casci's lap.

Casci watched as the woman from earlier approached them. She was bigger than all of them, and it was evident she was bringing an attitude with her.

"Um, you need to at least say excuse me when you bump into a bitch," she told Ariel with contempt.

"Ex-excuse me. You talking to me?" Ariel asked with her eyes closed.

"Yeah, bitch, I'm talking to you."

Reniya leaned forward, held her hand toward the woman, and told her, "My apologies. She's not too good when she's drunk."

"Well, y'all need to keep the bitch on a leash before she get her ass beat."

Casci rolled her eyes upward. It was apparent this confrontation was more about her being jealous of Ariel *and* the fact that the guy she and her friends were eyeing was looking at her.

"We got her. That's our bad," Casci told her.

"Casci, fuck that bitch. Big ass bitch mad 'cause she ain't getting pulled up on." Ariel set her bottle down and slid her hand into the pocket of her jeans.

"I got your bitch, bitch."

"Hey, hey. You need to take your big ass back over there," Detrick told her before stepping between her and Ariel.

"Nah, move, Detrick. Let me look at this bitch," Ariel spat.

Reniya stood also. "Sweetheart, don't get drug up in this bitch."

Before Detrick could stop her, Ariel came out of her pocket with a razor, and she slashed the big woman's face from her ear down the side of her face, while Reniya smashed the Cîroc bottle on the other side of her face.

Realizing that she'd been attacked, the big woman yelled. She tried in vain to close the gap on the side of her face to keep the blood from pouring out.

"I told you, our bad, bitch!" Casci stood, kicked the woman in the stomach, and looked toward the table where her friends sat. They all looked on in horror as their friend got jumped.

"Fat ass bitch don't know who the fuck she fucking with," Reniya grabbed a handful of the woman's hair and literally yanked a bundle from her head.

Seeing things unfold faster than he expected, Detrick grabbed Ariel's hand, took the razor from her, and stuffed it in his pocket. He then pulled Reniya off the woman. "Let's go, y'all."

"What them other hoes talking about?" Coffee asked with an upturned GTV bottle in her hand.

Once they were outside the club, Casci turned to Detrick and smiled. "Hoes don't know how to act when they get together, huh?"

"And we didn't even get you that private session with that Jamaican hoe," Coffee added.

"We'll just have to catch up with that bitch later. I can't be here when the cops roll up."

Casci, Coffee, and Detrick climbed into her Chrysler and pulled out of the lot.

"Did y'all see which way Reniya and Ariel went?" Casci asked. Knowing them, they weren't satisfied with the outcome of the altercation.

Reniya was wanting to get at least one of the big woman's friends, and Ariel wasn't done cutting her big ass up.

Casci thought about the fact that the group of women had been eyeing them since the moment they walked into the strip club. She thought about the fact that the only person who knew where they were headed was Detrick, and it could've been him who gave Marcus the heads up. Marcus could've easily had those women waiting for them to arrive. To where she felt Detrick should've wanted to see them drag a bitch, he was trying to keep her from getting cut up.

Casci looked in her rearview mirror at him. If Marcus was using him to set her and the girls up, she wasn't tripping. But if it just so happened that he had nothing to do with it, she wasn't going to bring it to anyone's attention. They'd deal with whatever and whoever came after them.

"Now we got some hoes to look out for, Casci," Coffee told her, thinking things through herself.

"Yeah. It ain't shit. Next time we cross paths, we're gonna just have to see what they talking about," Casci agreed. "All they got to do is step into the water."

"Sorry you had to see that shit, Detrick. I know you thinking the worst of us, but we really are good girls," Coffee told him innocently.

"Y'all some treacherous motherfuckers. Pretty and treacherous. That's what y'all are."

***

Reniya and Ariel pulled to the light and stopped. They'd stayed back a bit to see who all was associated with the women they'd got into it with just minutes ago.

Ariel nodded when seeing Trish walk over to the car that was parked near the rear of the lot. "I'm going to rock that bitch the next time I see her," she promised.

"I, at first, thought Marcus had something to do with that shit. But come to find out, Trish got a little crew from somewhere to come fuck with you. They didn't know you had piranhas in the tank." Reniya laughed. They watched as the paramedics loaded the big woman into the ambulance and sped off.

"I tried to cut that bitch's throat," Ariel told her.

"Next time, bitch. Next time."

Reniya lowered her window and frowned at the guy flagging them down. She looked the huge truck over, saw that he was driving money, and asked him, "What's up, baller?"

"Where y'all headed? What y'all trying to get into?"

Reniya looked at Ariel and smiled.

"Do what you do, bitch." Ariel was down.

Reniya turned back toward the guy and asked, "Where you from, nigga? I haven't seen you around before."

"Me and my niggas came up from Houston. We got a room at the Red Roof Inn."

"Well, me and my girl on our way to our room, and we could use a little company. It's her birthday, and I'm trying to show her a good time," Reniya lied.

"Well, what's up?"

"We're going to have to pass because we ain't trying to do the crowd thing tonight, if you know what I mean." Reniya winked at him.

"Um, let me come alone, then. I got money." He help up a stack of bills.

Ariel and Reniya looked from one to the other as if debating whether or not he was worth their time. That was all they needed to see, but they still chose to play the game.

"Aww, come on, ladies. It'll be fun," he yelled from the passenger's window.

"Follow us, then. Let's see what you talking about." Reniya raised her window, hit her blinker, and headed for the ramp. Since he was dying to give his money away, she was going to make sure they got paid.

Knowing the game that was about to be played, Ariel called her friend at the Travel Lodge Hotel, booked a room for the night, and made sure she had enough Visine to drop a horse. He'd be lucky if he saw some pussy tonight.

Chapter Eight

Marcus was awakened by the sound of his vibrating phone. Seeing that he'd missed a couple important calls, at least two from Detrick, he groggily rolled out of bed. He thought about the contractor's promise to have things back rolling. He couldn't wait to open the smoke shop. He'd already purchased over fifty types of tobacco, had cigars imported, smoking paraphernalia delivered, and was looking forward to the twenty pounds of Strawberry and Mango Kush he was about to push out of the shop. He'd been spending money at every turn, and having projected the estimated profit, he was anxious.

He made his way to his kitchen, debated what he wanted for breakfast, and decided to eat out. He dialed Detrick's number. Not only was it time to give him what he'd been waiting on, but Marcus wanted to hear about the night's events with the girls. His plan was to bump into Casci and them at the strip club, feign surprise, and go from there. But he'd gotten so caught up in his business transactions that time slipped by, and once he made it home, the much needed sleep took over him.

Detrick answered on the second ring. "What's up, bro? I just called you about twenty minutes ago."

Marcus pressed the speaker button, walked to his cabinet, and pulled a glass from the shelf. "Yeah. Matter of fact, you woke me up. How'd things go with the girls last night?"

"Yo, Marcus. Them hoes wild, man. I kick it with Coffee every once in a while, but I never saw her like I did last night."

Marcus smiled to himself. "Yeah?"

"Nigga, them hoes shut the spot down. Literally."

Marcus, at first, thought about the way each of them were known to dress. Provocative and sexy outfits were expected of Reniya, Coffee, and Ariel, at times. But he knew Casci would have to be begged into one of the outfits they were known for. He told him, "Yeah, I can only imagine what Reniya and Coffee wore."

"Nah, it ain't about what they had on, bro. Them hoes damn near killed a bitch in there."

"What?" Marcus's forehead creased, concern etched across his face. "Are they alright?"

"Yeah, they cool, but the hoe Ariel cut up had to be rushed to the hospital."

"Damn. I knew I should've went. I wouldn't have let that shit go down. Where were you?"

"Hell, I was standing right there. Before I knew what happened, words were exchanged, and that bitch Ariel came out her pocket with a razor and cut the other bitch face wide open. I did stop her from killing her, though."

"Who was the other bitch that got cut?"

"Hell if I know. They had to have been out-of-towners."

Marcus walked from his kitchen to his den area and snatched up the remote. The last thing Casci needed was to get caught up in some shit like that. "Casci wasn't in the shit, was she?"

"Like hell. She got up and kicked the shit out the bitch. More than once, I think."

"Fuck!"

Marcus thought back to the time he and the girls were at the movies, and he had words with a couple guys from across town. His attempts to dissolve the problem they had with him was seen as weakness. That led to him having to defend himself *and* the girls because they'd began shouting expletives themselves.

One of the guys slapped Casci, and before Marcus knew it, Reniya pulled a box cutter from her pocket and damn near slit the guy's throat. Punches were thrown, and shots rang out. When the smoke cleared and they were pulling out of the parking lot, one guy was shot multiple times, and Casci was the shooter. If nothing else, Marcus knew when one fought, they all ended up in the melee.

"And someone recorded the shit because it's all on YouTube already."

"Hey, um—meet me at the Waffle House in an hour. Let's take care of this issue."

Marcus ended the call and thought to himself. He had to get her away from the rest of the girls if they were going to talk and possibly bury the hatchet. They were short fuses, and all *one* of them needed to do was spark, and they'd all be set on fire. He'd have Detrick to set up a meeting. It was time to see if there was still any love between them.

***

Reniya and Ariel walked into the apartment at 10:40 that next morning, laughing and talking loudly. It was evident they were still high and tipsy.

Casci yanked the covers from over her head, thinking something was wrong. She'd been on the couch asleep, waiting on both of them. The calls went unanswered, when trying to reach them, and she was beginning to think they'd spent the night in jail.

Before she could question the two, Reniya flopped down on the couch next to her and began pulling off her shoes. Casci threw the covers back over her head.

"Rise and grind, bitch." Reniya pulled at the covers Casci was under.

"Reniya, I'm sleep." Casci's voice was muffled.

"Girl, we got to tell you about the shit we just went through," Ariel yelled from the kitchen.

"Can it wait?" Casci vainly held herself under the piece of cover Reniya hadn't pulled off her.

"That shit was crazy, huh?" Reniya looked back at Ariel and shook her head.

"But lucrative." Ariel laughed.

She held up a stack of bills and twisted them in her hand. Hearing all the commotion, Coffee walked into the living room in her panties and bra—a blue and gold scarf around her head. "Where the hell y'all bitches been?" she asked, seeing that it was damn near eleven o'clock in the morning. She walked to where Reniya wrestled with the cover Casci was under, looked from her to Ariel, and placed her hands on her hips. She smiled.

"Bitch, you should've been there. We met this nigga at the light, and—" Reniya began.

Ariel cut her off. "Cute nigga, nice truck, mind you."

"Anyway. The nigga pulled up on us, talking this and that, and waved a bunch of money at a bitch." Reniya continued.

Ariel raised the stack of cash she had again.

"What, y'all robbed his ass?" Coffee asked.

Hearing that, Casci came from under the covers and looked toward Ariel. She knew that wasn't her cup of tea.

Reniya continued. "Didn't have to. The nigga followed us to the Travel Lodge, got in the room, and turned straight bitch on us. I was planning on drugging his ass, tying him up, and leaving his trick ass for room service, but the nigga just wanted to pay us to fuck him."

"He was once of them fetish freaks," Ariel told them.

"Yeah. He begged Ariel to piss on him. Paid her two hundred dollars just to do that."

"That ain't shit. Tell 'em girl." Ariel walked from the kitchen and sat across from Reniya and Casci. She began checking her phone, inbox, and Facebook accounts.

"I told the nigga it was Ariel's birthday, and I wanted to do a little something for her. This nigga had a bag with all kinds of shit in it. He had his very own dildo and everything. He paid us to feel on each other while he sat in the chair and jacked his dick."

Ariel stood, held her hands a couple feet apart, and said, "And this nigga's shit was looooonnnng."

"I fucked him with a nine-inch dildo, and Ariel spanked his ass."

"Fuck y'all. You hoes lying y'all asses off," Casci told them.

"Where the hell you think we got all this money?" She then pulled a stack of bills from her clutch.

"Who was this nigga?" Coffee asked, eyeing the money they had.

"That's the tripped out part. He plays basketball for the Rockets now. The nigga got plenty of money, and he don't mind spending it on the shit he likes."

"Oh, don't worry. We told him we had friends who liked that fetish shit, and he can't wait to meet y'all." Ariel laughed.

"Y'all fucked a faggot?" Casci shook her head and tried to cover her herself a third time.

"It was just his fetish. The nigga was fine as hell, but his dick was too big. Other than that, he was straight as hell."

"Did he fuck?" Coffee frowned. She hated guys with big dicks. They did nothing for her.

"I mean, he jacked off—" Reniya began.

"That bitch lying. She sucked that nigga dick," Ariel told them.

"You nasty, bitch." Coffee shook her head in disgust.

"That don't make no sense, Reniya. Damn, bitch."

"Girl, I just had to see if I could swallow that motherfucker, but he paid a bitch five hundred dollars to try."

"Did you swallow the dick, or what?" Coffee probed.

"Bitch, I just told you I tried. I swallowed most of it, though."

"Y'all some nasty, trifling bitches. Y'all didn't even know that man." Casci pushed Reniya away with her feet.

"Well, these nasty bitches got paid for it," Reniya told them mater-of-factly.

"You fucked the nigga with a nine-inch dildo?" Coffee inquired, trying to visualize the event.

"I tried to stuff that motherfucker in his ass, too."

"I mean, what was he doing? Was he—"

"Bitch, he wasn't doing shit but taking that motherfucker and screaming for Ariel to spank his ass harder. Don't worry, we going to Houston real soon." Reniya nodded.

Coffee talked all that stuff about what she would and wouldn't do, but she was going to see. They were all going to see.

"Where's Detrick?" Ariel asked, realizing that Coffee was damn near naked.

"Um, home, I guess. Why?"

"I just thought he'd be the nigga you woke up to this morning, with all that touching and shit y'all was doing last night."

"That was all for the money, bitch. Don't play." Coffee snapped her fingers over her head and walked back to her room.

"Girl, guess what?" Ariel began.

"What, Ariel?" Casci peeped at her, hoping there wasn't more.

"We saw that bitch, Trish, talking to them hoes last night. We think she was the one who sent that bitch to fuck with Ariel," Reniya replied, knowing what Ariel was about to tell Casci.

"Yeah, me and that bitch had words at the motel the other day," Ariel told them for the first time.

"And you just now telling us?"

"I wasn't thinking the bitch would do some shit like that. But fuck her. I'm going to take it to that bitch's ass the next time I see her. I promise you that." Ariel nodded. Her mind was made up.

Casci smirked, knowing Marcus didn't have a hand in the incident. The possibility she was wrong had been proven. She sat up on the couch and asked them, "What y'all think about Detrick? I like him."

"He cool, but I still don't trust his ass," Reniya replied.

"Time will tell. I can tell he ain't used to being around no bitches like us, though," Ariel responded.

"Why you say that?"

"Cause niggas who know us would've known it was going down the minute that bitch approached us. Chris and Marcus would've stopped her from doing even that."

"Now I got to see where the nigga stand when money is involved," Casci told them.

***

Chris was coming through the apartments collecting ends and giving out fronts when he saw Reniya's Charger. He smiled to himself, seeing Ariel. He checked his watch and figured they'd most likely spent the night at the motel with Stacy and one of his buddies. He loathed the idea. Just knowing she was with him irked the hell out of Chris. Stacy might have gotten the best of him in the past, but that was about to change. One way or another, he was going to make sure Stacy stayed away from his girl.

He climbed the stairs, and once he was standing at the door, he fired up the blunt filled with Mango Kush. He was hoping Casci was up by now. He knocked.

"Who is it?" It was Ariel's voice.

"The police!"

The door swung open, and an agitated Ariel stood on the other side of the threshold. "Nigga, don't be doing that shit."

"How's my baby doing this morning?" He leaned down to kiss her.

Ariel stepped back. "Nigga, it's too early in the morning for that."

Chris saw Casci sitting on the couch, walked past Ariel, and let himself in.

"What's up, my nigga?" He handed Casci the blunt. "Here, hit this shit."

"You up kind of early." Casci took the blunt and blew the lit end.

"Making rounds." Chris looked back toward Ariel and nodded.

"Why you didn't bring us nothing to eat, nigga?" Ariel asked him.

"Why your fat ass ain't cooked nothing? Oh, yeah—you been laying up under that nigga all night." He rolled his eyes.

"Sounds like somebody jealous, if you ask me," she shot back.

"And it sounds like a nigga didn't even feed you when he finished fucking."

"Whatever, nigga. For your information, I wasn't even with Stacy last night." She walked over, snatched the blunt before he could get it from Casci, and put it to her lips.

"I heard about the shit y'all did at Butterflies last night," he threw out.

74

"Oh, yeah?" Reniya asked with a smile on her face.

"That shit all on Facebook. Somebody posted the shit this morning— early at that."

"You see ya girl open that hoe up?" Reniya asked.

"Nah. They must've started recording the shit seconds afterward. It shows you hitting her in the face with a bottle and Casci kicking her."

"Then they missed the good part." Reniya shrugged.

"Y'all asses going to jail if that bitch press charges." Chris watched Ariel.

"What the fuck you looking at me like that for? Fuck that bitch," she spat.

"It was probably behind that wetback ass nigga you be running behind."

"Sorry, Charlie, but it didn't have shit—" Reniya caught herself. It had everything to do with Stacy and the hoes he fucked with behind her friend's back.

"You ain't even got to tell me. I already know what's up," he assured her.

Chris saw Ariel check her phone. She smiled before answering.

"Hey, babe. Where you at?" she asked Stacy, while looking at Chris. She pressed speaker so she could prove that she wasn't with him the night before.

"Up ere trapping. Why you ain't been answering yo' phone?"

Ariel didn't feel like explaining her night, or morning, for that matter. She knew he'd most likely seen the shit from Facebook, so she lied.

"I was drunk as hell when we got home from Butterflies and I took me a shower and passed out. I just woke up, not too long ago."

Chris shook his head. Stacy's voice alone pissed him off, and hearing Ariel having to explain herself only infuriated him more. He said, "You ain't got to lie to that nigga."

"What was that?" Stacy asked through the phone.

"Boy, that wasn't nobody but Chris. He over here smoking with Casci," she continued to explain. Ariel gave Chris an evil glare. It was too late for her to switch off the speaker phone because that would've definitely got her accused of something.

"Why that nigga always over there? Ain't that nigga got some burgers to flip or some fries to drop?"

Ariel laughed.

Chris had had enough. He snatched her phone up and spoke directly into the mic. "Nah, nigga, I got your girl to fuck. That's why I'm always over here." He pressed end and handed Ariel back her phone.

Both Casci and Reniya shook their heads.

Ariel looked on with her mouth wide open. She couldn't believe Chris had just done that. "Nigga, why you say some shit like that?"

"Man, fuck that nigga." Chris pulled from the blunt they were smoking and handed it back to Casci.

"And what I'm supposed to do when—"

The ringing of her phone silenced her. She pointed at Chris, mouthed the words 'shut up,' and answered. "Yeah, baby, I—"

"Where that nigga at, Ariel? Where that hoe ass, begging ass nigga at?"

Reniya and Casci dropped their heads.

"The place I was when you first called, wet ass nigga. In your girl's ass," Chris went on, despite her stern warning. He mouthed the words 'fuck him' to her.

"It's funny you don't be having shit to say to my face, playboy."

"Well, fuck you, faggot ass nigga. You know what it is when I do see you. How about that?" Chris leaned toward the phone so his words could be heard clearer.

Casci, Reniya, and Ariel only listened and watched Chris. It was about to be some shit now, and they all knew it.

"Knock, knock, bitch ass nigga. It's time to answer the door."

"Bring your pussy ass on then. I'm in the Gardens, bitch." Chris ended the call. He was done talking.

Reniya stood, walked past Chris, and patted his shoulder. "Let me change clothes and put my Chucks on. I'm not going to let them jump you."

"I don't need no help with that nigga."

"That's what you said the last time." Casci laughed.

"And the time after that," Ariel reminded him.

"I slipped the last time, and the time before that was when his boys were there," Chris explained.

Coffee walked back into the living room. She was still wearing her panties and bra. "You did what, nigga?"

"Tell her what your dumb ass did, Chris." Ariel sat back and folded her arms. She looked up at him and shook her head.

"Well, just know that if you win, we're going to make this bitch give you some pussy," she told him.

"It ain't about no pussy. I just hate that nigga fucking her over."

Ariel half-smiled. She said, "You're crazy, Chris. You get to smoking that shit and you just don't give a fuck anymore."

"Fuck that river swimming ass Mexican. I got something for his ass. I know that much." Chris stood, pat his waistband, and headed for the door.

It was time he ran Stacy off anyway. Ariel was his girl, and after today, they'd all know it.

Chapter Nine
One Week Later

With Reniya and Coffee's help, Chris and Casci were able to move three of the four kilos Marcus had given her outside of the Gardens. By selling each of the ounces they had for $750, they were able to slash the going price by$100-$150. She and Chris reveled when counting the $81,000 cash for the third time. This was the most money either of them had seen in their lives.

After giving the girls their cut for making things possible, Casci and Chris sat at the foot of the bed in Coffee's room in thought of their own. Where Chris was excited about the next kilo he'd sell, Casci was looking forward to doing something else with the cash they now had. This wasn't something she planned on continuing. She had her mind set on opening up a fashion boutique of her own.

"You think that nigga, Marcus, will give us a deal on some more work?" Chris asked, his fear of the hustle pushed to the far corners of his mind.

"Detrick did say that he'd get more work, once I was ready, but I know niggas just be talking to make things sound like everything's alright," she told him.

Casci had seen personally how animosity formed when certain parties felt as if money was skipping over them. And now that she'd moved the work Marcus had given her, someone somewhere was complaining about coming up short.

"Well, let's see what the nigga's talking about. You already know he's going to go through ya boy, Marcus, so we should be good."

"I'm not trying to keep doing this shit, nigga. We had a good run, and the shit came without a loss. It ain't no promise the shit happens like that anyway."

"Bitch, I know you ain't freezing up on a nigga. You got me into this shit." Chris stood and walked toward Coffee's bedroom window and peeked out the curtain.

"Nah, nigga. I'm not bailing out on you. I'm just saying, I'm not trying to keep doing this shit. The money is to be invested so we won't have to keep doing this shit." Casci remembered all the girls she left in the Gatesville Prison. The ones who couldn't back away from the hustle. The very ones who made it a life's journey of stepping on stone.

"Well, plug me in with the nigga. A couple of more runs like this, and a nigga will be sitting real nice."

"Yeah, that's what half of them hoes in prison thought, too," she responded.

"Come on, Casci. We in this shit now. Let's push this shit to the limit." Chris turned back to face her. He pleaded with his eyes, but then jumped, hearing a bang on the room door.

"Hey, y'all better not be fucking on my bed," Coffee yelled through the gap under the door.

"Bitch, ain't nobody fucking," Casci yelled back.

"Y'all sure have been in there a long time."

"Sure have," Reniya added, letting them know she was present also.

Casci got up, walked over to the door, and opened it. She and Chris were fully dressed and she wanted them to see that. When she asked Coffee if she and Chris could use her room, it was for business, not pleasure.

"Ouu, bitch, who y'all done robbed?" Coffee asked, seeing the stacks of bills across the bed.

"That's from the stuff Marcus gave her," Reniya confirmed. She leaned against the door post and crossed her arms.

"We hustling. That's where we got all this money from," Chris responded.

"Nigga, y'all gave me five hundred funky dollars, and y'all made all that?"

"You already know I'm going to bless your game." Chris pulled out his wallet, searched until he found a couple of Sonic coupons, and handed them to her. "Here. These are good for a double—"

"Gray ass nigga, I don't want no damn double nothing from no damn Sonic." Coffee snatched the coupons from him and tossed them behind her. She put one hand on her hip and held the other out toward him.

"Damn. You just going to bleed a nigga already. Let me at least get my dick sucked before you bite my head off." He dug into his pocket and pulled out another $300 hundred and handed it to her.

"I'm going to do more than suck your dick of you don't break bread, nigga." Coffee smiled when seeing him fold. She'd already told Reniya she was going to get a bigger cut of the money she helped them make. The calls she made to some of the guys she knew was more than rewarding.

"Why you ain't fucking with Casci? This is mostly hers than mines."

"Cause, nigga. You been owing that bitch for the longest." Coffee walked over, opened her drawer, and put the money up with the rest of the cash she kept there.

"Um, can we finish doing what we doing?" Casci laughed, seeing the expression Chris was giving Coffee.

"I can't stand your black ass, Coffee." Chris pushed her shoulder as she passed.

"Understand, nigga. You can't understand my black ass." Coffee slapped her own ass, walked out, and closed the door behind her.

Chris sat on the other side of Casci and smiled at her.

"If you was a nigga, I'd suck your dick, Casci. You know that?"

"Yeah, I bet you would." She laughed.

"You got to let that hate shit go, sis. That nigga putting you on. I could see if he wasn't doing shit for you, but he is," he told her, knowing she still felt some type of way about Marcus.

Casci remembered the way Marcus used to sit with her, plotting and planning. She'd been his little sister for as long as she could remember. This was the same way things started with Marcus. They'd started out hustling, just as she and Chris were. Despite the same hustle, they wanted different things from it, just as she and Chris were understanding now. She looked over at him. This was something she couldn't afford to do again. It was the very thing she promised herself she wouldn't do.

"I'll tell you what. I'm going to give that nigga Detrick thirty thousand dollars, and whatever he give me in return, I'm going to let you do your own thing and we'll just split the money," she offered.

"That means I'm going to have to pay them hoes in there more money." Chris fell back onto the bed and covered his eyes with his forearms.

"Are you going to do the shit or not, nigga?" Casci asked, while stuffing the money into the Polo Sport backpack she had.

"Hell, I ain't got no choice," he mumbled. "Make the call."

Casci smiled to herself. She was going to give Chris the benefit of the doubt. This would show where he was when it came to money. Money made people do things they normally wouldn't do, and experience taught her that was something she needed to know sooner than later.

* * *

The phone call from Stacy came early this morning. Ariel knew that was so he could see if Chris could be heard in the background. Him telling her that he had a surprise for her had her jumping in her car and making her way to the hotel where he told her to meet him.

The moment she walked into the hotel room, she knew it was about to be on. Where Doom was normally around, Stacy was alone and the tune of Johnny Gill's "Perfect" was playing on the small stereo on the counter. Rose petals were scattered from the door all the way to the bedroom door and candles were lit, giving the room a nice fragrance.

Ariel smiled sheepishly.

"I can run you some bath water if you haven't already bathed," he offered, after closing the door behind her. Stacy pat her on the ass and leaned down to kiss her cheek.

"Are you going to bathe a bitch, too?" She turned to face him.

"I'm about to do more than that, so it's up to you."

"Oh, really? What is all this about, Stacy?"

Stacy relieved her of her phone and clutch, and began undoing her blouse.

She allowed him.

"It's all about you, babe."

Ariel let her blouse fall to the floor and turned so she could unclasp her bra.

He placed a trail of kisses form her earlobe to her neck.

She smelled the alcohol on his breath, reached down, and palmed the bulge in his boxer/briefs.

Chapter Ten

Once it was understood they'd head out to meet Detrick, Casci slung the sporty pack over her shoulder, and she and Chris headed out. The minute she and Chris stepped out of their breezeway, she spotted the back Jaguar at the far end of the parking lot. Not only did it stand out amongst the rundown and average automobiles around it, no one in the entire complex owned such luxury. With so much money on her at the time, she thought of the possibility that she was being watched, and Detrick was the one behind it. But he'd already proven her wrong when it came to thinking the worst of him.

She threw Chris the keys. "Here, you drive," she told him, before walking to the passenger's side of the car. If it was the cops, it would be Chris going to jail, instead of her. And they'd have him out in no time."

***

Ariel showered and redressed while Stacy made a couple calls. She had a couple clients scheduled for the day, and she wasn't about to reschedule.

Stacy was sitting on the edge of the bed when she stepped out of the bathroom. One of the calls he'd just received informed him of the whereabouts of Peanut, and he couldn't wait for Doom to arrive.

"When are you going to put that dick on me again?" she asked. Ariel walked up and stood between his legs. She began rubbing the sides of his face.

I'm going to fuck with you in a couple days. Me and Doom have to take care of some business and ain't no telling when I'm going to be back in pocket." Stacy set his phone on the bed beside him and pulled her close.

"And don't fuck off that scene you recorded. I want to look at it."

"I got you. Ain't nothing going to happen to it." He held up the SD card.

"Well, let me get out of here before I end up with my ass in the air again." Ariel leaned down and kissed his lips.

"Oh, hey. Who that nigga scoring from? I hear he hustling out the Gardens," he asked her.

"Who, Chris?"

"Yeah. Who that nigga fucking with now?"

Ariel slung her bag over her shoulder and told him, "Him and Casci fucking around. That nigga, Marcus, be having Detrick bring her work. He dropped off some a while back and they been moving that shit like crazy."

"Oh, yeah?" Stacy regarded her with raised brows. It was nice to know that Chris was making a little money.

"Casci was talking about selling him the Chrysler Marcus gave her, and he's been saving money for it."

Stacy stood, grabbed Ariel by the waist, and told her, "Find out what they paying. I might have it for cheaper." Now that he knew Chris was hustling, he wanted to know what kind of numbers he was messing with, and if stepping on Chris was worth his time.

"Alright. I'll see what's up."

They walked out to her car hand in hand. He slapped her ass, when she went to open the driver's door.

Stacy thought about the fact that most of the guys that stopped scoring dope from him were now getting work from the Minez brothers. The thought of them trying to push him off the block came to mind because he wasn't pushing their work. He knew how the Minez brothers operated and he wasn't about to become another of their workers.

Now that the oldest brother, Hector, was living down in Miami, the younger brothers were using the niggas in the hoods to move their product. Now that he'd closed a couple of his spots because of his feud with J-Rod and his cousin, other niggas were making money. And Chris just so happened to be one of them.

Stacy leaned into the window, kissed Ariel, and headed back inside. He had some things to do.

***

Marcus watched as Casci and Chris pulled out of the parking lot. Casci looked in his direction several times, and each time, his pulse quickened. She had indeed gained a little more weight, but she was just as beautiful as he remembered her. The smile that came across his face was because she looked nothing like he imagined she would after serving so much time in prison. He'd seen a couple of other women walk out with teeth missing, their hair cut off, and looking as if they'd been to prison. Casci on the other hand, showed none of the signs that she'd just gotten out of prison, and he was sure it was because of the money and drugs he'd given her.

He shook his head, seeing the way she was dressed. It was like old times. He twisted his lips and shook his head, seeing that she was rolling with Chris. Chris was a peon to him, and he didn't want Casci getting caught up with a nigga who wasn't going to have her back.

The minute the Chrysler pulled out of the lot, his phone began vibrating. It was Detrick. "What's up, homie?"

"Hey. Just got a call from Casci and she's ready to re-up."

Marcus smiled. "Oh, yeah?"

"She says she's going to play with thirty thousand. You ready for her, or what?"

"Yeah. I'll tell you what. Have her meet you at the detail shop in three hours. Give me time to stop by the house, and give you time to situate things on your end."

"Bet that. Three hours. Let me call ya girl and let her know what's up."

Marcus ended the call and inhaled. It was time. One thing he knew how to do was read Casci. If there was going to be blood shed between them, he would be able to pick that up in the first few minutes of being around her. Hoping things were about to fall in his favor, Marcus headed to the detail shop so he could swap cars. He didn't need her knowing that he'd been watching her at any point.

***

Chris was styling and profiling in the Big Body 300 and it was amusing the hell out of Casci. His head bobbed along with the beat that pounded in the rear of the sedan.

"All I need now is a couple more hoes in this bitch," he yelled over the music.

Casci passed him the blunt she was smoking on and nodded. "Nah. All you need to do now is pay me for this bitch."

"What about you? What you gonna drive?"

Casci shrugged. "I'll cop me something when the time is right. I don't want this big ass car. I need something like a Miata, or one of them sports coupes."

"You need a truck, Casci. You can't be no boss bitch running around here driving no little ass shit like that."

Casci's phone vibrated. She smiled, seeing it was Detrick.

"Yeah?" she answered.

"Meet me at that same detail shop in three hours."

Casci hung up and looked over at Chris. Detrick's tone alone told her that Marcus himself would be there.

"Three hours. He wants us to meet him at the detail ship in three hours," she told him, before looking out the passenger's window.

"I hope these niggas ain't on no bullshit, Casci." Chris tried passing her the blunt, and she refused it.

It was at that moment that Casci realized she wasn't ready. Despite the gun she had, the vendetta she avowed to, and the years of waiting for this moment, she wasn't ready to end her friend's life. People made mistakes, and those mistakes shouldn't have to cost at all.

***

Reniya reluctantly phoned Jingles. He answered on the second ring.

"Hello, pretty lady. How's everything going for you?" he asked.

"I'm pissed, I'm broke, and I need to bust a nut. Can you help me with those three problems?" Reniya looked over at Coffee and twisted her lips.

Coffee mouthed the words, "Take one for the team, bitch."

"Come by and find out," he told her in a sexy baritone.

"My pussy has been throbbing all day, and I need to be done right," she told him.

"Baby girl, you already know Daddy knew what to do with that young pussy."

Reniya put her finger on the phone's mic and told Coffee, "He sound like a damn pedophile."

"Girl, just bait the hook," Coffee whispered.

"I want some of that tickler and everything, Jingles."

Coffee drove while her friend baited the hook they were dropping into the waters. With Jingles being the only millionaire they knew personally, it was agreed that they'd keep him holding the bag. Reniya might've complained when it came to laying up under him, but never once complained when it came to the things he did for her, or them, for that matter.

"Baby girl, just bring me some of that young pussy. Daddy going to put you to bed. When I'm through eating that ass, ain't going to be nothing but the platter you sat on."

"See, nigga, you gonna have a bitch climbing the walls." Reniya rolled her eyes.

"I can tie you down, if that's what you like. Umm-hmm. I can introduce you to some of this bondage shit."

"As long as my shit get ate, I wouldn't give a damn if you rolled me up in a big ass tortilla."

Both girls chuckled under their breath, hearing the big man try his best to sound sexy and inviting. Not only was she wiring him up to do all he wanted done, she was wiring herself up to do what needed to be done. One of the ways Reniya baited him was acting as if his dick was just too big for her. That way, he spent most his time with his tongue between her ass. He loved the idea of coaching her when it came to the dick.

"Just bring me some of that young ass puss. I'm going to have things laid out for you."

"I'll be there in a few hours. Swallow one of them damn pills, nigga, because it's about to go down."

Reniya ended the call and smiled.

"That nigga gonna eat a bitch alive."

"It's for the team, so it's all good," Coffee told her. "It's all good."

Chapter Eleven

Stacy and Doom parked down the street from the spot where Peanut was holed up. The tip he received had proven true. The first time they passed the spot, they questioned the validity of the tip. But after parking and watching for a minute, Peanut himself walked out on the porch smoking a blunt. They watched as he looked up and down the block before walking back inside.

Doom had begun loading hollow point bullets in the Mac-11 he had and Stacy filled the clip to the assault rifle he was holding. Neither of them knew how many people were inside, or if there was anyone else. All they knew was that when they got there, it wouldn't have mattered if the US Military was there; they were going to drop everything and anything moving.

Stacy thought about the repercussions that would come with them gunning down Peanut, and not J-Rod, but it was a chance they both agreed to take. They'd sat for right at an hour, hoping J-Rod would show, but no such luck. They'd get at him when they crossed paths again.

"This for Black," Doom told him before tucking the Mack-11 under his left arm.

"Yeah. This one's for Black," Stacy agreed.

They both climbed out of the truck and made their way toward the spot Peanut was hiding.

***

Chris and Casci were sitting in the parking lot of the detail shop thirty minutes early. If something foul was at play, she wanted to be able to see it before it was time. She counted the money again, so things would be right on her end.

"You see that Jaguar parked on the side of the building?" Casci wanted to see if Chris was on point.

"You talking about the black one?"

She nodded.

"Yeah, looks like the same one that was in the parking lot in the Gardens when we left." Chris looked around the parking lot at the selection of high-end cars. This had to have been the spot all the real heavy hitters got their cars and trucks detailed.

"Just making sure you on point, nigga. You've got to be aware of your surroundings."

"Motherfucker, I work at Sonic. Niggas be trying to rob that bitch all the time, and I be making sure I know when a play is about to be ran."

"Well, this ain't no Sonic. If a nigga hit us, we got to be ready to roll with that shit." Casci looked over at him, seriousness etched across her face.

"Yes, ma'am."

"Nigga, I'm serious. What you gonna do if three carloads of niggas surround us right now with fully-automatic rifles, talking about 'where it's at?' What the fuck you gonna do?" She grilled him.

"Hell, I'm not going to let a motherfucker just take my shit." He matched her seriousness.

"See, that's why motherfuckers get killed right there. They try to save the product and money instead of saving their own asses. That's dumb shit, Chris."

Casci remembered that night she shot Rosa. It was because she'd done the exact things Chris talked about doing. It was because of that action Casci reacted.

"Look at that motherfucker right there, Casci. That's got to be a hundred thousand dollar Benz."

Casci's heartbeat began racing, seeing the foreign luxury car turn up into the lot and head toward the back. She knew it was Marcus, and seeing Detrick climb out of the truck he was driving, she inhaled, closed her eyes, and shook her head. She had to still her nerves.

"Let's go see what this nigga talking about," Chris told her.

"Um, stay back just in case. I need you to watch my back." She watched as Marcus climbed out of the 550 Benz. He looked in her direction. The powder-blue linen slacks, white shirt, and dark blue loafers showed her that he'd stepped his game all the way up. He was no longer the jeans, T-shirt, and Jordan's guy she grew up with.

Her door opened, and Detrick was standing there offering her his hand.

"I'll take the money to the back and get everything ready."

"Oh. I thought you were being a gentleman." Casci smiled.

In her mind, she walked in behind Marcus, put her pistol to the back of his head, and pulled the trigger. It wasn't until Chris asked, "You sure?" did she realize Marcus had already walked in ahead of her and the money that came with them was taken in the opposite direction.

"Yeah, I'm sure."

Casci entered the rear office of the detail shop. Marcus closed the door behind her. Her eyes wanted to behold him, but instead she walked to the far end of the room and stood at the office window.

Marcus walked to where she stood, his arm slightly brushing her shoulder. He sighed deeply.

"Is this another one of your spots?" Casci asked, making conversation between them. She resisted the urge to face him.

"Nah. Just a place to meet with people I fucks with."

Casci tsked. "You mean the people you fuck over?"

Marcus clasped his hands behind him. "I deserved that."

"Oh, you deserve so, so, so much more."

"You know the saying, 'May we always get what we want and none of what we deserve.'"

Casci was taken aback. Where she once used the saying in reference to the things she did, she was now feeling them. Those words would be the same ones she had to eat.

"I never in my life thought it would be you, Marcus. Ariel, yes, but you...never." Casci turned to face him.

"Casci, I...I fucked up. I fucked up, and I couldn't take the shit back, man." Marcus pat his chest while talking, emphasizing that *he* was at fault.

"And you think you giving me all this shit makes it right?" Casci reached up, pulled the shades from his eyes, and set them on the desk behind her.

"I know there's nothing I can give you to make you feel any different, Casci. I also know there's nothing you can take from me that will make you feel any better." Marcus looked deep into her gray eyes.

Casci sighed.

"I missed you like hell, too. Not a day goes by where I don't think about you. When I heard that you were out, my world flipped upside down in a matter of seconds. I had to see you. But first, I had to see where you were at mentally," he confessed without blinking.

Casci pushed past him, walked across the office, and took a seat in the chair adjacent to the desk. "You had to see where I was at?"

"I know you, Casci. I knew your heart. Yeah, I had to see where you was at." Marcus pulled the other chair across the room and sat in front of her. He sat down, leaned forward, and placed his hands on her knees. "I've had my eyes on you since I first heard. I knew all about the shit you and them crazy ass girls been getting into. Butterflies got new metal detectors and everything at the doors now." Marcus smiled for the first time.

"You broke that heart, Marcus. I'm not that same person anymore. I'm—"

Marcus grabbed Casci's hand and lowered his head. "I'm sorry, sis. I truly am. You tell me how to make this shit right, and I'll do it. I'll do whatever it takes to have you back."

Casci saw the hurt in his eyes. She heard it in his voice. This was the guy she looked up to as a brother. This was the same guy who betrayed her. Marcus was now a guy she could never trust again.

***

Coffee nodded, seeing Jingles' Rolls Royce parked off to the side of the Royal Suites Hotel parking lot. There were only two Phantoms in Oak Cliff with huge twenty-four-inch rims under them, with one being tan, and Jingles having the maroon-colored one. It wasn't like he could hide his whereabouts. And if this was what he called being inconspicuous, he was sadly mistaken.

"Um, call me in an hour and act like it's some important shit going on." Reniya pulled her phone off the wireless car charger and said, "If he ain't got the pussy by then, he out of there."

"Whether now or later, you're still going to have to give the nigga some pussy. Let me go up with you. I don't have shit to do. We can work his ass together," Coffee suggested.

"All the nigga want to do is eat my pussy," Reniya reminded her.

"And?"

"So you're just going to sit and watch this nigga eat my pussy?" Reniya gave her a look of question and confusion.

"I might as well. You know he a trick. Let's play his ass."

Reniya looked toward the hotel entrance. "Let's go."

Jingles opened the door to the suite, wearing one of the hotel's courtesy robes, the thick cigar perched between his lips. The smile he greeted Reniya with widened when seeing Coffee. "Ladies, ladies. Come in. Come in." he stepped aside.

"I figured I'd bring you a treat, being that you're always good to me," Reniya lied.

Jingles laughed a hearty sound. He closed the door and hurried to grab the unopened bottle of champagne. "Drinks?"

"Please," Coffee accepted. She kicked off her shoes and slid her bare feet across the thick carpet.

Jingles spilled the drink he was pouring. His attention was distracted, seeing her feet and French pedicure. "Shit!"

"Don't get nervous now, nigga." Reniya took one of the glasses and handed the other to Coffee.

"I knew I had one bad bitch coming, but two of you. I'm going to have to keep my eyes open." He laughed.

"These rooms are nice," Coffee exclaimed as if she'd never been to that particular location.

"Yeah. For three-fifty a night, they better be. There's a Jacuzzi right through that door, a fireplace around that corner, and a huge bedroom down the hall." He pointed.

"Ou, I like this." Coffee spun around like a little girl in fantasy land. The sundress she wore raising with each twirl. She'd already pulled one side of the panties she wore between her ass cheeks, and by the way Jingles was smiling, she knew it was just a matter of time before she was knee deep in his pockets.

Reniya smiled. She liked the card her friend was playing. She jumped right in.

"Girl, your panties all in your ass." She walked over, raised Coffee's dress up, and pulled out the wedgie. She slapped her chocolate ass. "With your fat ass."

"Is my ass too fat for you, Jingles?" Coffee pranced toward him, spun to where her ass was inches from his legs and raised her dress.

"Not at all, young lady. Not at all," he responded, admiring the young, chocolate tender in front of him.

"Niggas be saying it ain't firm enough. Is it firm enough, Mr. Jingles?"

Jingles placed the cigar in his mouth and palmed her ass with both hands. He parted her cheeks.

The bulge behind his robe became evident. He looked toward Reniya. "Come here, baby girl. Let me see whose ass is the firmest."

"Hers might be the firmest, but my pussy the tightest." Reniya grabbed Jingles' hand and pushed it between her legs. You feel that motherfucker right there? You feel that?"

"Baby girl, baby girl, let me get y'all out these clothes." He undid the belt to his robe and freed his eight-and-a-half-inch dick.

Coffee looked down with her mouth open and her eyes wide. "Look how big and thick it is," she lied. "I don't know if I can handle all that."

"I told you the nigga was packing," Reniya added, stroking his ego more.

"Ladies, ladies. It ain't the size of the wave. It's the motion of the ocean."

Knowing what needed to be done. Reniya walked over, grabbed Jingles' dick, and pulled him toward the living area.

Coffee pulled the dress she wearing over her head and followed.

They were about to give this trick a real treat.

***

Chris paced the parking lot in thought. He'd already smoked one of the blunts he and Casci pulled up with, and was wanting to fire up the second. Not only were his thoughts on the amount of drugs they were about to leave with and how he was going to handle moving them with and without the girls' help, but he was thinking about Casci. She'd already told him that he was pretty much on his own with this batch, so he knew she wasn't really trying to get dope money. But then there was the fact that he went out and bought the guns she really wanted. Whatever the case, he was going to ride with her through whatever and whoever.

Casci was the only person who gave him the time of day, when it came to him trying to make a move. For years, he saw these same guys, who were hustling, but never once did any of them take him under their wing, school him to the game, or even try to put him on money. He'd walked around these same guys, rubbed shoulders with the same circles, and even entertained some of the same women, but he was always looked at as that scrub nigga who was always around bad bitches. Chris didn't owe anyone but Casci, and it was about time he made his mark in the streets.

He looked towards the building, seeing Detrick walk from the service area with the same Polo back pack Casci gave him. He walked to meet him.

"Here's the package, man."

He smiled. "What we looking like? What he give us?" Chris walked the pack to the Chrysler and placed it in the backseat.

"That's three, so let Casci know she own ten thousand."

"That's all?" Chris closed the rear door and looked back toward the building. "That nigga really breaking bread, huh?"

"Yeah. I ain't never seen the nigga drop out like this. He and Casci must go way, way back."

Chris thought of just that. He thought about the fact that, if it so happened Casci and Marcus hooked back up, he'd really be on his own. Marcus was in a whole other league, when it came to hustling. Casci would easily choose Marcus over him.

"What's taking them so long?" Chris checked the time on his watch.

"So Casci done talked you into this shit, huh?" Detrick asked.

Chris thought about the person who really got him into the mess he was in: Ariel. He only wanted to show her that he was about the life she praised. If only he had the type of money Stacy had. If only she could see that he'd take care of her just as good. Those were his thoughts before he saw himself as a game player.

His phone was now summoning him to people and places where money was exchanged. His name was one many associated with the likes of Casci, Reniya, and Coffee. Niggas weren't pulling up with either of them if they weren't sitting on money. Chris was now acknowledged by the same guys who walked by him without a thought of who he might be.

"I'm beginning to think I'm the one talking her into this shit again," Chris replied. There was no way he was about to say his like for Ariel and his hate for the nigga she fucked with was the reason.

"It was only a matter of time before she stepped back off the porch." Detrick nodded toward the row of luxury cars parked out front. "Niggas don't pull up in this motherfucker if they ain't fucking around out here in these streets. It's damn near one million dollars sitting in this lot, and let Marcus tell it, Casci supposed to have something showcased here, too."

"As long as she wants, I'm going to ride this shit out with her." Chris made sure they were looking into each other's eyes when he made the statement. He let it be known that she was the one calling the shots.

"All I can say is be careful out here. Not everybody agrees with a bitch making the moves they should've been making." Detrick smirked, looked toward the group of guys standing at the far end of the building and shrugged. "Some of them niggas paying twenty-three thousand dollars just for one of them bricks. If they knew Casci was getting them for less than ten thousand, you'd better believe it would be some shit."

Chris sized up some of the guys he knew personally. Some were known to slide on the ski mask and some were known for sending niggas who did. Casci's words found him. He gave a shrug of his own and told Detrick, "Prey and Predators, homie. It's understood."

"As long as you understand that, then you good," Detrick replied, before walking to his truck and climbing in.

Chris turned back toward the building, checked his watch, and rubbed his hands together. "Don't trip, Casci. Don't trip," he stated to no one in particular.

Chapter Twelve

Once they were a couple of houses from the spot Peanut was hiding, Stacy pulled the black bandana up over his mouth and nose. He nodded towards the back of the house and waited until Doom was in place before he eased up the stairs. Music could be heard through the flimsy wooden door, and the thought of Peanut entertaining company entered his mind. He and Doom already agreed that whoever else was inside was just at the wrong place at the wrong time.

When he was sure no one was onto him, he knocked on the door twice.

"Look out, Peanut!" Stacy raised the rifle waist level.

"Who is it?" asked the voice on the other side of the door.

Stacy squeezed the trigger, sending a spray of lead through the wooden door. He took a step back and kicked in the door with all his might. The guy that answered the door was shoved forcefully to the wall behind him. His chest and stomach eaten by the bullets from the assault rifle. Stacy saw two other guys hit the floor, game controllers in hand. Either of them couldn't have been a day over sixteen years old. He looked around the room for Peanut.

"Where Peanut? Where he at?" Stacy waved the rifle back and forth in front of him.

"In the back, man. He in the back," they yelled in unison.

Stacy looked down at the guy that answered the door a second time. His lifeless eyes still staring at the holes that riddled him. These youngsters were apparently just playing a video game. There were ounces of dope on the table, unrolled blunts, a couple of bottles of MD 20/20 and two small caliber handguns. Before he could question them any further shots rang out from the rear of the house.

"Stacy! Look out, Stacy!" Doom had done the same to the back door. There was another guy that had the same fate as the guy that answered the door with Stacy.

"That ain't Peanut. That ain't him!" Stacy ran back towards the front of the house, kicked in the door to one of the bedrooms, and fired a series of shots inside. Nothing.

Doom had walked through the kitchen and was standing in the front room where Stacy had two of the youngsters lying face down. He kicked one of the guys in the side and stomped his head.

"Where that nigga go? Huh? Where that bitch ass nigga go?"

"He was in the back, man. I promise," Pleaded the youngster.

Doom pointed the Mack-11 and fired three consecutive shots into the back of youngsters head and neck.

"He in attic! He ran up in the attic," the other youngster cried, seeing that both of his friends were dead.

Both Stacy and Doom looked upward. The sounds of broken glass could be heard.

"Fuck! Let's go, nigga. Let's go," Stacy yelled.

Stacy hurried and grabbed the drugs that were sitting on the table. He was sure money was there, but they didn't have time to search for it. Just as he was putting the rifle under his arm, more shots rang out. Doom had placed the barrel of the Mack to the back of the surviving guy's head, and filled it with hollow point bullets.

He followed Stacy outside. They looked up and down the block. Doom pointed at the figure that was running away from the house. It was Peanut.

"There that bitch right there," Doom took two steps in that direction.

Stacy grabbed his arm. Neighbors had begun peeping out of windows.

"He ain't going far. We got him," Stacy told him before making his way back to where they were parked.

"That bitch mines, homie." Doom told him, while they hurried down the block with concealed guns.

They were more than sure Peanut knew exactly who they were now. Now that blood was shed from each end, it was war, and whoever happened to step on the field had better be ready.

***

Casci sat and listened to Marcus explain things from his point of view. She watched him melt in front of her. He went from being a strong, confident boss player to a scared little boy on the run. This was the Marcus she knew. She closed her eyes, denied the tears that threatened to fall, and shook her head.

"I've been going through hell out here, Casci. When Reniya and Coffee kicked me to the curb, I was thinking it was you, and that's what you wanted. I begged for your information, tried to send you money whenever I saw one of them, and even tried to explain things to them. But them bitches threatened to kill me the next time I came around."

Marcus looked from the floor to the ceiling. "And I knew them hoes would do it. I didn't have shit, Casci. Wasn't nobody fucking with me, and when Hector said that I was either going to hustle for them or he'd have you killed, I did that. Because of the shit I did to you, I became they bitch. Half the shit I make goes to them. Hell, I bought that house Alex live in. For five years, I've been paying for Rosa's therapy, the customizations to her cars, and anything else she come up with. The only thing I haven't given that bitch is some ass."

"So Rosa still fucking with them niggas?"

"That bitch married Alex, but I'm the motherfucker taking care of her. The bitch call, I come running. She complain about some shit, they come running."

Casci wiped the tears from his eyes with her thumb.

"Why, Marcus? We was supposed to do this shit together, man." Casci fought back her own tears.

"The money and the hate I had for that bitch. You had already told me you didn't want to keep hustling, and I was scared that I wouldn't be able to do it without the money."

"I—I'm. I would have never done you like that, Marcus." Casci pulled her hand from his. She leaned back and crossed her arms.

"Even now, you all the family I got, Casci. I can't lose you again."

Casci lowered her head into her hands. When she did look at him, the tears had fallen. She stood. "You left me to die in there, nigga. You let me die, Marcus," she cried.

Marcus stood, grabbed her by her shoulders, and pulled her to him He held her as tight as he could.

"I'm sorry, Casci. I'm sorry, sis. Just tell me what I got to do. Please. Please."

"I just need some time, man. I got to sort this shit out."

"Whatever you need, I'll give you. Whatever I got is yours, Casci. It's yours," he assured.

While Casci covered her eyes and hid her face in his chest, all she could see was him. All she could remember was them together.

Yes, she was all he had left.

***

"Take that dick, bitch. Make him work," Coffee told Reniya from the chair adjacent to the circular bed she and Jingles were on.

"I can't take it like that." She moaned, feeling Jingles raise her leg.

"I got you, baby girl. Daddy gonna make it good for you," Jingles said, while stroking her with slow, winding strokes.

Reniya squirmed under him. She bit down on her lip with each thrust, sucked air through her teeth, and clawed at his back. The minute he buried his face in her shoulder, she looked over at Coffee and winked.

"You like that, baby girl? You like that?" he asked when he thought he was hitting her spot.

"Oh, shit, yeah, that's it. That's it," Reniya yelped.

"Work that shit, nigga. You got to work me harder than that," Coffee told him.

The more she coached, the harder Jingles went.

"This that young pussy, baby girl. You got to stroke and stir it like hot coffee," he told her.

Reniya acted like she was running from the dick. She knew how to stroke his ego.

Jingles raised off her and looked back at Coffee. He smiled. "Come on over here. Let me taste that motherfucker you got."

"Give me a thousand dollars." Coffee stood, walked to the foot of the bed, and began stepping out her panties.

Reniya closed her legs, rolled on her side, and began rocking. "Girl, that nigga fucked the shit out of me."

"Do me like you did her." Coffee raised her foot and tossed her panties toward him.

"One thousand dollars, huh?" Jingles crawled to where she stood.

"Uh-huh." Coffee batted her eyes, put a finger in her mouth, and covered her pussy with her outer hand.

"I'll give you five hundred now and give you the rest when you come back to the club." Jingles kissed her stomach, grabbed her arm, and began pulling her onto the bed.

"Promise?" Coffee pouted.

"That's a promise, baby girl. I make damn hear five thousand a day at the club. I got over one hundred thousand in my office safe right now. One thousand dollars ain't going to hurt me."

Coffee let him pull her onto the bed. She opened her legs and laughed.

"The two of you trying to break a nigga."

"You take care of us, we'll take care of you," Coffee assured him.

Reniya climbed off the bed and slowly walked toward the bathroom, acting as if he'd just knocked her back out.

"You alright, baby girl?" Jungles asked, seeing Reniya grimace with each step.

"Yeah, I'm good. It's been a minute since I've been fucked like that, is all," she lied.

"Do me right, Jingles. Do my shit right."

Coffee pushed his head between her legs. She gave Reniya the thumbs up.

"This motherfucker taste like peaches, baby girl."

"Wait until you taste this ass," she replied before raising both her legs.

Feeling the warmth of his tongue, she closed her eyes. Knowing that both her feet were in his pockets, Coffee squirmed and moaned her pleasure. She could definitely get used to this.

"Suck that pussy, nigga. Suck my shit right," she coached him.

***

Chris was standing by the Chrysler smoking his second blunt when Casci walked out of the detail shop. Her eyes were red from crying, so he rushed to her side.

"You alright, Casci? What that nigga do?" Chris pulled the Glock he was carrying from his waistband.

"I'm ready to go, Chris."

Chris looked from Casci to the doors of the building. As soon as he saw Marcus walk out, he ran up on him. "What the fuck you do to her, nigga?"

Marcus only watched her as she climbed into the passenger's side of the car. He ignored Chris.

"Now, nigga," Casci yelled from the car.

Chris hurried to the car and sped off. He looked over at his friend, and once they were out of the lot to the detail shop, she turned to him and smiled.

"I'm a bad bitch, ain't I?" Casci checked herself in the compartment's mirror. "I had to go Hollywood on his ass."

Chris frowned. "Bitch, I thought you was crying for real."

"Gotta play this shit, nigga. I ain't practiced all these years for nothing." She laughed.

"What that nigga talking about?"

Chris relaxed when seeing that it was all for show.

"A bunch of bullshit. A whole bunch of bullshit," she replied. Casci laughed to herself when thinking of some of the things Marcus said.

"We got three from his ass." Chris nodded toward the back seat.

"We got a lot more coming, too. If you fuck me over, Chris, I'm going to burn your ass alive, nigga." Casci looked over at him. She leaned toward him. "Alive, nigga."

"Yes, ma'am." Chris smiled, checked his rearview, and hit his blinker.

"Where we headed now, clown?"

"I'm taking you out to eat. I got a couple more coupons, and they expire tomorrow." He laughed.

"Cheap ass nigga. I want a bacon cheeseburger, fries, and a limeade, and one of them shakes."

Chris shook his head, thinking how trifling Casci was. She'd fooled the hell out of him. Now that he was thinking about it, it was the same thing all of them did, when it came to the games they played.

Chapter Thirteen

For three days Casci had to sit and listen to the girls go off on her for actually putting herself in the presence of Marcus. None of them trusted him, and despite her being out and receiving gifts and money from him, they still weren't feeling him. Everything he'd done so far was a part of a bigger scheme, when they told the story.

"I'm not saying I trust the nigga, I'm just saying we need to see where this goes," Casci told them.

"Just last week you wanted to kill the nigga, now you talking about seeing where the shits going. Fuck that nigga, Casci," Reniya spat.

"That bitch is up to something, she just ain't telling us," Coffee concluded, hearing the knock on the door.

"You know how the saying goes, keep ya friends close, and ya enemies thinking they closer."

Coffee looked through the peep hole, turned to face the girls and whispered, "Speaking of friends, here's ya new bestie now."

Coffee smiled, after opening the door. Detrick stood outside with bags in his hands. "Hey, Coffee, is Casci here?"

"Yeah, come on in, nigga," Coffee stood to the side.

"I go some more shit for Casci," He told them. He carried the bags to the table by the kitchen entrance and sat them down.

Both Reniya and Coffee began going through each of them.

"She don't want this shit, so tell that nigga he can keep his money," Reniya told him, seeing the contents inside.

Coffee laughed and said, "Ou, bitch. I like these hoes right here." She held up a pair of Retro Jordan's.

"That nigga still thinking she some body. All this nigga shit he went and bought." Reniya held up over a dozen pair of silk boxers, boy shorts, and sports bras. There were several Adidas and Nike warm-up sets, three pair of Jordan shoes, two pair of Shell-Toe Adidas and a week's worth of Cargo shorts of every color.

Coffee kicked off one of the house shoes she was wearing and tried on one of the shell-toes. "That nigga spent a grip. I can say that, though."

"All that's missing is some damn Dickey jeans. He could have at least bought the bitch some Gucci or some shit like that."

While they sorted through the items sent, Casci smiled. She'd rather he bought her exactly what he did, instead of the shit the girls were trying to dress her in. She looked over at Detrick and gave him the thumbs up. Marcus had done just fine.

"Why you looking at me like that," Detrick asked Reniya, seeing her stare at him as if he'd wronged her.

"So the nigga using you to deliver the shit because he know if he brings his ass through here, we ain't going to accept the shit."

Detrick threw his hand up. "Hey, I'm just the delivery man. I get paid whether she accepts the shit or not."

Casci stood, yawned and told them, "Let me jump in this shower right quick. I'll be right out, Detrick. Don't let them hoes take all your money." She told him with a smile. The last time he was there, she was sure she'd saved him. This time he was on his own.

"Take ya time, bitch. He looking like he ready to spend some of that money he been making," Coffee told her.

"Yeah, take ya time, Casci." Reniya pulled several pair of silk boxers from the bag and walked towards her room.

***

Ariel was awakened by the kisses Stacy was planting on her face and neck. He took her left nipple into his mouth, when she turned to face him.

"Move boy, I haven't even brushed my teeth yet." Ariel smiled, feeling him spread her legs.

"I'm not worried about no damn teeth. I want some as that hot ass pussy," he told her, before positioning himself between her thighs. He went down, and kissed her stomach.

"And leave my stomach alone, nigga." She pushed his face.

"I like this pudgy ass stomach."

Ariel raised her knees, grabbed his chin, and pulled his mouth back to her breast.

"Hold up." Stacy then pulled her to the floor, beside the bed, and after pushing one of the pillow under her ass, he raised her legs. He entered her slowly.

"Am I going to be able to go to work today, babe," Ariel asked. She threw her legs around his waist and began throwing the pussy back. She matched his stroke with a roll of her own.

"I'm still thinking about it." Stacy cupped her shoulders with both hands, buried his face in her neck, and began grinding into her. His pace quickened, hearing her moan.

"Shhiiit, what's gotten into you this morning?"

"You like that shit, nigga? Beat this pussy, babe."

Just before he reached his climax, Stacy pulled out of her and stood.

"Nigga, why you stop?"

Instead of answering, he bent down, scooped her up, and carried her into the living area of the hotel. He sat her on the couch and spread her legs again. He sucked her juices from her pussy.

"Oh, you on some more shit, huh?" Ariel threw one of her legs over the back rest and the other over his shoulder.

"Just making sure this pussy loose and wet by the time you get back to that nigga."

"Move, nigga." Ariel pushed his face away. "I told you I wasn't fucking that nigga."

The minute she twisted herself from under him, Stacy pushed her towards the arm of the couch.

He entered her from the back.

"Naw, don't stretch the pussy now." Ariel tried to push back.

Stacy pinned her by cupping his hands around the arm of the chair. He then began biting her upper shoulder. "Throw that ass back," he instructed her.

"Uuugghhhhh, nigga." Ariel bucked backwards until his thighs slapped against the back of hers. She rolled her hips, tightened her pussy's grip, and gave it to him the way he liked. The way she loved to.

"He fuck you like this, bitch? That nigga blow your shit out like this?" He asked with hard forceful strokes. He grunted with each.

"You can't fuck with this pussy, nigga. Make a bitch bust. You got to fuck me harder than that," she taunted him.

Stacy raised himself, reached around, grabbed her throat and pulled her to him. He fucked her harder and faster.

"Oohhhhh, shit yeaaahhh," she screamed her pleasure. Her insides exploded over and over again.

Stacy released her neck, grabbed both her ass cheeks and squeezed them as hard as he could. He closed his eyes as tight as he could.

"I... love... you, girl." He released deep inside of her, leaned forward, kissed her cheek, and collapsed beside her.

Ariel stood over him, placed both her hands on her hips and said, "I need some money, Stacy."

"How much you need now?" he asked, still trying to catch his breath.

"Give me $1,500."

"$1,500? Damn, bitch." Stacy sat up, put his back to the couch, and looked up at her.

"Yeah, nigga. Every time I try to go to work, you talking about pussy. I got to get paid somehow."

He pulled her down into his lap. He kissed her lips. "I got to take another trip out to Houston, babe. I got some shit going on and I might be gone for a couple more days."

"You going down there to see some bitch," Ariel playfully punched his face. "Let me find out, Stacy."

"Girl, please. I ain't got time for none of the shit. I be about my money when I go down there."

"Well, I'm just glad you ain't really fucking around in the city because these niggas out here getting killed every day." Ariel wrapped his arms around her and leaned back onto his chest.

"Yeah, that's what I'm hearing," he told her.

"I heard some hoes at the salon talking about four teenagers just got killed three days ago at some trap house. Some grimy ass nigga killed some kids for some drugs," she told him with a tinge of disgust.

"That's some fucked up shit, huh?"

"Hell yeah. Niggas ain't got shit to do but rob each other for crumbs." Ariel grabbed his hand and began fingering the huge ring he wore on his index finger.

"I wouldn't be surprised if that nigga Peanut was behind that shit."

"Speaking of him, ain't nobody seen that nigga. Word is, no one knows if he's dead or alive."

"Somebody going to get at him. I've been looking for that nigga myself, and I can't even find him," he lied

"Well, you just make sure you all right out there." She held out her hand, "And give me my money. This pussy ain't free."

Stacy laughed. He nodded "Well, I got about $500 more I need to get out of this bitch." He lay her down and climbed on top of her.

"And I better nut, too, nigga." Ariel loved the way Stacy sexed her. She loved the fact that she was able to keep his dick hard, and she loved the money she gave her.

***

Chris was sitting in the parking lot of the Razors hair salon, waiting for Ariel to show up. She didn't go home the night before, and he had a pretty good feeling she was with Stacy. He'd called her several times already, but was sent to voicemail. He wanted to talk to her about the discussion they didn't get to finish. Something Detrick said stayed on his mind. Now that he'd thought about it, he was wanting to know if there was a chance he and Ariel could hook up.

Just days after receiving the drugs from Marcus and the task from Casci, Chris had already sold a quarter of a kilo and was supposed to be meeting up with another guy that talked about having $7,000 to spend.

He checked his watch again. He knew, if she wasn't there by now, there was a possibility she wasn't coming. And being that he wanted to get at her privately, he headed to meet the guy with the money to spend. He'd go straight to the Garden's from there.

***

While they rode, Casci and Detrick smoked and talked about the game as they knew it. He asked her if she'd be willing to put money into opening a business, instead of continuing to change everything in the drug game. Detrick might have sold drugs and done some of anything when it came to the streets, but he was also making moves to better his situation.

"Boutiques, I want my own boutiques," Casci told him. "High end clothes."

"Boutiques?"

"Hell yeah. You see how these hoes spend money on that high ass shit," Casci told him, matter-of-factly.

"Real talk. Real talk." He handed her the blunt.

"And look at all the money these trick ass nigga spend on these hoes."

"Oh, so we tricks for liking the hoes we fuck with to look good? He asked. He looked over at her with a smile.

"Hell yeah, y'all some trick ass nigga. But hey, who ain't?"

"It ain't tricking when you know what you giving it to a hoe for, Casci. Tricking is when a bitch successfully put you in the game for money, and you fall for that shit. Just because a nigga give a bitch something, don't mean he ain't seeing what's happening. He might cut for a bitch and look at it as an investment."

Casci nodded her understanding, released a thick stream of smoke from her nose, and held the blunt in front of her. "This got to be some good shit. I'm sitting here agreeing with a nigga on what a trick is," Casci laughed.

"Call it what you want to, Casci. Call it what you want to."

Casci looked towards him, seeing the huge 550 Benz parked in a circular driveway. Detrick pulled in behind the car and parked.

"He's in Miami for the next few days," he told her. Her expression speaking volumes.

Casci followed Detrick through the foyer, watched him punch in the security code, and walked into a spacious living area. She frowned, "Who that nigga live with?"

"Why you ask that?"

"Cause that nigga ain't decorated this motherfucker." Casci looked around at the furnishings, the décor, and the neatness of everything. "Ain't no way that nigga living here alone."

"As far as I know, he does."

Detrick stepped out of his shoes, before stepping onto thick white carpet. Casci did the same. She followed him into the kitchen area and took a seat on a bar stool.

"Take a look around, Casci. That nigga ain't coming back for another two days."

She watched Detrick pour her a glass of Minute Maid juice. She took it and climbed down from the stool. Casci immediately recognized several pictures of her and Marcus together, back in the day. There were several of all of them together in the courtyard in the Garden. Casci pointed. "This nigga got these old ass pictures?"

Detrick followed her from the kitchen, through the living area, and into the hallway, where the majority of the pictures were hung.

"That nigga always talk about you, Casci."

"Yeah, I bet he do.'' Casci stopped at the picture of him and her at AT&T stadium. She tsked. They were both wearing number 8 jerseys. Casci turned, "This was when—"

Detrick leaned down and kissed her lips.

Casci pushed him back. "Nigga, what the fuck?"

Detrick stepped into her, grabbed her by the waist, and pulled her to him. He kissed her again. He slammed her back into the wall, and held her there.

"Detrick, you tripping, nigga," Casci said weakly.

Detrick found her tongue and began sucking it. He reached for the seam on the t-shirt she was wearing and began pulling it over her head.

Casci held her hands up to allow him. Once her shirt was thrown to the floor, she threw her arms around his neck. She stepped out of her sweats, when he pushed them down.

Detrick grabbed her short but thick frame by the ass and lifted her until she wrapped her legs around his waist. He walked her into Marcus' bedroom, fell across the bed with her, skillfully undid the buckle to his own pants, and pushed them down around his ankles.

Casci reached down and pushed her panties until Detrick pulled them off completely. He kissed her passionately. He felt between her legs. Casci was wet. He parted her legs with his knees. With closed eyes, Casci reach between them, grabbed his dick, and placed it at the entrance of her pussy.

"Don't hurt me, nigga."

Detrick entered her slow. The thickness of him caused her to arch her back and the length of his dick had her biting down on his neck. Detrick knew it had been a while since she'd been penetrated and was as gentle as he could be. Her pussy gripped him tighter with each stroke. Her moans had him gauging how deep he went, how fast he fucked her, as well as told him when he was hitting her spot. She went from biting his neck to sucking and kissing the side of his face.

Casci raised her legs more, inviting him deeper. She gasped, arched her back, and clawed at his, when feeling him hit the bottom of the pussy.

For the next thirty minutes there was no talking, no question to ask, no answers to give, only pent up frustration and a release of pleasure. They changed positions after every explosion that rippled through her body.

Loving the way she received him, Detrick flipped Casci onto her stomach and entered her from the back. She arched her back, spread her legs, and looked back at him while he stroked her. Once she was able to take all of him, she rolled her hips, matched his rhythm, and watched his facial expression shift.

Detrick pulled out seconds before he came. A thick hot shot of cum covered her ass and back. Casci reached back, smeared it on her ass, looked him dead in the eyes, and began sucking her fingers clean. He leaned over, covered her mouth with his, and sucked her tongue. It had been five long years since she'd been penetrated by a man, and she enjoyed every minute of it.

***

Coffee was sitting in the living room thumbing through channels and Reniya was thumbing out text after text. They'd been trying to come up with a plan for most of the morning. One possibility they couldn't get past was coming up on the cash Jingles bragged about having in the safe in his office at the club.

"That nigga was probably lying his ass off," Reniya told her friends.

"If it ain't $100,000, it might be close to it. That nigga just might be sitting on something like that." Coffee leaned over, grabbed a lighter, and fired up the blunt she was holding.

"Evening if we do put the lick together, we're still going to need all hands on deck, and you know Ariel ain't built like that."

"We need a nigga on our team," Coffee told her.

"I already know Casci gonna be down. That bitch think she's slick." Reniya sat her phone on the table and walked over and sat beside Coffee.

"Well, who else. It's got to be somebody easier than Jingles."

"Stacy! Ariel told me about all the money he and that nigga Doom be keeping in the motel. He been pulling money from his other spots and keeping it in the motel they are at." Reniya stood, walked to the window overlooking the parking lot, and smiled.

"But how will we get it?" Coffee dumped ashes from the blunt into the ashtray and held it up for Reniya.

"That nigga been wanting to fuck us. All we got to do is get them niggas away from that motel and have someone run up in that bitch." Reniya pulled on the blunt with one eye closed.

"And just in case a motherfucker seeing what they ain't supposed to be seeing, we have a nigga do the shit. That way, if word get back to them, all they know is that some nigga hit they spot." Coffee smiled at the outlook she had.

"We need a motherfuckin' nigga on our team. Uugghh!" Reniya spun around. The knock at the door halting their conversation.

Reniya went to answer the door. It was Chris.

"What y'all in here doing?" he asked, walking past Reniya.

She and Coffee looked at each other. "Hell naw," they shouted in union.

"Hell naw, what? What's up?" Chris looked from one to the next with question etched across his face.

"What the hell do you want, Chris?" Reniya closed the door behind him and walked back into the living room.

"Casci ain't back yet?" he asked them. "Ariel ain't checked in either?"

Instead of answering the questions he was sure to ask, Coffee patted the couch beside her.

"Here, sit down. Let a bitch run something by you real quick."

Reniya took a seat on the arm of the couch next to him. "And you'd better not tell nobody, not even Casci," she told him, while handing him what was left of the blunt.

"Y'all in here fucking around, huh?" Chris leaned away from Reniya. He looked over at Coffee and shook his head.

"Shut your dumb ass up, nigga!" Reniya snatched the piece of blunt she'd given him.

"Damn, gorilla looking ass girl. I was just fucking with y'all."

Coffee pushed his shoulder from one side and Reniya pushed his head from the other. He was known to fuck up something good, and telling him of the good licks they had lined up might just be their fuck up. All they knew was they needed a nigga on their team. And they needed one now.

Chapter Fourteen

"If that nigga find our we robbed him, I'll really have to kill his ass." Chris stood, walked over to the window, and looked down into the parking lot.

"Hell, the way you talked to that nigga last week, you're going to have to do that anyway. Word on the street is—"

"Ain't no damn word on the street." Chris turned, pointed at Reniya, and walked toward her. "Both of y'all trifling bitches just trying to start some shit."

"Believe what you want to, nigga. Motherfuckers ain't in the fifth grade no more, Chris. Niggas ain't knowing paper off shoulders anymore to prove who's the baddest. Niggas dropping niggas off out here for much less. And you already know that nigga Stacy ain't the one to slap-box with. You got to murder that nigga, or he's going to murder you. Point blank," she told him while winking at Coffee.

"But hey, if you want to be one of those niggas out here ducking and dodging niggas because you know they coming for your ass, then that's what you do. You in the game now, nigga. Chasing Casci got your ass tagged and now that niggas know you trying to move a little something, they coming," Coffee added as if it was nothing but common logic.

Chris closed his eyes and placed a hand on his lip and rubbed his head with the other. He walked back toward the window.

"Let's get this money, nigga. We ain't out here to play with these niggas, and we damn sure ain't to be played with." Reniya set the bottle down and stood. She walked over to where Chris stood and grabbed his hand. "Now come on in here so I can give you some of this pussy."

"Move, girl." He pulled his hand from hers. "Don't nobody want none of that salty ass pussy. You bitches are some sharks."

"Sweet and salty, nigga. You gotta lick ass too, remember?" She laughed.

"I mean, how? How do y'all even know the nigga got some money like that?"

"Because, ya girl friend just bragged about getting fucked on one hundred thousand dollars." Reniya reached for her phone.

"That bitch might be lying too."

"If you was able to, would you fuck her on a bed full of some money? Niggas we fuck with ain't got no reason to lie, Chris. This nigga on money for real-for real."

"I'm going to have to kill that nigga. Y'all know that?'

Reniya shrugged.

Coffee continued to thumb through channels.

"Or y'all trying to get me killed. I don't know what to think when it comes to y'all," he told them evenly.

"Well, then, just stay in your lane, Chris. When these niggas start pulling up on you, slapping you on the ass, whispering in your ear and telling they homeboys how they gonna fuck you, you don't say we didn't try to put you on game." Reniya went back to scrolling through her phone's gallery.

"Your bitch ass ain't ready for the shit we trying to do," Coffee spat in disgust.

"Y'all some black-heart-having ass bitches. What we gonna tell Ariel? We start walking around here with oney like that, she's going to put two and two together."

"That's why we keep on making sells and helping you and Casci sell that shit. She already be telling that nigga Marcus be giving y'all work." Coffee watched him.

"And once the nigga dead, we'll just start giving her money. And you can start fucking her."

"Let me think about this shit. Y'all ain't talking about stealing no damn clothes or sunning our of the liquor store with a purse full of drinks. Y'all talking about killing a motherfucker."

"Two motherfuckers. Hi and Doom's funky ass."

"Let me think about this shit." Chris walked toward the door.

"Don't take all day, scary ass nigga. You running around here with that gun for nothing. With your bitch ass." Reniya walked him to the door. She slapped him on the ass as he was stepping out. "Pretty ass nigga."

"Snake ass bitches!" he yelled over his shoulder.

Reniya walked back over to where she was sitting and smiled. "Pussy been making niggas kill each other for two thousand years."

"It's also been the reason they live." Coffee held her palm toward Reniya.

They high-fived in celebration. There was no doubt Chris would be their guy.

***

Detrick led Casci into the bathroom, ran some water for their shower, and sat her at the edge of the his and hers sink.

"You already know I got to taste the pussy," he told her before kneeling between her thighs.

Casci smiled, shook her head, and scooted to where he ass was hanging off the sink. She leaned back on her elbows. "You better not tell—"

Detrick cut her off. "Don't worry, Casci. I know what time it is." He kissed the insides of both her thighs, rubbed his lips and chin across her pussy, and spread her legs wider. He licked her asshole.

"I just don't want you to think this shit is going to happen again," she managed to get out. Casci closed her eyes when feeling his war, soft tongue caress her clitoris.

"Umph-umm." He moaned.

"And this shit don't come between me and my cousin, Detrick."

Detrick munched on her pussy, massaged her inner thighs, and once her legs began to shake, he swallowed her juices.

***

After a hot shower, Casci walked back into the room to find Detrick standing by the window on his phone. He'd straightened the bed and dressed back into the clothes he wore.

She waited until he ended his call before asking him, "And that nigga trust you enough to leave you with access to his house?"

"Matter of fact, this is the, like, second or third time I've been here." Detrick reached into his pocket. "You like it or what?"

"Yeah, the nigga got a nice set-up. I'm not going to lie, but—"

"Well, he wanted me to give you these." Detrick handed her the set of keys Marcus had given him.

Casci laughed. "Yeah, right."

"He told me to tell you that he knew you ain't feeling sleeping on that couch and whenever you want to, you can just come here, get your head right, or just chill."

Casci looked at him with question.

"Here." He pushed the keys toward her.

Casci continued to towel herself. She looked around them and smiled when Detrick handed her her panties.

"And you'll be here to take the pussy again, huh?" She Snatched them from him and slid them on.

Detrick helped her dress. "I was praying that shit worked out the way it did, because I don't know what I would have done if it hadn't."

"Oh, so you been planning this shit?" Casci sat on the corner of the bed and watched him. "Did he tell you to do that too?"

"That nigga would kill me if he found out I did some shit like that. And you know it." Detrick smiled, walked over, and sat beside her. "I owed you that."

"Really?"

"Remember I promised you a good time at Butterflies?"

Casci laughed. "And you think that was it? Nigga, you ain't no bitch." She nodded toward his lap. :And you damn sure ain't got no pussy. So technically, you still owe me."

"You really a cool chick, Casci. You ain't like Coffee and Reniya and them."

"Yeah, I'll bet."

Once she was dressed, took a look around the house, and was standing on the patio overlooking the oblong-shaped pool, she held her hand out. She really hadn't decided what she'd do as far as accepting Marcus' invitation, but she was going to consider it. And although she hadn't found the place he kept money, she was more than sure it would be close by.

"So, what's in Miami?"

Detrick looked down into the waters of the pool. His expression turned sullen. "He goes to pick up his work from Hector. If you haven't figured it out yet, all these niggas get they work from Hector."

"Oh, yeah?" Casci thought back to the conversation she and Marcus had in the back of the detail shop.

Marcus' words were, "That bitch call, I come running" and "Because of the shit I did to you, I became they bitch."

"He ain't really told me, but I know them motherfuckers holding something over his head. Why ain't nobody killed them hoes yet?" Casci frowned.

"Them Minez brothers deep, Casci, and they hiding behind one of them cartels down there in Miami."

Casci nodded her understanding but still didn't see why they had such a hold on the city.

"Marcus ain't the only one. That nigga J-Rod work for them hoes. Snoop Deuce be scoring from them, them Northside Niggas run hits for

116

them, and Dre P got them blood niggas ready for whatever. Hector dun' masterminded the whole operation. He ain't easy to touch, Casci."

"So, when we do make a move, we going to war with the Minez brothers and all the motherfuckers banking off them?" Casci watched Detrick, trying to read him.

"And some of us going to die too," he replied.

Casci had thought about just that for years. She'd even thought about the many people she once knew that died at the hands of the Minez brothers.

"That's all in the game, ain't it?" Casci turned and walked back inside. Her mind was made up.

Detrick followed her inside. He told her, "He's already put money on them niggas Stacy and Doom heads for the shit they did to them kids at one of their spots. Don't let that shit happen to you."

"Shit happens." Casci shrugged, pushed the key to the house in her pocket, and stepped into her shoes. It was time she got back to the Gardens.

Detrick sighed, stepped into his shoes, and nodded. Marcus's description of her and the person she was spot on. Niggas would go to war for her. And by the way things were looking, he'd be somewhere in that line-up.

***

The minute Ariel walked into the salon, she knew she was the topic of choice. Not only did the talking stop, but Mildred was the first to approach her.

"Girl, have you heard about all this shit your man is in?"

Ariel walked over to her station, set her purse and phone in the second and first drawer, and looked at her with surprise. "Who? Stacy?"

"Yes. Stacy." Mildred waved the question off and pointed toward a woman sitting under the dryers. "Him and his boy dun' went and shot up some trap house."

Ariel looked from Mildred to the woman under the dryer. "Shot up some trap house?"

"Four teenagers got killed, and now some cartel is looking for them. Girl, stay away from him."

Ariel stammered. "Um, I haven't seen Stacy in about a week. The last I heard, he went out of town," she lied. She'd heard about the shooting. She and Stacy even talked about it, and thinking about the way he'd been acting lately, it was easy for her to see he was running or hiding from someone.

His calls to her requesting she meet him at the hotel. The way he and Doom were hiding out at that rundown motel, and the fact that he was in possession of so much money. Ariel shook the thoughts she was having, He was spoiling and pampering her because he couldn't afford to have other women he was fucking to sell him out for whatever him and Doom's whereabouts would reward them.

"Well, just be careful around him, Ariel. I'd hate for something to happen to you because of some shit he's involved with."

"Oh, you don't have to worry about that. I barely see him as it is," she lied.

Now that the blanks were filled, she couldn't wait to confront him.

Chapter Fifteen

Marcus had checked into the COMO Metropolitan Hotel two days ago and was still yet to get word on the whereabouts he was meet with Hector. Being that his trip was one he had to fund himself, he was shelling out over $500 a night. And since Hector was no longer wanting to meet at their long time spot in Atlanta, Georgia, he was shaving to travel all the way to Plantation Florida for the kilos of cocaine the Minez brothers had for him.

He hated the way things were between him and the brother Hector. Despite him being the reason the younger brother Alex and his now wife Rose lived a lavish life, he was still treated like a peon. There was no respect between them, and Marcus also knew the only reason he was still alive was because he was making over a million dollars a year and had been for the last three years. And a large portion of that money went to Hector Minez. Not only was Marcus expected to sell drugs for the brother, he was responsible for their passage back to Dallas. He took $250,000 to Alex once a year for them to do as he pleased and another quarter of a million was the percentage he was paying for the drugs Hector gave him on consignment. With the money he was able to put up. Marcus bought a building and invested in a smoke shop. His plan was to have several in a few years.

He walked toward the door when hearing a knock, It was time.

"Let's go."

Marcus looked from one of the heavy-set Mexicans to the next. "Do I need to lock—"

"Move, *puta!* We no have all day."

Once downstairs, Marcus was led to a tented Yukon. He climbed in. Things had definitely changed since the last time he was there.

***

Detrick pulled into the Gardens and headed for the rear of the complex. He looked over at Casci. "Marcus' house doesn't seem like a bad spot to chill out at all, does it?"

"These motherfuckin' complexes are home, Detrick, but yeah, I'd love to have something outside of these wall one day."

"Let's just hope we live that long, Casci. How about we do that?"

"Yeah, why not?"

Detrick pulled behind Reniya's Charger and stopped.

"You coming up or what?" Casci reached for the door handle.

"Nah. I have some shit to got to do."

"Oh, so you just gonna fuck a bitch down, drop her off, and be done with it, huh?"

Detrick laughed. "Nah. Any other bitch would have had to find her own way home."

Casci punched his arm. "Just remember what I said, nigga."

Detrick made the zip the lip motion and acted as of he was throwing the key out the window.

"And you still owe me that Jamaican bitch." Casci climbed out the truck, closed the door, and headed for the stairs. She wiped the smile from her face.

***

Reniya was standing in the window looking out over the parking lot when Detrick and Casci pulled back up. In only a month's time, she was seeing Casci do what she and the other girls were still yet to do. She and Coffee talked about stepping their game up, but Casci was doing the shit. It was time they did the same.

"here's Casci and Detrick," she told Coffee.

"Is he coming in or what?' Coffee stood.

"Nah. Casci coming up alone."

"Good, 'cause I don't feel like parading around in no little bitty ass panties right now."

Reniya walked over and opened the door before Casci could. "We thought we were going to have to come looking for you."

"Girl, that nigga trophied a bitch, put me on some killah ass weed, and snitched on y'all hoes."

Coffee laughed from where she sat. "Yep, sounds like him. The only thing he didn't do was fuck you silly."

"Or, did he?" Reniya asked, immediately picking up on Casci's aura.

"Bitch, please. I don't even know that nigga." Casci walked past her, grabbed a juice from the 'fridgerator, and went to sit beside Coffee. She reached for Reniya's phone, yet jumped when feeling Reniya's chin over her head.

"And the bitch smell like soap."

"Bitch, get from over here." Casci smiled. "Damn."

Coffee tilted her head and frowned. Casci was definitely acting like a woman who's just gotten fucked. She couldn't stop smiling, and she was apparently thirsty, having drank half of the juice in one swig. "Casci got some dick!" she yelled. "This bitch just got fucked, Reniya!" Coffee jumped across the couch all on her cousin. She wrestled her.

"Ouu, bitch, ya bull daggin' ass finally fucked."

"Will y'all move? Y'all act like I fucked Idris Elba or somebody." Casci pushed Coffee off her, drank the last of her juice, and set it on the table. She smiled at them. "Y'all better not say shit neither."

"Did he eat that ass?" Reniya asked, happy for her homegirl.

"Did he?" Casci closed her eyes. "Nah, the question is, did he fuck you in the ass? 'Cause if so, I'm not sucking that nigga's dick ever again."

"No, he did not fuck me in my ass, bitch. He actually took the pussy. Before I knew what was happening, I was naked and eight inches of dick was stretching my pussy open."

Reniya smiled. "Bitch, you sound like one of them hoes who got caught cheating on the husband or something. Talking about, 'before you knew what was happening.' You sad, Casci."

"You didn't get paid? Bitch, you tripping. Don't start giving these niggas no pussy for free, Casci. I wouldn't give a damn if it was Idris Elba."

Casci dug into her pocket and pulled out the set of keys Detrick had given her. She held them up, "I get houses for this pussy, bitch."

Reniya spread her legs and dropped her ass low. "Beat a bitch's ass, suck a little dick, make a lot of money, we lit!"

Casci sat back and just watched her girls celebrate. She loved seeing them happy. These were the members of her family, and nothing would come between them. Especially no nigga.

***

Marcus covered his eyes when stepping out the Yukon. The ride offered him the luxury of seeing the latest porn movies on the screen inside, but the curtain limited his view of the scenery around them.

His eyes widened when he was led through huge French doors. The vaulted pine, plant ceiling, the saturnian marble floors, and the Aztec décor were all new to him. Not only did Hector Minez move not another house, he'd moved up in the game.

"Ahh, Marcus. Come in. Have a seat," hector instructed.

Marcus couldn't take his eyes off the Ashanti look-alike. He nodded at her. "Hector, I see you're doing pretty good down here." Marcus sat across from his host.

Hector waved the women away, and once he and Marcus were along, he told him, "I live like this because of the stupid shit you motherfuckers do. I pay eight hundred and forty thousand dollars for a million-dollar home. You the reason I live like this, Marcus." Hector's smile vanished. He leaned forward, grabbed his cigar from the ashtray, and lit it. He blew a thick cloud of smoke in Marcus' direction, openly disrespecting him. "I hear that pendejo Casci is out, eh?"

"Yeah, she out on an early parole. I spoke with her just recently." Marcus leaned away from him, looked over at he burley Mexican guards standing at the entrance of the lounge area.

"Oh, she no kill you?" Hector laughed. "That bitch! Does she know you the reason she still breathes!"

"I didn't get to talk to her for long. It was in passing. But yeah, I'm still alive." He looked at Hector. "Look, I didn't come here to talk about her. I came to get my shit so I can leave Florida as soon as possible."

"No, my friend. You come here because I send for you, and you leave when and if I want you to leave, eh?"

Marcus looked back toward the entryway.

"Lucky for her, you work for me." Hector stood suddenly, slammed his cigar on the opague glass table, and pointed at him. "All you motherfuckers work for Hector Minez!"

Marcus looked away. It took all of him not to speak his mind.

"Maybe I want you to kill that *pendejo*. Eh? Maybe Hector make you kill that bitch."

"Look, man. We already agreed on that shit. We leave her out of it." Marcus looked Hector straight in his eyes and told him, "I move your dope, I make your money, and I take care of your little bro and his wife. So leave her alone."

Two of Hector's man made steps in their direction when hearing Marcus' tone of voice and seeing him eye their boss. Hector stopped them with a have of his hand. He smiled, fell back down into the chair, and said, "Double."

"Double what?"

"I want double, or you and that bisch die, eh? You together robbed me, so you together pay me. I hear about your prices, Marcus. I know you making a lot more than you give me. You handle it. Put that bisch to work." Hector waved the guards over.

Marcus stood. "Raise my package, I pay you double."

There was no answer. One of the guys grabbed Marcus' arm and pulled him toward the exit. The Uzi he and the other guard carried gave him little to no choice.

"I'll have Alex oversee the delivery of that double, Marcus."

Chapter Sixteen

Chris had just finished a $7,500 transaction with another one of the guys Reniya hooked him up with and decided to stop and grab a couple boxes of the Philly Titan Cigars. Casci had told him that she was expecting a couple ounces of mango Kush, and he was going to be ready.

He pulled the Chrysler around the gas pumps and parked closer to the side of the building. He liked the way people gawked at the customized 300. Marcus had put a pretty penny into the upgrade, and he was sure.

He parked, allowing the heavy baseline of the Young Jeezy track to vibrate the glass of the building, and slowly opened the car door. He pushed the Glock he had between the seat and the armrest compartment before climbing out. Chris was just about to enter the building when a familiar voice halted him.

"What's up, playboy?"

Chris faced the guy who addressed him. Stacy and Doom were walking out of the building. Stacy had the hood to the hoodie he wore over his head, halfway covering his face. Doom was wearing dark shades, and both his hands were in the pockets of the jacket he wore. Chris was slipping, and this was the first time he'd ever felt this way.

He looked from Stacy to Doom, seeing the hand grip of the pistol he was holding in his pocket, and looked back to Stacy.

"What's all that shit you was talking over the phone?" Stacy walked within inches of Chris—their noses damn near touching.

"You want to drop this nigga or what, Stacy?" Doom asked, while making his way around Chris.

"I'm not about to do no bumping with you, nigga." Chris thought of the words Reniya and Coffee used when it came to dealing with Stacy. He took a step back, just in case a knife was pulled. The pistol he had was left in the car, and although people were walking back and forth through the lot, he was still vulnerable.

Stacy took a step forward, closing the distance Chris created between them. "Nah, this bitch ass nigga was just trying to impress them hoes," Stacy told Doom. "You didn't really mean that shit, did you, faggot ass nigga?" Stacy's forehead lightly tapped Chris's.

Knowing he wasn't in the position to do anything, Chris turned his head.

"That's what I thought, hoe ass nigga." Stacy raised his hand from the pocket of his hoodie. He held it out in front of Chris. "Drop out, nigga. You already know what time it is."

Chris reluctantly took another step backward, but this time, he bumped into Doom.

"Ain't nothing but dick back here, weak ass nigga. This what you want?" Doom pushed the barrel of his pistol into Chris's back.

"Drop out, hoe ass nigga. I heard you out here trying to make a little noise." Stacy went into Chris's pocket and pulled out the wad of cash he'd just made. "Yeah, looks like he's finally begged up on something," Stacy told Doom, before sticking the money into his own pocket.

"How them hoes gonna feel when they find out your pussy bigger than theirs?" Doom laughed.

"Yeah, I might just swing by the Gardens and give it to Casci myself. And let her know that you'd do better selling ass than dope." Stacy pushed Chris aggressively, knocking Chris back a step. "Next time, playboy!" Stacy held his middle finger up, while yelling over his shoulder.

Chris looked toward the Chrysler. He thought about going to get the gun he had and putting a couple slugs in both of them, but thought better of it. People were still walking to and from. There were just too many witnesses.

With no money on him now, he walked back toward the Chrysler. Once he climbed in and closed the door, he slammed his hands on the steering wheel.

"Bitch," he screamed, causing several people to look in his direction.

He looked in the direction Stacy and Doom went, looking for Stacy's truck, and saw that they were now riding around in a Ford Mustang, with heavily tinted windows.

Chris slowly pulled past them and headed for the Gardens, Casci's words reminding him of the game he was now in. "You've got to be aware of your surroundings and what the fuck you gonna do." Now that he'd done the total opposite of what he swore he would, that mistake wouldn't be made again.

***

Stacy and Doom climbed into the tinted Mustang and sat there. They watched Chris until he pulled out of the lot, and fired up a blunt of the fruity Kush they had. Doom pulled out the Ruger he'd pushed into Chris's back and placed it in his lap. He scanned the area continually as Stacy tended to the weed.

"I should've knocked his punk ass out, and took that damn car, huh?" Doom asked Stacy.

"That nigga ain't gonna last here anyway. These hungry ass niggas gonna bend all the rules when they get word that he tryin' to make some noise in the game. He a street nigga, but he's in over his head, fucking with that bitch, Casci." Stacy pulled on the blunt, coughed, and pulled again.

"She gon' to get that nigga killed, huh?" Doom pointed at a car full of Blood gang members.

"Yeah, I see them," Stacy told him, while reaching for the FN rifle on the back seat. He checked the hundred-round clip before locking it into place.

"You think they working for that hoe, Hector?" Doom asked. He unlatched the safety feature on the 9mm Ruger.

"Never can tell, fucking with these niggas now a days. Everybody want the bag now."

They watched as the group climbed out and filed into the gas station. None of them once looked in their direction.

Seeing there was no threat of danger, Stacy put the sports car in gear and pulled out of the lot. "Let's go find this bitch ass nigga, Peanut, and get this shit over with."

Doom nodded, all the while looking in his rearview mirror at the group of guys that came within inches of their deaths.

***

Reniya and Coffee ran their play by Casci. They both wanted to rob Stacy and Jingles, and needed her on board. Casci, at first, spoke against it, not wanting them to do anything stupid. But the more she protested the idea, the more she realized they were going to attempt it without her.

"I'm just saying. Y'all need to think this shit through first, because niggas ain't trying to take no losses like that." Casci looked at her cousin with raised brows, hoping she understood what came with what she and Reniya were suggesting.

"Bitch, that's why we got you, to help us think this shit through." Coffee walked from the sofa to the kitchen.

"Just think of what we ain't thinking of, Casci. The ins and outs and shit." Reniya leaned forward on the couch, placed both her elbows on her thighs, and watched her.

"Bitch, we chasing the bag, too," Coffee spoke from where she was standing.

Casci nodded. "I understand that, but—"

"'But' my ass, bitch." Reniya stood and said, "These niggas fuck with you, Casci. You ain't been out a month, and you already sitting on money and dope. That nigga really paying you not to rob his ass. Hell, we know you about that shit, so help some bitches out." Reniya pushed Casci's leg with her knee as she passed.

Casci hated when her girls pouted. She hated seeing them go without, and she couldn't stand seeing them abused in any kind of way.

She sighed, closed her eyes, and told them, "Marcus went to Miami to get some more work. He should be back in a day or so."

"How much work?" Coffee walked back into the living area. She looked at Casci with all seriousness.

Reniya did the same. "How much work, Casci?"

"Forty keys."

"Forty keys?" Coffee swung at the air above Casci's head before repeating, "Forty keys?"

"Bitch, what the fuck you waiting on?" Reniya asked her, knowing Coffee was wanting to get at Marcus anyway.

"And the nigga done gave you the keys to his house. Let's go by there and wait on his ass," Coffee told her. She looked toward Reniya.

"Hell yeah. We'll be sitting in the dark when his punk ass walk in the door."

Casci looked at them. "Then what?"

"Then we smoke his bitch ass," Coffee said simply.

"I'll pull the trigger, if you won't. Fuck that nigga." Reniya shrugged. It was simple as that.

"You bitches need to calm down. I'm thinking about long-term. The nigga dropping out already. And if I play the shit right, we can get a three-way split on the work he's bringing home. How y'all know he's taking it to his house? He might be dropping the shit somewhere else, and we go jump the gun and don't get shit. Then we end up killing that nigga for nothing. Y'all bitches got to think." Casci stood, walked over to the widow, and turned back to face them. "We got to think long term now."

"I still say we surprise his ass, just in case. If he got the work, we kill him. If not, we act like we wanted to surprise him and give him a threesome because of the way he's been breaking bread with you." Coffee looked at Casci.

"Sit your black ass down, girl. That nigga wouldn't fall for no shit like that. This is still Marcus we are talking about."

Reniya threw her hands up in defeat. "Well, we need to come up with something. It's too much money out here for us to be without, Casci. Fuck it, I'll start selling some dope. Tell that nigga to give me a kilo."

"I'm not saying we ain't going to bleed these niggas. We just got to think this shit through. We need alibis and all kinds of shit. But most importantly, we need a nigga like Detrick on our team."

Coffee shook her head. "Hell nah. We can let the nigga fuck all day long, but we ain't about to put that nigga in our business, Casci. Fuck that shit."

"Damn. If we can win for forty kilos of dope, we'll be rich in no time." Reniya's thoughts took her to a place she'd always dreamed of going, a place far away from the Gardens.

"If we go fire that nigga shit up, he's going to know I had something to do with it," Casci told them.

"And what about that nigga Stacy? We know he siting on some bread. All we gotta do is get him and that skinny ass nigga Doom away from the motel and run through that bitch like the laws just hit it," Reniya told them.

"Now, it's going to look funny if a bitch was seen running out that motel room and speeding off in some car," Casci said.

"Let's just fall up in that bitch and gun they as down. We got some heat, and ain't nobody going to care about them niggas." Coffee went over to the couch and pulled the AR-15 from under it.

Reniya then slipped her hand between the cushions of the couch and pulled out the Glock Casci kept there.

Just as they were about to replace the guns, the front door swung open. Both Reniya and Coffee raised the barrels toward the guy standing there with a pistol in his hand.

Casci yelled, "Wait!"

Chapter Seventeen

Stacy drove by J-Rod's spot and stopped at the top of the street. He at least hoped they'd see a sign telling if Peanut was or had been hiding out at this particular spot. Now that word was out that they were the ones behind the shooting where four teenagers died, they weren't about to take any chances, when it came to the people they normally associated with. Stacy was still able to spread some money, and them finding out where J-Rod was now setting up his operations only took a couple of racks. To them, it was money well spent.

"I say we just run up in that bitch and do what we came to do," Doom told Stacy. They'd been sitting at the top of the block for thirty minutes and had yet to see any movement in or outside of the house.

"Naw, what we need to do is sit and wait for his ass. I don't want to expose our hand with these niggas. The last I heard, them niggas was talking about we were out of town somewhere." Stacy passed the Kush filled blunt, leaned against his door, and slumped lower in the seat.

"That nigga might even have some money up on that bitch. You see ain't no traffic coming in or out." Doom watched the block carefully. "This might be where he lay his head at night."

Stacy nodded. This had to have been a spot he came to get away, or the one he kept all his work and money. Unlike the spot where they caught up with Peanut the first time, this house was in a much nicer neighborhood. These weren't trap houses. These were really homes.

"That is what am banking on. That is why we need to slow this shit down." Stacy reached for his vibrating phone, saw it was Ariel calling, and told Doom, "Be quiet right quick." He lowered the volume on the radio and answered. "Hey, babe, what's up?"

"Where are you at, nigga?"

"I am in Houston, why?" he could tell from the tone of her voice that she was doing more accusing than asking.

"Don't lie to me, Stacy. Where are you?"

"Man, I don't have time for all these questions and shit, Ariel. I am trying to take care of some business so that I can get back to the road." Stacy looked over at Doom.

"Nigga, do you know what is being said about you and that crazy ass nigga you are running with. Huh?"

"What is it now, Ariel, because I ain't been fucking with no hoes," he told her, as if that was what she was accusing him of.

"This ain't got shit to do with no hoes, Stacy. Don't play me for no fool. I know you had something to do with that shooting the other day."

Stacy sighed. "What the hell are you talking about, woman? I ain't shot anybody." He reached for the blunt Doom handed him and took a pull. He wiped away the ashes that fell onto the floorboard.

"You think I am stupid, huh? You think I am one of them dizzy ass hoes you be fucking with, nigga?"

"Ariel, I am trying to take care of some business. I'm going to call you as soon as I get back to the highway," he told her, seeing J-Rod drive into the garage of the house they were watching.

"Motherfuckers out looking for you, Stacy. I can't believe you lied to me about that shit. I—"

Stacy cut her off. "Ariel, I have to go, babe. I'm going to explain everything to you later. Bye." He ended the call, checked the rearview mirror to see in the opposite direction, and sat erect in the driver's seat.

"There was another car in the garage," Doom told him. He checked the magazine a second time, loaded it into his Ruger, and slid it into the pocket of his jacket.

"For all we know, it's ten motherfuckers in there, so let's do this shit and get out."

"Yeah, this might be the last time we catch this nigga like this," Doom replied, reaching for his door handle. He slowly climbed out and left the door slightly open.

***

Ariel called several more times, and each time she was sent to voicemail. She couldn't believe the things she was hearing at the salon. The things they'd done and the things people were talking about doing to them were horrendous. Then there was the fact that he'd been playing her for the information she had.

"Punk ass nigga," she yelled, being sent to voicemail the third time. People always warned her about the things Stacy did and now she had no choice but to listen.

***

Chris froze, seeing the guns pointed at him. He raised his hands. "Nigga, you almost got your ass smoked," Reniya told him. She lowered the handgun she held.

Casci walked towards him, pulled him inside, and closed the door. She frowned, seeing the welled up tears in his eyes.

"What the hell is wrong with you?" She walked back around him. "What you do, Chris?"

"I'm going to kill that bitch ass nigga." Chris closed his eyes, walked over to the kitchen counter, and wiped his face." I swear to God, I'm going to kill that bitch."

Coffee walked over to the window and peered out of it. She made sure no one had followed him. "What happened? What the fuck you crying for?"

Chris looked skyward in order to keep his tears the check. He told them, "That bitch ass nigga robbed me."

"Who? Who you talking about?" Casci watched him.

"That nigga Stacy, they caught me up in the gas station and beat me for the money I just made off of that quarter of a kilo I had."

"They beat you, for what now?" Reniya frowned.

"They got me for the money I just made, deaf ass girl," Chris went off.

Coffee laughed at him so hard she fell onto the sofa. She pointed at him, unable to speak for laughing.

"Fuck you, black ass man!" Chris held his middle finger high. He rolled his eyes and looked down at Casci for comfort and understanding.

Casci looked away to conceal the smile that was forcing its way onto her face.

"I am serious. Y'all think a nigga bullshitting. Them punk ass niggas hit me up, right there in the middle of the fucking parking lot." Chris pointed towards the ground, emphasizing his point.

"Weak ass nigga," Coffee yelled between breaths. "Your ass..."

"Black ass motherfucker think this shit funny. See if your crab worm built ass laugh when I smoke them niggas."

Coffee continued pointing at him, while she laughed.

"Nigga, you quick to slap a bitch. But when these niggas get at your ass, you run home, crying like a little bitch," Reniya went off.

"Leave him alone, Reniya. You see the nigga shook up," Casci told her. She grabbed Chris' arm and led him to the couch in the living room. "Where the Kush at?" she asked Reniya.

"Punk ass run around here talking like you a killer, and you let some niggas pull your pockets." Reniya threw the gun on the couch and grabbed her phone. "Let me see if somebody posted that shit yet."

"Bitch, I'm not playing with y'all," Chris yanked his arm away from Casci and looked at them. The tears finally falling and his voice cracking.

Coffee laughed harder, causing Casci to laugh and Reniya to look at him with raised eyebrows. "Nigga, you better sit your ass down and breathe before I call them niggas over here," she told him, before laughing herself.

"Aw, shit," Coffee sat upright so she could see him better. She wiped the tears in her eyes and smiled. "My bad, Chris. My bad, nigga."

"Fuck you, with your ashy ass. Chinese looking ass can't even apologize to a nigga."

"Okay, okay, tell us what happened from start to finish," Casci told him.

"Naw, naw, hold up right quick," Coffee stood up, stretched the cramp in her stomach, and walked towards the kitchen. "Let me get something to drink first."

Chris waited until she was in the kitchen before he ran everything down, just as it happened. He saw the disappointment in Casci's expressions, the humor Reniya was seeing, and could hear Coffee muffle her laughter, while hiding in the kitchen. Now that he was able to see what they were seeing, he could do nothing but laugh himself.

"And when I tried to step off of the nigga, Doom pushed the barrel of the pistol he had in my back, talking about, 'it ain't nothing but dick back here.' I started to spin around and knock all them diamonds out of his mouth," Chris told them.

Coffee's laughter grew louder. Casci lowered her head and Reniya just shook hers.

"Why you didn't run up in the store?" Reniya asked.

"Motherfucker, how I'm going to run when the niggas was sandwiching me?" Chris gave her an incredulous look.

"You should have screamed, HEELLLP MEEE," Coffee yelled from the kitchen. She was on the floor now.

Chris closed his eyes, and a smile crept onto his face. "That foggot ass girl gonna make me put my foot right up her ass."

"Ain't nothing but dick back here, pretty ass nigga," she told him mocking Doom's tone of voice.

Casci laughed.

"You might as well put that gun up and get you a bottle of mace," Reniya told him.

"You've got to man up, nigga. I told you, you've got to be aware of your surroundings at all times," Casci smiled at him. She wasn't upset with him at all. He needed to experience a loss.

"Yes, ma'am," he agreed sarcastically.

"Nigga, you the one got slapped with dick," Reniya told him, knowing he was trying to be funny.

"Ain't no room for slippers in the game, Chris. Niggas out here making examples out of niggas like you," Casci got serious. "What if them niggas would have took your life, instead of some money?"

"By the time I looked up, it was too late," he confessed.

"Your girl ass was too busy trying to look good and be seen. I wish they would have made your ass get naked in front of all the people. The shit would have gotten real then." Reniya wasn't letting up. She needed him to be and do more, when it came to what they were trying to pull off.

"Will you shut up," Chris looked towards Casci. "Will you tell the bitch to shut up?"

"Ain't nothing but dick back here, bitch ass nigga," Coffee yelled from the kitchen, a second time.

Chris jumped up, ran towards the kitchen, and found Coffee on the floor. He wrestled her until he had her arms pinned and he was straddling her. He pressed his knuckle in her ribs.

"Shut... Shut your black ass up," he told her, while tickling her.

"Ain't... nothing but dick—"

Reniya looked over at Casci and rolled her eyes. She told her, "Now we got to harden his weak ass up. I told that bitch that nigga wasn't right."

"Chris! Chris! Come on so we can put this shit together, nigga." Casci lit up another blunt.

"This bitch in here trying to make me touch her pussy," he told them.

"Nigga, get your big ass off of me." Coffee tried in vain to free herself.

"Promise you gonna shut up. Promise."

"Okay, okay. I promise. I promise."

Chris rolled off of her, saw her ass in the air, and slapped it hard.

"Ouch, boy!"

"Big booty ass, girl."

***

Once Doom was standing where he was blocking the view from anyone on the inside to see who was on the outside, Stacy rang the doorbell. The mack-11 they used in the previous murder was concealed under his arm. He nodded at Doom, hearing someone approach the door. Doom frowned, hearing the female voice.

"Who is it?"

Chapter Eighteen

While Casci, Reniya and Coffee sketched out the plan to rob Stacy and Doom, Chris stood with his arms folded. His right hand stroked his chin from time to time. He looked over at Reniya, glanced in Coffee's direction, and shook his head. Hearing that he'd be the one to search the motel, where Stacy was said to have kept the $100,000, he walked to the window.

"And if the money ain't there?" he asked them.

"It's there. Where else they going to keep it? Ain't nobody fucking with them niggas right now. And I'm more than sure they ain't fucking with many people either," Reniya told him.

"As soon as you get the money, you hit up Casci, and she's going to text me," Coffee said, looking over at Chris.

Casci stood, inhaled as deeply as she could, and smiled. The plan they came up with did sound much better than it actually was, and for the first time since she'd been out, she prayed nothing rolled back in their direction.

"Chris, man, you are going to have to get out," Casci told him. "Being that we don't know if they have someone watching the room, you got to make it look as if everything is normal. Don't go looking around and all that shit."

"Motherfucker, I know what to do."

Coffee walked over to him with her fist out. "Lock that shit in, nigga."

"Yeah, nigga, lock that shit down." Reniya also walked toward him—her fist clinched outward also.

"I'm going to do my part. Y'all just make sure y'all do what y'all supposed to do. If y'all got to suck some dick, fuck, get fucked in the ass, then that's what y'all do." Chris dapped both of them up and looked over at Casci.

"Alright, nigga. You locked that shit down. So if you don't take care of your business, I'm going to pop a cap in your ass." Reniya raised her Glock.

"And you are going to swear to say you planned this shit by yourself," Coffee added.

"Motherfucker, y'all ain't the ones who got to worry about getting caught and shit. All y'all got to do is suck some dick." He looked toward Reniya.

Casci looked back at the three of them. She saw nothing but confidence in each of their expressions, and nodded. She knew this was only the beginning of it. Once the lights came on and it was time to act, most people froze. There was no turning back now. "But first, let's go see what that nigga Marcus got for us."

"Pretty ass nigga finally jumping off the porch," Reniya told Chris, as she handed him the duffle bag with the AR-15.

"Off the porch and into some shit." Coffee laughed.

Once the girls were seated in the car, Chris turned toward Casci and asked, "And just how much do I get off these licks?"

"You need to worry about not getting a slug in your ass, nigga. Because if I end up sucking a dick for nothing, I'm definitely going to have your ass face down and ass up," Reniya told him in all seriousness.

"Nigga, you know we going to bless your game." Coffee smiled at him.

"Cause I'm telling y'all right now, if y'all fuck over me, I'm gonna—"

"Nigga, you ain't going to do shit but thank a bitch. Now, let's go before this nigga get back." Reniya pushed the back of the headrest.

Casci rubbed her hands on the knees of the warm-up she was wearing. It was time.

***

After wrapping J-Rod's body in two of the trash bags they'd gotten from the kitchen, and sealing them with gray tape they found in the garage, they dragged him into the master bedroom and threw him in the tub. They agreed to do the same thing to Peanut, once he got there. It would be days, maybe months, before they were found, and once they were, Stacy planned on being long gone.

He and Doom would set up shop in Atlanta. Along with the $100,000 they already had, they had now come up on another $180,000 and twenty kilos of cocaine. They were more than sure they'd make something happen wherever they landed.

Stacey was standing in the kitchen, looking out the window, when an all-black F-150 pulled into the driveway. He signaled for Doom to be still, just in case the driver or the occupants could see movement.

"Is that him?" Doom asked from where he sat. He slowly reached for his Ruger.

"Can't tell. The motherfucker tinted up." Stacey watched the driver's side of the truck.

J-Rod's phone rang. Doom held it up, showing Stacy that it was from an unlisted caller.

"That's got to be him, man." Doom placed the phone face down and closed his eyes. He wanted Peanut bad.

"And it could be someone else. Whoever it is apparently is seeing something they don't normally see because they ain't getting out the truck."

"Let's just light they ass up from here." Doom slowly crept to where he could see outside.

"Nah, we can't risk no shit like that. For all we know, Peanut probably sent someone to see what was what before he came himself. This nigga ain't stupid."

For what seemed like forever, Stacy stood as still as he could, all the while, watching the truck sit idle less than twenty yards from where he and Doom waited. If there was a truck filled with guys awaiting word to surround the house, they were fucked. The last thing he wanted was a shootout with a bunch of guys while being trapped in a house they knew nothing about.

The phone rang again.

"That's got to be him, Stacy. That bitch probably called the nigga and gave him the heads up."

"Nah, if she'd done some shit like that, he wouldn't have even came," Stacy assured him.

Stacy clutched the handle of the Mack-11, seeing the driver's door open slightly. And just as it opened, it closed and began slowly backing out of the driveway.

"Shit!"

"The nigga must feel something ain't right." Doom slowly stood, and once the truck was heading in the direction it had just come from, he ran toward the garage door.

"Doom!" Stacy yelled, hoping his friend wasn't about to chase after the truck.

"The plates. I just need to see the plates," he yelled over his shoulder.

Once the truck disappeared down the street, Stacy wasn't taking any chances. He wasn't about to get caught slipping.

They grabbed the money and drugs and headed out the back door. Doom grabbed the chrome AK-47 with the wood handle that set behind the back door and concealed it under his arm. They might not have caught up with Peanut, but their stop wasn't in vain.

"Don't worry. We'll get his ass," Stacy told him while they walked back to their car with packs over each of their shoulders and automatic rifles under their arms.

"We should've set that motherfucker on fire, Stacy. Fuck them niggas."

Stacy looked over at his friend and smiled. He told him, "If anybody was seeing something, they most likely saw that bitch speeding away from the house, so we good. What we should've done was left some dope and money scattered around the house so it'll look like a drug deal gone bad."

"Let's go have some fun, homie."

Stacy pulled his vibrating phone from his pocket and frowned when seeing it was a text from Reniya. "I wonder what this bitch want?" he asked himself before typing a response.

"She probably looking for Ariel," Doom said after being told who the caller was.

"Or, she could be looking for this dick." Stacy laughed.

He knew that wasn't true. He'd tried too many times to fuck with Ariel's closest friends. It had to be something else.

***

By the time Ariel walked into the apartment, the girls had been long gone. Casci had texted her to let her know that they were going to stop by Marcus's house. She even told her that if everything went well, they'd have a little something to celebrate.

Hoping that things were alright on Stacy's end, Ariel called him several times. After being sent to voicemail each time, she plugged her phone into the charger and headed for the shower. She had some early clients, and she wasn't about to schedule them in later than they already were. She'd just get at Stacy later. That was if he was still alive.

Chapter Nineteen

Despite the long hours on the two-day stay at the COMO motel, Marcus was still furious when he pulled into his driveway. Not only did he have to wait two days to even see Hector, but the meeting lasted every bit of twenty minutes. On top of that, throughout the conversation, there were insults on top of insults, and then the eventual threat on his life.

He'd met with Hector many times, and although there was no love between them, there was never the level of disrespect he'd just experienced. And for Hector to throw it in his face that his stupidity was the reason the Minez family was living lavish and reneged on the agreement they had concerning Casci, it showed Marcus that he'd eventually renege on everything else they came to agree on, and the start of it was the *double* Hector now wanted.

It didn't have to be said that Hector wanted Casci dead. It didn't have to be said that Marcus would meet the same fate once the Minez brothers found someone to replace him. Marcus knew the only reason he was still alive was because he took care of the youngest brother and his wife. Marcus knew about the guys in the city who worked for the Minez brothers. He also knew he was making the lion's share when it came to the money being sent to Florida. Marcus was a valuable asset for now, and that was something he had to use to his advantage.

After pulling into his driveway, and gathering both his luggage and the package Hector gave him, Marcus walked into his home, punched in his security code, and pulled his luggage into the foyer area. Once he stepped out of his suede loafers, he made his way to the kitchen. It wasn't until he flipped the light switch near the kitchen's entrance that he saw the familiar face sitting on the stool in front of his island counter.

Marcus froze, seeing the 9mm Glock in her hand. He lowered his head and closed his eyes. "Do what you gonna do," he told her with his head downcast and his eyes still closed.

"Tonight just might be the best night of your life, nigga," she told him before placing the Glock on her lap.

Marcus opened his eyes and raised his head. It was then he noticed another figure leaned against the wall at the far end of the kitchen and another walk up behind him. Marcus frowned. "Chris?"

"Hey, man. This ain't nothing personal." Chris shrugged, the AR-15 in his hands raising slightly.

Marcus looked from Chris back to Reniya, who was now palming a Glock. It had been a minute since he'd last spoken to either of the girls, and that was only because they'd threatened his life. But for Chris to be on the hit, it confused the hell out of him. He and Chris never had any beef. And every time Marcus stopped by the Sonic restaurant, it was nothing but love on both their parts.

"So, Casci sent y'all to do her dirty work?" He looked across the room at Coffee. His heart fell.

Reniya looked up at him. "We didn't want shit from you then, and we don't want it now,"

"See." Marcus raised his hands for emphasis.

"I'm not trying to have that shit, motherfucker. You found a way to break bread with Casci. We should've had your ass robbed a long time ago. That's what we should've done." Coffee scoffed.

"He's going to come for us eventually, Casci. The son of a bitch know we ain't got the kind of money he's asking for. He know me and you ain't breaded up to be able to pay double, and he know I'm not going to be the one to do you."

"So, hold up. Let me get this shit right," Chris spoke from where he stood in the doorway. "He wants you to kill Casci or pay him double of what you're already paying?"

"Yeah, something like that." Marcus looked from him to Casci.

"Well, pay that shit, weak ass nigga." Reniya pointed the Glock at him and continued. "If that motherfucker comes to Dallas looking like he's fucked up about Casci, I'm going to shoot his ass myself."

"You ain't the only one," Coffee added.

"Between him and his brother, Alex, I'm giving them two hundred and fifty thousand apiece. And now that Hector wants double of what I'm paying him, I'm looking at seven hundred and fifty thousand out of what I'm making now. I can't live off that shit. I just got the renovations done on the smoke shop. I'm still paying on this house, and—"

"A smoke shop?" Coffee cut him off.

"Casci, I hope you ain't believing this nigga," Reniya told her.

As long as Marcus was in the game playing on the level he was, he had to have some major money put up. Not only that, but he was giving her the same spiel he gave over five years ago.

"What the fuck I got to lie for, Reniya, huh?" Marcus stood.

Chris stepped forward, the rifle in his hand extended toward Marcus. "Chill out, man."

"And you need to stop pointing that thing at me, nigga." Marcus pointed his finger at Chris. "This ain't no game, Chris. You go down this road, ain't no U-turn, nigga, and it ain't no backing out of it. So when you pull ya strap on a nigga, you make sure you ready to pull that trigger."

Chris didn't bulge.

Marcus looked from Chris to Casci. "Casci, you'd better get this nigga."

"Chill, Chris." Casci waved him back.

"Nah, don't chill. Let's smoke this nigga and be done with this shit." Reniya stood, pointed the Glock she held at him, and nodded at Chris.

"Reniya! Reniya," Casci yelled before standing and grabbing the gun from her. "Chill out, bitch, we got shit to do."

"I'm tired of these niggas, Casci. All these motherfuckers do is lie, play on bitches, and think the shit gon' keep going unanswered. I'm finna start killing these hoe ass niggas!" Reniya stormed past Casci, pushed past Marcus, and headed toward the kitchen.

"Damn, what's wrong with you?" Chris asked as she passed him.

***

With so much money and drugs in the motel room, both Stacy and Doom were careful with the people they allowed to know of their whereabouts. They'd made a few calls, as far as the work was concerned, but for the most part, they agreed to hold on to it until they set up shop in Atlanta. After a couple of blunts, some drinks, and looking at several of the videos of Ariel he'd recorded, Stacy was feeling himself. He walked into the restroom and called her.

Ariel answered on the third ring. "And he finally calls?"

Stacy smiled to himself. "Hey, babe. I just got back to my phone and saw that you'd called several times already."

"Nigga, I'm not going to play with you. You know what the fuck you doing."

Stacy held the phone away from his face with one hand and placed the Kush-filled blunt to his lips with the other. "Babe, I owe you an apology."

"You damn right you do, Stacy. What the fuck, nigga? Where you at anyway?"

"Me and Doom pulling up to the motel right now," he lied.

143

"Now what's all this shit I'm hearing about you and these shootings and shit?"

"Babe, why don't you come by here so we can talk face to face? I need to see you." Stacy used his sexy voice to lure her.

"No. I have to get up early in the morning, Stacy, and I'm not about to fuck with you tonight."

"Please, Babe? I need some." He pouted.

"Nigga, do something else because that shit ain't going to work. I told you I have some shit to do early in the morning."

"You must got that nigga over there or something." Stacy hoped that would get her to make the trip.

"Bye, nigga. If a nigga was over here, I sure wouldn't be on the phone fighting with your ass."

"Oh, so you gonna make me come over there?" Stacy hopped up on the counter, pulled the half-ounce of the fruity herb from his pockets, and began emptying out another leaf so he could roll up.

"And don't bring your lying ass over here tonight. I just got out the shower, and I'm about to climb into my bed while it's nice and quiet."

Stacy frowned. "'Quiet? Where them loud ass homegirls at?"

"In the streets somewhere, and I want to be sleep by the time they crawl through that door."

"Well, then, let me come by for thirty minutes. I promise I'll leave."

"Bye, Stacy. What you need to be doing is explaining that shit you out there doing. I can't believe you had something to do with some kids getting killed, nigga. Here I am bragging about my man, and you out there doing some grimy shit like that. You know how that makes me look, Stacy?"

"Babe, listen. You already know them hoes at that salon don't know what the fuck they be talking about. If I would've shot some fucking kids, I would've been in jail right now, Ariel. Some shit went down, some motherfuckers got shot up, and everybody pointing the finger everywhere. Why the fuck would I have killed some kids, Ariel? Tell me that."

"They said you was trying—"

"They? Who is 'they,' Ariel?" Stacy placed the phone on the counter beside him and fingered a nice lump of Kush into the emptied leaf.

"Motherfucker, *everybody*!"

"Ariel. Ariel, I'm going to swing by there tomorrow. Stop believing everything you hear them hoes talking about in the damn salon. Them hoes don't know shit."

"I'll be at work tomorrow, so to make sure you bring me some lunch when and if you do come by there."

Stacy ended the call with her and rolled and sealed the blunt he'd made. He looked through his contacts until he was looking at the most recent text from Reniya. He tilted his head to the side when thinking of what she could possibly want.

"Doom, call a couple of them West Dallas hoes over here," Stacy yelled from the bathroom.

"Nigga, is you crazy? Them treacherous ass hoes ain't coming over here." He laughed.

"Fuck it. Let's get a couple of these crackhead hoes, then." Stacy laughed, fired up the Kush-filled blunt, and walked into the room with Doom.

"Motherfucker, that's worse than fucking with them West Dallas hoes. Just chill. Something is going to come through. I feel it," Doom told him before reaching for the blunt.

***

Reniya and Coffee looked on as Marcus explained all that was said in his meeting with Hector Minez. They regarded each other with disbelieving expressions, when hearing how Hector was now living, because it was just a few years ago he and his brother were all living in a three-bedroom house. When relaying to them the fact that he alone had been making well over $900,000 a year, Reniya dropped her head, and Coffee stood.

"Motherfucker, you *been* making that kind of money, and me and the girls been out here selling ourselves short just to get by?" Coffee walked toward him with balled fist.

Casci grabbed her wrist before she could do anything rash. "Coffee, we ain't here for that," she reminded her.

"I tried to get at y'all for years. I tried to break bread with y'all but…" Marcus looked over at Reniya, whose head was still down. "I tried but—"

"*But* my ass, nigga." Coffee fell back onto the couch and crossed her arms.

"Reniya know I'm not lying." Marcus continued looking at her.

Despite all they'd been through, his betrayal, and the falling out they had, this was still his family.

"I'm in here, Marcus," Casci told him from where she sat in the den. "Come in here so we can sort this shit out."

Marcus walked over to his refrigerator, opened it, and pulled out a bottle of spring water. He watched Reniya as he walked by her and made his way into the den. He paused when seeing Casci sitting there. He sat across from her.

"I'm more than sure you've found my money by now," he told her, before taking a sip of the water he held.

Casci nodded.

"I just brought forty kilos back from Florida, and they're in the luggage in the foyer," he added.

"I know."

Marcus sighed, threw his head back, and closed his eyes.

"We ain't here to rob you, Marcus." Casci spoke barely above a whisper.

"Then why are you here?" Marcus's eyes found hers.

Casci held up the keys she was given. "I thought I'd accept your invitation."

Marcus laughed, she didn't.

"This shit gets better and better by the minute," he told her.

"So, how was your trip?" Casci asked.

Marcus watched as Reniya and Coffee walked over toward them. Reniya sat next to him, and Coffee sat next to her cousin. Chris stayed standing in the doorway, the riffle he held resting at the ready.

"About the same as this one."

Reniya sat to where she was looking right at the side of his face. She told him, "What did you expect, nigga?"

Marcus looked over at her and smiled. "It's good to see you, too, Reniya."

"You already know if it was up to me we wouldn't be having this conversation, don't think for one minute I agreed to this meeting and talking shit. Because I didn't."

"Well, thank you for listening to whoever agreed on it." Marcus looked over at Coffee and shook his head.

"What the fuck you smiling at me for?" Coffee went off.

"Black is definitely beautiful when it comes to you, girl."

"Yeah, whatever." Coffee rolled her eyes.

Marcus knew about the crush she at one time had on him, and if it wasn't such an age difference between them, they would've definitely been more than good friends. However, their loyalty was to Casci, and that was something he had to understand and respect.

Chapter Twenty

"And if I have to fuck this nigga for free, I'm going to burn your ass too," Coffee told him.

"Shh. Y'all, shut the fuck up. I'm calling him now." Reniya walked to where Casci stood and sighed. She whispered to Marcus, "How much money you got on you?"

"Why?"

Before she could curse him out, Stacy came on the line.

"What's good?"

"Hey, nigga. You holding some of that Mango Kush or what?" Reniya looked from Casci to Marcus and rolled her eyes.

"Yeah, yeah. What's up?

"We trying to get about half a pound tonight." Reniya shrugged, hoping that was a big enough sell for him to get bolted.

"Who is 'we'?" he asked

"Motherfucker, you got it or not, Stacy? I don't have time to be answering no million damn questions." She went off.

"Okay, okay. Damn you acting like—"

"Nigga, a bitch trying to get fucked up and kick it."

"Where you at, Reniya?"

"We in Desoto for right now. Why, what's up?"

"I'll tell you what. Meet me and Doom up at the Royal Suites in about thirty minutes."

"Man, I'm not about to get caught up in that hot ass hotel, Stacy. Pick somewhere else," she told him, knowing the Royal Suites wasn't too far from the motel they were staying in.

"Um, okay. Meet us at the Deluxe Inn by South West Mall."

Reniya sighed loud enough for him to hear. Her playing the vanquished roll worked damn near every time when it came to niggas and their demands or her. "We walking to the car now. How much is this going to run us?"

"Since it's y'all, bring $1,100."

"Eleven hundred? Damn, nigga."

"Reniya, look. This is some of the best shit in Dallas right now. I'm not going to fuss over you."

"That's a new one." Reniya gave Marcus and Casci the thumbs up.

"Where is Casci?" Stacy asked.

"The hell if I know. She bent a couple corners with Chris's working ass," she told him, while looking at Chris with an apologising shrug.

"That hoe ass nigga tell y'all I caught up with him at the gas station?"

"Aw, yeah? That nigga ain't told us no shit like that. What happened?" Reniya looked toward Chris and shook her head.

Chris was seething by now, and looking toward Marcus and seeing the disappointment on his face, he slowly nodded.

"Yeah, well, fuck Chris. Meet us at the Deluxe in thirty, nigga."

"Oh, hey, Reniya."

"What's up?"

"Is Coffee coming with you?" This nigga Doom want to know.

"Is the shit going to get any cheaper if she do come?" Reniya asked. She looked over at Coffee.

"Hell yeah, the shit gets cheaper," Doom yelled into the phone.

Reniya yelled Coffee's name as if she was at a distance instead of a couple feet away. After relaying the message, she laughed and told Stacy, "Yeah, you know that bitch coming."

"Let me get you a package together, Reniya. I'll see you in thirty."

Reniya ended the call and looked at Marcus. "Why the fuck y'all still here?"

While she and Coffee made their way to her Charger, Marcus and Chris hurried to the rental car he'd been driving. Casci jumped into the driver's seat, while Marcus climbed into the front passenger seat, and Chris climbed into the back.

"I'm going to text you some bullshit emoji when we're done," Casci told Reniya.

Coffee yelled from where she was, "And hurry up because I don't need this nigga trying to fuck me all night."

***

Stacy looked toward Doom and smiled. Not only had he tried unsuccessfully in the past to sex both of Ariel's friends, but he knew this was about to be another attempt. He walked across the small motel room and searched the wooden table for the pills he saw just days ago.

"What are you looking for?" Doom asked, seeing him reach for the small pouch.

"Them hoes want a half-pound of the Mango Kush. I'm going to throw in some of the XO's, too."

"Oh, you want to drug them hoes, or what?" Doom watched him with anticipation.

"Hell nah, I'm not doing shit like that." Stacy frowned, looking at his friend and shaking his head.

"We can just take the pussy once we get them on these pills, Stacy," Doom said seriously.

"Nigga, all you got to do is pay them hoes and they gonna fuck anyway," he told him, not even giving his idea any thought.

"Man, if we can get these hoes on tape sucking that dick, we can sell the footage to one of them Porn Hub companies."

"Nigga, help me put this shit up so we can go. You tripping now."

Stacy walked into the bathroom and began emptying the water out the tank behind the toilet. He used a thick rubber hose to siphon the water, and once it was empty, he stashed $150,000 in it. After replacing the lid and adjusting the soap basket atop, he moved into the room area and put the twenty-three kilos of cocaine into the springs under the two beds. He felt it would be wiser to put the money in one place and the drugs in the other. The Kush he and Doom were smoking influenced that decision.

"Just in case we get lucky and spend the night with them hoes." He told Doom after making sure nothing could be seen in the event one of the motel room keepers stopped by.

"Let's just go tell them hoes that we're going to be out for the night, but we'll be back in the morning sometime," Doom figured.

"Nigga, you know them hoes don't give a damn about that. Them no good motherfuckers know we be hustling out this spot. They ain't going to do nothing but try to charge a nigga for an extra day. Tomorrow, we'll get a room somewhere else. Keep the shit moving until we find that nigga Peanut and get ghost."

"Yeah, that makes since." Doom pushed $20,000 into his pocket.

"Nigga, what the fuck are you bringing all that money for?" Stacy looked at his friend.

"Once I start making it rain on that bitch, she ain't going to have no choice but to let a nigga fuck. Either way, I'm fucking that hoe Coffee tonight. I've been trying to fuck with that hoe for a minute, nigga." Doom snatched up the pack filled with exotic and slung it over his shoulder. "And I'm not even going to use no rubber."

"You fucking up now, nigga. That bitch fine as hell, but I wouldn't risk no shit like that. The bitch got some good head, a little tight pussy, and can't take no dick."

Doom nodded. His mind was made up. "Hold up. Let me take a shower right quick."

"Yeah, and clean your ass…because we fucking these hoes tonight, nigga."

Stacy smiled. That was what he hoped also. With Ariel at the apartment and out of the way, it was worth a shot. If nothing more, he'd just try his best at talking her into on a hand job. Something had to be given, though.

***

Casci drove the car along the shoulder of the highway until they were able to see the motel from where she pulled to a stop. She hit the head lights.

"Why we stopping here?" Chris asked them.

Marcus looked over at Casci because things didn't need to be explained to him, and he wasn't about to do anything.

"Because from here, I can see what needs to be seen. Once you two hit up the spot, all you have to do is just start walking up the service road, and I'm going to scoop you up down a ways. That way, the car don't get seen, and you don't get seen getting into the car."

"Oh."

"Nigga, you sure you ready for some shit like this?"

Casci half-turned in her seat and faced Chris. "This ain't the same as flipping no burgers, Chris."

"I'm as ready as I'll ever be. These niggas don't know who they fucking with," he told them, remembering the way they clowned him at the gas station.

"These niggas will definitely kill you if they ever found out you had something to do with they spot getting robbed, Chris. This ain't no pocket change, nigga. We trying to hit 'em for all they got."

"Yeah, that's the only way to move, ain't it?" Chris looked out of the window and pointed to the parking lot. "There the Mustang they were in the last time I saw them."

Casci looked at her watch. "What's taking these niggas so long to leave?"

It had taken them right at twenty-five minutes to drive from where Marcus lived to the motel, and they were still there. The lights could be seen in the room, so she knew they were still there.

"They might've changed their minds." Chris came back.

"Nah, them niggas ain't about to pass up the chance at some pussy." Marcus pulled a black ball cap from his pocket and handed it back to Chris. "Here, put this on."

"What I need this for, nigga?"

Marcus closed his eyes and dropped his head. Chris was constantly questioning him about what he knew so little about. Marcus was the one who'd spent his days and nights doing exactly what they were about to do, whereas Chris was only known for selling a little dope and flipping burgers at Sonic.

"Motherfucker, just put the damn hat on. Cover your facial features a bit. You'd be surprised at how motherfuckers get identified just from the shape of their heads, and the structure of their jaw line and ears, and shit."

"Ain't everybody going to be in their room?"

"Nigga, that's complex. It might be somebody on the second floor, looking out of their window, waiting for a ride when we stumble up in that bitch." Marcus looked back toward Casci with a raised brow. "Casci, really?"

Casci shrugged. There were things Chris did...

"Just follow my lead, Chris. That's all you have to do." Marcus sighed, pulled the ball cap over his eyes, and sat back in the seat.

"What are we waiting for, nigga?"

Instead of answering, Marcus just crossed his arms and closed his eyes. It had been a while since he got his hands dirty, but he knew the importance of patience.

"We waiting until they leave, Chris. Right?"

"Oh, yeah, yeah."

Marcus scoffed, shook his head, and continued looking out the window at the motel across the way.

"I hope these niggas ain't moved the money." Chris rubbed his thighs with anticipation.

"Five minutes. Y'all get in and get out. Whatever you ain't found in five minutes, fuck it," Casci told the both of them.

"We going to break they ass." Chris smiled.

Marcus turned, looked Chris dead in the eyes, and told him, "Robbing motherfuckers while they ain't home is bitch shit, but it's still a part of the game. When you really trying to look at a nigga, you take it to his ass, whenever and wherever."

"Oh, really?" Casci looked over at Marcus with a questioning expression of her own.

"You know what I mean, Casci."

"What happened if them niggas circle back and walk in on us?"

"That's what you got the big gun for, Chris."

"Okay, here we go," Casci told them when seeing the door to the motel room open and Doom step out.

***

Reniya pulled into the lot of the Deluxe Hotel and the parked near the office building. She and Coffee scanned the parking lot for familiar rides.

"Where this nigga at?" Coffee asked.

"Hold up," Reniya said, while pulling out her phone and sending Stacy a short text.

"And tell that nigga to hurry up." Coffee checked herself in the compartment's mirror. "Man, I hope this shit work out."

"Why wouldn't it? We know what we got to do, and Marcus ain't going to fuck up. So—"

"I just can't help but think something ain't going to go right. This a hundred grand we talking 'bout."

Reniya chuckled. "Yeah, this ain't like peeling a nigga for a couple grand or a couple hundred from his wallet." She smiled to herself.

"Bitch! I'm sitting here shaking, and I'm not even doing nothing." Coffee shook her head.

"Just chill. It's about to get real." Reniya sent the text and set her phone on the charger. She leaned her head back and closed her eyes.

"What are you going to do with your cut?" Coffee asked.

"Sit on it for a while, then eventually use it to put on places to make more," Reniya told her.

"Shit, I'm buying a car. Then I'm going to treat myself out."

"And that's when niggas start putting two and two together and realizing that just the other day you was a boosting bitch. And right after some niggas get robbed, suddenly, you became some boss bitch." Reniya shook her head.

"I need a car though, Reniya."

"Not right off, Coffee. Nigga's eyes are going to be wide open, and when they see shit they ain't used to seeing, they start pointing the finger, bitch. Just ride this shit out like we supposed to. If nothing else, we throw Marcus under the bus. Have niggas thinking he spoiling us like he spoiling Casci."

"How much that nigga getting anyways?"

"Who, Marcus?"

"Yeah."

"Fuck that nigga. He ain't getting shit. This little shit he doing just on GP." Reniya hurried to grab her phone when hearing the ping and seeing its face light up.

Coffee sat and watched in silence.

Reniya deflated when seeing the text.

"Is that him?"

"Hell nah, this Jingle's trick ass."

"What the fuck he want now?"

Reniya laughed and said, "'Baby Girl, Baby Girl, bring daddy some of that young pussy.'"

"If this shit goes right, we just might need to pay that nigga a visit." Coffee adjusted herself in her seat.

"Hot ass." Reniya rolled her eyes and smiled.

"Let me call Casci and see what the fuck taking this nigga so long."

"The way that nigga massage a bitch pussy, he'll get a couple dollars out of me."

Reniya nodded in agreement.

The phone rang twice before Casci answered. "It's on bitch."

"Where them niggas at girl?"

"They walking across the parking lot right now. That nigga, Doom, got a small pack, so the money here."

***

Once Stacy and Doom climbed into the Mustang and pulled out of the parking lot. Marcus and Chris climbed out of the rental and made their way down the service road. Marcus stopped when they made it to the payphones.

"What's up, man?" Chris looked from Marcus to the motel room door.

"Just making sure they don't circle back around, and making sure it's no movement inside." Marcus pulled his cell phone out and dialled Casci's number. "You can't just go running in a spot, nigga. What the fuck's wrong with you?"

Chris huffed and pulled the cap he was wearing lower over his eyes. He continued looking toward the door and window of the room Stacy and Doom had not too long exited.

"Casci, you going to get this nigga killed. This nigga…"

"They gone, nigga. I followed them a ways up and circled back around. Take care of your business."

Marcus pushed his phone down into his pocket and nodded at Chris. "Let's get in, nigga. Five minutes and we out."

Chris watched as Marcus walked up to the window and began to grey tape the corners. He frowned.

"What—"

"Just look and learn, nigga." Marcus crossed tape over the window and pulled out a small hammer. He tapped the corner of the window once. It shattered and held its form, quietly. He looked back at Chris and smiled. "Like I said. Look and learn, nigga"

Chris watched as Marcus kicked the window in and climbed through. He followed, seeing that no one was looking or even walking by. He gave his eyes a second to adjust to the darkness and reached for the room light.

Marcus stopped him. "Ain't nobody supposed to be in this room, Chris, not even us."

Instead of arguing with Marcus, Chris walked over to the bed and yanked the covers back. Marcus went straight to the vent. Seeing nothing there, he walked into the bathroom.

"Where in the fuck can a motherfucker hide one hundred thousand dollars?"

"Check the mattresses, feel for inconsistences in the form, and go from there," Marcus told him, before disappearing into the bathroom.

Chapter Twenty-One

As soon as Marcus and Chris disappeared into the motel, Casci phoned Detrick. It was time to take the game to the next level. With Chris being such a novice when it came to the game she played, she hoped Marcus would be the one to put him up on it. Either he'd do that, or Chris would get caught slipping in the worst way.

Detrick answered on the third ring. "Hey, you."

Casci could hear the smile in Detrick's voice. She shook her head because she knew he'd most likely thought she was calling for other reasons than she really was.

"What's up, nigga? What you got going on?" Casci continued to watch the area where Marcus and Chris went.

"Nothing. Just waiting on this money."

"Say, what's the bounty on them niggas Stacy and Doom now?" Casci closed her eyes.

Snitching was not her thing, but she needed to put both security around Chris and Marcus, and distance between her and any possibilities that she was in on the hit.

"Hell, last I heard, it was at seventy-five thousand."

"I know where they at, and I know what they getting in," she told him. If anyone was neutral in the ordeal, it was Detrick. It wasn't like Stacy was the nigga his girl was fucking with.

"Good, because motherfuckers was asking me about they asses the other day. What's up?"

Casci ran everything to Detrick, just as she'd planned. The Southern Motel, the black 2017 Mustang, and the fact that it was thought that they were hustling out the spot. That along with what Detrick knew was more than enough for him to agree to her terms.

"And all you want is fifty thousand?" Detrick sked her.

"Yeah. You can pocket the rest, or pay them niggas. That's on you."

"I'm glad I ain't never fucked over you or them girls. You cold-hearted, Casci."

Casci felt those words like he wouldn't believe. There was no turning back now. She told him, "That's exactly what motherfuckers need to learn right now."

"Well, I'll swing through your spot tomorrow and bring you your ends."

Casci frowned. "That fast?"

"Girl, that nigga Hector ain't doing no playing. He's got the money at two or three different spots. I'm just going to make a call to Alex, and after that, I'm going to pick up our shit."

"Um, yeah. That's a bet then. Get at me later." Casci ended the call and placed her phone back in the pocket of her cargo pants. "Damn."

With all that was going on, even if it was found out that she was behind the scenes making moves, Stacy and his partner would be out the way.

***

Stacy pulled into the parking area, saw Reniya's Charger, and headed in that direction. The minute he pulled alongside her, he smiled, showcasing his iced-out grill

"My bad, Reniya. My bad," he reported before climbing out of the Mustang.

"Nigga, you the one told me thirty minutes."

"I know. I know. I had to take care of some other shit right quick." Stacy looked toward Coffee and shook his head.

"Where the shit at?" Reniya pulled out a wad of bills and began counting them.

"Nah, we ain't about to do this shit here. Let's go inside. We already got a room and everything." Stacy looked around the area and made sure no one had seen him. He threw the hoodie over his head and started walking toward the glass doors.

"Motherfucker, we got shit to do, Stacy. You ain't said shit about going into no damn room."

"Reniya, will you come on? I'll make it worth y'all while," he said with his usual diamond-encrusted smile.

Doom walked over to Coffee and gave her a light hug. "Hey, chocolate ass girl."

"What's good, nigga?"

"Shit. By the looks of it, you doing all the good." He sized her up with his eyes. His smiled resembled Stacy's, showing off tens of thousands of dollars in diamonds and dental work.

"Looks can definitely be deceiving then." Coffee subtly looked toward Reniya.

"Will y'all come on?" Stacy yelled from the entrance.

"Yeah, come on in here and let me holla at you for minute, Coffee." Doom reached for her arm and led her toward the glass doors.

"Fuck it." Reniya gave in. She rolled her eyes upward, hit the alarm of her car, and followed Coffee and Dom inside, suppressing the smile on her face as best as she could.

Once inside the hotel room, Stacy threw his keys onto the table in the living area and pulled the hoodie he was wearing over his head. He walked into the kitchen area. "Y'all want something to drink?"

"Nigga, hurry up and weigh this shit up so we can go." Reniya walked over, fell onto the couch, and pulled out her pone. She was anxious.

Stacy looked toward Doom, hoping he was having more luck with Coffee. All he needed was some time to warm up to Reniya, he was sure. He also didn't want to put too much pressure on her. There was no need in getting dissed by Reniya and canceled by Ariel. He had to play his cards just right.

"Hey, I need to talk to you about some business anyway," he told Reniya.

Reniya continued to type and scroll through her phone. For those who looked in her direction, she was only doing what the average person did when messing with their device, but Reniya had gone into her Messenger app, and was recording everything that was being said. In the past, that was a mistake she'd made when it came to trying to show Ariel how niggas was. It was always his word against hers and Coffee's. But if push came to shove, this time, she'd have more than enough proof to show her friend.

"Oh, really?"

"Yeah. I know you be trying to get money, and I might just have something for you."

"Nigga, you ain't sitting on bread I like that. How you gonna have something for me?" Reniya set the phone on the table in front of her.

Doom and Coffee sat on the other side of the suite, near the patio. They were passing a Kush-filled blunt back and forth amongst themselves.

"Let me blow you a charge," he told her.

"Yeah, give me a headshot." Coffee handed him the blunt.

Doom got on his knees and crawled up to her. "Here, open your legs right quick."

Coffee was sitting on the edge of the huge ottoman. She smiled inwardly because of the game he thought he had. She decided to help him out.

"Give me a second, nigga." She then pulled his shirt over his head. Once she was lying back on the ottoman, she pulled him onto her and pulled his shirt around the both of their heads. "Do you know what you're doing, nigga?"

"Um, hell yeah," he told her.

Doom took the blunt's cherry into his mouth and blew a continual stream of smoke into her nostrils and mouth. The shirt she had around their heads kept any smoke from escaping.

Coffee coughed, opened her legs, and continued the charge. She laughed, thinking of the money she'd soon have.

"This the shit, huh?" Doom asked when hearing her laugh under the charge.

With their bodies touching, he positioned himself to where his middle was pressing against hers. He slowly began grinding into her.

"Umph-ummm, boy. What you doing?" Coffee asked, but made no attempt to stop him.

"Come on, Coffee. Just let me feel that motherfucker." He then began grinding into her harder.

"Nigga, that ain't doing shit for me." Coffee gently pushed his bare chest. She wanted to see his next move. If it included money, she'd be game.

"See what you did now?" Doom raised himself, grabbed his crotch, and showed her his dick print.

"Nigga, I ain't done shit. You did that," she argued but never took her eyes off the bulge in his denim jeans.

"I'll give you a grand for the pussy." Doom reached in his pockets and pulled out wad after wad of cash.

"Damn, little boy. Where you got all that from?" Coffee stared at the money with wide eyes.

"I got way more than this. This ain't shit but throw away money."

Coffee bit her bottom lip. She shook her head. "I don't know about that, Doom. You cool and all, but you just a little boy." Coffee took the blunt they were smoking and held it in between her fingers. She knew what was next.

"Two thousand. I'll give you two thousand dollars for the pussy."

"Nigga, how old are you?" Coffee frowned. It was then she realized she didn't even know how old he really was.

"Nineteen."

"Nineteen? Nigga you don't even know what to do with this pussy." The games had begun, money had been exposed, and it was time to perform.

"Let's find out then." Doom stood, grabbed her hands, and led her toward the bedroom.

"Reniya. Let me see what this little boy is talking about right quick," she announced, before she and Doom disappeared down the short hallway.

***

Marcus checked under the sink twice, and he knocked on the wooden walls of each shelf. Once he was certain that nothing was out of the ordinary, he checked the ceiling, then the toilet. He removed the soap basket on the lid of the tank and removed the lid itself. He shook his head when seeing the plastic.

"Amateur ass niggas," he told himself, before carefully pulling the plastic from around and under the tank floaters and levers.

"Look out, Marcus."

"Motherfucker, who is Marcus?"

Marcus closed his eyes and shook his head. For all they knew, it could've been a listening device in the room. Two-way radios weren't uncommon in the game he was used to. Neither were camera phones. That was another reason Casci said five minutes. Chris had so much to learn and not enough time. Hell, he'd already jumped off the porch.

"I can't find shit in this dark ass room," Chris told him.

"Here I come. Just hold up."

Marcus held the plastic in both hands and hurried into the living part of the room. He snatched up one of the pillowcases and pushed the plastic inside.

"What's that? Is that the money?" Chris beamed.

"Feels like it." Marcus noticed that Chris had made a mess of the bed and heater. "You check under the bed?"

"Yeah, that's one of the first places I looked."

Marcus scoffed, pushed the mattress over, and raised it to where he was able to push it against the wall. He did the same to the box spring, and that's when Chris saw something he hadn't before.

"What the fuck is that?" he pointed.

Instead of answering that, Marcus snatched up another of the pillows and pulled it out of the case. He sat the makeshift bag he was holding by the door and began stuffing the bricks of cocaine into the second pillow case. Chris watched him.

"Motherfucker, go check the window. I don't need you standing over me."

Chris hurried to the window and peeked out into the night. Only a couple of people were walking about, but no one was paying attention to the window or the room they were in. He repeatedly looked back to ensure Marcus wasn't doing anything he shouldn't have been doing.

"The window, nigga!"

"What you doing?"

"Here, let's go," Marcus told him after stuffing the case with the bricks.

"Let's check the walls and shit."

"Nigga, let's go. We got more than we came with." Marcus reached for the door knob.

"I know them niggas got some more shit in here, man. Jewelry or something." Chris walked over to the dresser.

"I'm out, nigga. You tripping now." Marcus threw both bags over his shoulder and exited the room. He wasn't about to argue with Chris, and he damn sure wasn't about to go against the code he went by. Marcus was walking up the service road when Chris ran up beside him.

"Nigga, why you leave me?"

They both slowed their walk when seeing in the headlights behind them.

"That's Casci."

"Look at what I found behind the dresser, nigga." Chris held up a diamond-encrusted medallion.

It hung from a thick and heavy link necklace.

Marcus turned, snatched the chain from Chris, and threw it in the field across the way. "What the fuck is wrong with you, nigga? What the fuck is you gonna do with that? Huh?"

Chris looked in the direction his prize went and frowned.

Once they were both in the car, Marcus threw both the bags in the back and threw his elbow on the passenger's window. He looked over at Casci. "You really trying to get me killed, ain't you?"

"How did it go?" Casci pulled away from the shoulder of the road and headed back to Desoto, just in case someone did see the car the two guys who'd just left the motel jumped in.

"This nigga don't know what the hell he doing, Casci. These plays you running are too big for him." Marcus finally smiled. "We hit they ass hard, sis." His words caused that same smile to vanish, and for Casci to look at him with an expression that reminded him that he was no longer that to her.

"Where we headed now?" Chris asked the two of them after looking in one of the pillow cases and seeing more cocaine than he'd ever laid eyes on.

Casci sent the 'thumbs up' emoji text to Reniya. It was time to start things out.

***

With Doom and Coffee in the back room, Stacy had some alone time with Reniya. His approach was all the way off, and he was nowhere near the milestone he'd wished to see by now.

"I'll tell you what, Reniya. I'll pay you. I'll give you what you want. You know how bad I've been wanting to fuck with you."

"Nigga, you over there full of that shit. You tripping." Reniya sat back, crossed her legs, and folded her arms.

Stacy walked over, sat next to her, and squeezed her thigh. "It was always you, and you know that. The only reason I started fucking with Ariel was because you wasn't trying to give a nigga the time of day."

"Nigga, you tried to fuck me and Coffee. Remember that?" Reniya leaned away from him.

"Okay, I was tripping back then. I just wanted a bad bitch on my team."

"Ariel *is* a bad bitch."

"Yeah, she pretty as hell, but Ariel ain't no bad bitch like you. You got the height, the looks, the body, and everything."

Reniya rolled her eyes. "Nigga, whatever."

"I'm serious, Reniya. I could use a bitch like you on my team."

Reniya looked toward the hallway and yelled, "Bitch hurry up. This nigga out here tripping."

"Okay, look." Stacy pulled several bands from his pocket and sat next to her. "Let me taste it."

"And then what?" Reniya watched him.

"That's it." Stacy threw his hands up.

"Nah, nigga. I'm talking about with Ariel. I'm not about to fight that bitch behind your dizzy ass."

"I'm not going to tell her shit. For all I know, she laying up with some nigga right now. Hell, she might even be fucking that pussy ass nigga Chris."

"Don't play. You know she ain't fucking with that nigga."

Stacy stood. He wasn't going nowhere. "Well, just sit there and watch me jack this motherfucker." He then undid his pants and pushed them down to his ankles. He watched her with his eyes. "You just scared of this motherfucker right here," he told her while stroking himself.

"Nigga, don't shoot that shit on me." Reniya uncrossed her legs, leaned back, and watched him.

"Open your legs some. Let me at least see the pussy." Stacy sat close to her and pulled her thighs apart with his free hand.

The ping on her phone got her attention. Reniya swiped her screen, saw the emoji, and swiped it back to its previous setting. It was on now.

"I'll tell you what, nigga." Reniya stood, stepped out of the shorts she was wearing, and began slow wingding to the songs she played in her mind. She was about to give him his very own lap dance.

"Aww, hell yeah." Stacy reached forward, grabbed a handful of Reniya's ass, and pulled her to him.

"Don't get that shit on me, nigga."

***

Coffee was sitting on the bed, and Doom was standing in front of her with his shirt off. He'd already handed her $2,000, so the pussy was already paid for.

"I'm going to show you what this little boy can do," he told her, before pushing his pants down and stepping out of them.

"Nigga, you ain't fucking me with that big ass dick." Coffee climbed farther onto the bed. She acted as if she was running from the dick.

"Girl, I know what I'm doing." Doom climbed onto the bed and grabbed her ankles. "I'll be gentle. I promise."

Coffee allowed him to pull her to him. She kept the smile that was creeping onto her face at bay. Doom was just too damn skinny for her. Both of his thighs were barely the size of one of hers. His dick was long, but it was skinny. It was the skinniest dick she'd ever seen.

"Nigga, you trying to hurt a bitch with all that." She nodded toward his dick.

Doom pulled her to where she was lying under him. He raised the shirt she was wearing and kissed her stomach. "Your black ass ain't had no dick like this," he told her.

Coffee raised her middle when feeling him pull at the waist of her shorts. She pulled her own panties down when he pulled at the top she wore.

She looked up at him, hearing Reniya yelling from the living area. It had to have been time. Doom gently licked her nipples before taking her breasts in his mouth.

Coffee sighed, grabbed a handful of his hair, and pushed his head down between her legs. "Lick that pussy like that."

While Doom licked and sucked her pussy, she thought about the lick they'd just hit. She laughed to herself when thinking of the fact that they now had two niggas on their team. Those were the missing pieces of the puzzle when it came to their come up.

After she'd cum once, she pulled him onto her, wrapped her legs around his waist, and let him have his way. She wrapped her arms around his neck and held him to her so he couldn't see the expressions she made. She twisted her hips and rolled her eyes when he called himself digging deeper. She moaned quietly at first, and once he'd found his rhythm, she stroked his ego even more. She attempted to close her legs.

"Nah, open them legs back up, girl. You take this dick!" He grunted.

Coffee allowed him to pin her with one leg up. She smiled to herself for a second time because the little boy was about to pay her out the ass.

"Make me cum, nigga. Make this pussy cum," she encouraged him.

Coffee thought of the many times she and the girls sat around talking about niggas and their sex game. She thought about the time Ariel mentioned about a nigga having a booty dick. She half-chuckled to herself because now she knew exactly what her girls were talking about. Doom's dick was so skinny that all it was good for was to fuck a bitch in the ass.

And when thinking of that, Coffee told him, "Let me turn over. I want to feel that big motherfucker in my ass."

Doom had been stroking and grinding as hard as he could, and he was grateful for the break. He was determined to show her what the "little boy" could do.

Chapter Twenty-Two

Chris stood and watched in awe while Casci and Marcus counted the money. He lifted several of the bricked kilos, thought about the weight of them, and frowned because something so small rewarded him so much. He counted twenty-eight bricks and knew exactly what he was going to do with his cut.

"I got one hundred fifty thousand. What you get?"

Casci looked up at Marcus and nodded. "One hundred fifty thousand."

"Them motherfuckers was making a little noise, huh?" Marcus smiled, leaned back on the couch, and closed his eyes.

"And twenty-eight kilos," Chris added.

"That's what I'm tripping on because twenty of them are packed exactly the way mines are," Marcus told the two of them.

"Okay, what's that supposed to mean?" he asked, not understating why it was an issue.

"Because the shit I got, I had to go to Florida to get, and I know Stacy and the nigga, Doom, ain't fucking with Hector."

"Maybe they got the shit from someone who does." Chris shrugged, looked over at Casci, and gave her a prosaic expression.

"If them niggas was moving work like that, I would've known," Marcus sighed and said. "Them niggas must've robbed somebody who does fuck with them Mexicans."

"So. And?" Chris questioned him with raised brows.

"It just means we have to be careful with this shit. We don't need word getting out that we're sitting on another motherfuckers work, 'cause they might just come looking for it."

"I mean, what's the problem? You say these are packaged the exact same way yours are. No one will be able to tell the difference anyway." Chris looked toward Casci for affirmation.

"Motherfucker, how many of these things have you bought, or sold, for that matter?" Marcus raised himself, sat with his elbows on his knees, and looked at him.

"Hell, I've moved a couple."

"That's the motherfuckin' problem. You ain't moving shit. You ain't scoring the shit we're looking at, but you over there bumping like you know what the fuck is going on out here. Niggas ain't out here selling this shit to any or everybody. And the motherfucker scoring it damn surely ain't buying it from no any and everybody.

"You start putting out packages niggas know you ain't been having, niggas are going to start talking about it. And when you can't answer the questions they asking, you get fucked. Simple as that." Marcus reached for one of the familiar bricks and held it up. "You see this logo—this stamp? It's only a few of us in the hood who run these, and you ain't one of them."

"Well, I am now," Chris told him defiantly.

"Nah, what you going to do is keep working at that damn Sonic. We gotta do this shit right."

"I quit that shit."

"You quit? Why would you do some stupid shit like that, Chris?" Marcus looked toward Casci. "Did you know that?"

Casci shrugged.

"Well, you're going back. I'm tied up in this shit now, and I'll be dammed if I let you, Coffee, or Reniya's scandalous ass get me crossed up."

"Motherfucker I got niggas calling me right now for work. I'm out here doing numbers too, nigga, and I'm not about to stop that just because you scared."

Marcus stood, walked within inches of Chris, and told him, "Nigga, these motherfuckers out here will slit your throat for half of one of these bricks, and I damn sure ain't Ariel. I'll have your ass stuffed in a five-gallon bucket and sold to some old motherfucker who spends his life sitting in a boat fishing."

Marcus stared at him unblinking. Chris took a step backward and looked down at Casci. She only watched the both of them.

"Casci, you'd better get ya homeboy," Chris told her.

"That's between y'all. I know my dick ain't as big as neither of yours."

Marcus shook his head. "It ain't got shit to do with whose dick is the biggest, Casci. It's all about the motherfucker with the most experience, and this nigga don't know shit about these streets."

"Keep thinking that, Marcus. Keep thinking I'm some bitch or something." Chris turned and walked toward the kitchen area.

"You got a problem with what I said, nigga?" Marcus began walking toward the kitchen also.

Casci grabbed his arm. "Hey, chill out. Y'all chill the fuck out. If money do this to y'all, then maybe y'all don't need any." She looked up at Marcus, knowing those words would find him, even in his anger.

Marcus threw his hands up in defeat. He went back and sat down across from Casci.

"This was Reniya and Coffee's lick. If anybody do some bitching, let it be them. We're supposed to be making sure this shit goes forward, not backward," she told the both of them. Casci stood when hearing the doorbell. "I got it."

Chris leaned against the counter and scoffed. "You got me fucked up, Marcus. You need to know that."

"Let it go, pretty ass nigga. Let the shit go, man."

"What the fuck you mean? You sitting here trying to clown me in front of Casci and think—"

"This ain't got shit to do with Casci. It's about staying alive, nigga. You got caught slipping, so that's exactly what you won't be doing. And I'll be damn if I fail because of some stupid shit you do."

"Like you don't and haven't done some stupid shit. You already fucked over Casci one time. I don't trust you."

Marcus stood. "Bitch ass nigga, I don't give a fuck who you trust." Marcus pointed at him. "You roll with the program, or you get rolled over. I'm not playing, Chris."

Reniya and Coffee entered the room, followed by Casci.

Reniya clapped her hands to accent her voice. "Hey! Hey! Hey! What the fuck?" She walked to where Marcus stood and looked up at him.

"Get ya sister before I dick him down." Marcus never took his eyes off Chris.

"I got ya sister swinging, nigga." Chris wasn't backing down.

"Come on, y'all. You niggas tripping now." Coffee walked to where Marcus stood and stopped. Her eyes went to the table in front of them. "Ouuuu, bitch!"

Reniya's eyes followed Coffee's. A smile crept across her face. She laughed. "Ohh, shit." She turned, threw her arms around Marcus, and squeezed him.

"Ain't this a bitch?" he told her before wrapping his arms around her also.

It had been years since he'd even touched her. To see her overjoyed because of something he partook in put a smile on his face as well.

"I knew you was going to pull off that shit, nigga," she said excitedly.

Coffee walked over, grabbed two of the $10,000 stacks, and knocked them together. "How much is it?"

"That's one hundred fifty right there," Casci told her before sitting back down where she was before they arrived.

"One hundred-fifty thousand?" Reniya looked from Marcus to Casci.

"And twenty-eight bricks," Marcus added.

"Ohh, we lit, bitch. I told you, Casci. I told you," Reniya exclaimed. She pushed away from Marcus, went to sit in Casci lap, and kissed her. "Bitch, come here." Reniya continued to plant kisses on Casci's face and head.

"Fuck all that. What's the cut?" Coffee asked, while holding the stacks of $100 bills.

"You, Reniya, and Ariel get fifty thousand apiece. This one is for y'all," Casci told them.

Chris pushed away from the counter and walked to where they were. "And where my cut?" He looked from Reniya to Casci.

"Motherfucker, fuck you," Reniya said. "You already getting most of the dope, nigga. What the fuck—"

Marcus cut her off. "Nah, I'm going to sit on most of that shit. Some of the bricks are packaged the exact same way as the ones I went to pick up in Florida. And I know them niggas Stacy and Doom ain't fucking around with the people I'm fucking with. I wouldn't be surprised if them niggas robbed somebody for them."

Reniya shrugged, looked back at Chris, and told him, "Nigga, you going to be alright. Marcus is going to make sure you straight."

"Marcus? I don't trust that nigga. How we know he ain't going to up and disappear with all the work? How we know he ain't going to fuck over us like he did Casci?"

Marcus was just about to cross the room when Coffee and Reniya stepped in front of him.

Coffee told him, "Check that shit, nigga, 'cause he's right. How we know that you ain't just saying that shit, so you can float with all the dope?"

"Really?" Marcus looked from her to Reniya, who only looked at him with twisted lips. "Really?"

"We ain't falling for that shit this time, Marcus," Coffee told him flatly.

Seeing things taking a turn in a direction she didn't want them to go, Casci asked them, "And what took y'all so long anyway?"

That question put another smile on Coffee's face, and caused Reniya to flop down beside her. She knew they had a story to tell.

Coffee threw the stacks back on the table and pulled $2,500 from her pockets. Reniya reached for the handbag she was carrying and pulled out two baby wipes containers.

"She let that nigga fuck," Reniya told them.

"And she let that nigga jack off on her," Coffee said.

"Wait, who did that?" Casci looked from her girls to Marcus and shook her head.

"That bitch let Doom fuck." Reniya sat back, crossed her legs, and began looking through her phone.

"I came like a motherfucker, too. All the while he was grunting and sweating, I was thinking about this money."

"That nigga, Stacy, just wiped his shirt out on a bitch. And once I got that text, I gave him a lap dance. I let him squeeze on the ass, suck the pussy, and everything."

"You fucked Stacy?" Chris asked from where he stood.

"Nah, nigga. I said I let him suck the pussy and jack off on me." Reniya rolled her eyes.

"And you fucked Doom?" Marcus asked Coffee, the frown he wore showing his disgust.

"Y'all should've seen that nigga, too. He really thought he was serving a bitch. Talking about, 'take this dick, bitch. Take this dick.'" Coffee walked over behind Chris and grabbed him by the waist. She imitated the way Doom was thrusting. "Take this dick, bitch! Take this dick."

Chris only shook his head. He told her, "Girl, if you don't get your nasty hands off me."

Casci laughed when seeing Chris push her hands off, and she continued to chase him as if she was really hitting him with the dick. Casci loved seeing her girls happy. They did some questionable things for the sake of it, but for the most part, she knew Marcus needed to hear firsthand the way they were now having to live because of something he'd done. He'd left them to fend for themselves, and they'd become the girls he claimed to despise.

"What about you, Casci?" Coffee asked.

"I'm good. I should have something coming through in a day or so." Casci waved her off.

"I got Casci and Chris. Y'all just do what y'all supposed to do." Marcus looked from Reniya to Coffee and said, "And don't go spending-crazy."

"Can I buy me a car, at least?"

"Not right now, Coffee. Let me see where everything is, and I'll take you to cop something myself." Marcus began separating the money. "And I'm going to put Ariel's cut up until this shit dies down," he continued.

"Yeah, make it look as if you're just trying to make the shit right with her," Coffee surmised.

"Well, at least we didn't kill his ass for the money." Reniya stuffed her cut into her handbag.

"Not yet, anyway," Chris told them, while giving Marcus a mean stare.

Reniya picked up on the statement and told him, "Nigga, stop tripping. You know we're going to make sure you alright. All you got to do is sit back and ride. You got some bad bitches in you corner now."

"Ain't that truth," Coffee added.

"Don't let this shit come between us, nigga," Reniya told him, before looking over at Marcus.

Casci's thoughts went to the deal she and Detrick had going. Whether or not he'd fucked her over was the question she continually asked herself. She really didn't know Detrick. But if Marcus was fucking with him, there was a good chance he was a standup guy, and she was going to give him the benefit of doubt.

"This is just beginning, y'all." Reniya high-fived Coffee and pulled one of the cornrows on Casci's head.

"Beat a bitch's ass, suck a little dick, make a lot of money, we lit," Coffee began the chant. She looked toward Chris and Marcus. "Repeat after me, bitches."

"Don't start that shit, Coffee." Marcus pointed at her.

"That's why your black ass got AIDS now. You fucked that sick ass nigga, Doom." Chris's statement halted her chant and made Casci laugh.

"AIDS?" Coffee's mouth fell open.

"That's why he paid you all that money. Bitches ain't giving that nigga no pussy," Chris added.

"Girl, that nigga fucking with you." Reniya hoped.

"Nasty ass, fucking all these niggas without rubbers. Her ass going to end up with something," Marcus told her.

"Nigga!" Coffee threw a stack of bills at Chris. "Don't be fucking with me like that," she admonished him.

"Stop fucking all these strange ass niggas, then."

"Y'all hitting them like this, I'm the one ain't going to get no dick," she told him, before reaching for the stack of money.

"Nah, keep selling the pussy. Niggas see you riding in something nice, all they can say is that they contributed to it," Reniya encouraged her.

"Just wrap it up, bitch. Make 'em wrap that motherfucker up," Casci agreed. Now that they were game players, they had to play harder.

"Let's hit Jingles' perverted ass next. We know he sitting on just as much," Reniya suggested.

"Jingles?" Marcus looked over at Casci.

Coffee walked past him, her knee brushing his. "You scared?"

"Jingles? Motherfucker, we're going to kill that nigga and the big ass niggas he got on payroll."

Marcus shook his head. "Nah, not him."

"Then we do the shit without you," Reniya told him.

"Yeah, nigga. We got Chris." Coffee beamed. She winked at him.

Marcus lowered his head and sighed. He already knew what it was. There was no turning back. If Casci wanted to go to the end of the earth for her girls, he'd be right there with her.

Casci smiled and shrugged. She told him, "It'll be like taking candy from a baby."

***

From the moment Stacy and Doom climbed into the car, the conversation had been about the girls. Each of them had finally gotten what they wanted, and the excitement was heavy in the air.

"I told you, nigga. I told you I was going to fuck that bitch." Doom beamed. He fired up the Kush-filled blunt and took a long, hard pull from the herb.

"Nigga, you ain't do nothing to that girl." Stacy smiled.

He was happy for his friend. Coffee was not only older than Doom, but had more popularity *and* was the prettiest girl he'd ever sexed. She was one of the ones he'd been trying to fuck for the longest.

"Bullshit. I had that hoe bent up. She kept running from the dick, and I put that pound game on her." Doom closed his eyes at the memory. "I'm telling you, nigga, that hoe can't take no dick. I even fucked her in that fat ass of hers."

Stacy pursed his lips. There was no way he was going to believe Coffee gave that ass, too. "You had me believing that bullshit for a minute, nigga, but you went too far talking about you fucked her in the ass."

Stacy exited the freeway and drove down the service road. They'd already stopped to get something to eat, and now they were headed back to the Southern Motel.

"I should've recorded that shit, man. Niggas ain't going to believe this shit." Doom smiled. "It cost me twenty-five hundred, but I fucked the shit out that bitch."

"Yeah, well, I finally got to fuck Reniya, so I'm good, too."

"Yeah right. You can tell someone else that shit because I know for a fact you would've recorded that shit."

"I didn't have time to set up my phone. We all got to the room at the same time, remember?"

Doom shook his head. "That ain't going to stop you. And you know them hoes wasn't falling for that watered down ass shit you was trying to pull. You see they declined them drinks you tried to give 'em."

"Nigga, you don't know. You was in the other room. I fucked that bitch. I…" Stacy fell silent after turning into the lot of the motel. The first thing he noticed were the two dark-colored trucks parked at the far end of the parking lot. They were parked side by side.

"I'll bet you that hoe pussy ain't better than Coffee's," Doom wagered, not picking up on his friend's silence.

"Look." Stacy pointed. He brought the Mustang to a full stop. He hit the bright lights in his attempt to better see the trucks.

"Who is that?" Doom asked. He looked toward their room door and pointed. "The window."

"This shit ain't looking right, bro." Stacy checked his rearview mirror. "Shit!"

Doom quickly reached in the back seat for the assault rifle they had laying under a huge towel.

A series of shots rang out from where the trucks were parked. Stacy ducked, seeing the fire blast from several guns.

"Go, nigga, go," Doom yelled, before holding the FN out of the window and returning fire.

Bullets could be heard slamming and piercing the exterior of the car. The continual thump of lead against fiberglass had both of them ducking for cover, not being able to see behind or in front of them. Stacy threw the sports car in gear and floored it. The car jerked backward, wildly— its twenty-two inch Yokohama fires hitting the pavement.

Stacy could only guess where they were in reference to the entrance of the motel and the service road they'd turned off of. But once he was sure they'd backed back far enough, he swung the car in the other direction. It wasn't until the car jerked from hitting the curb that he looked up, straightened himself, and geared the car into first. He caught a glimpse of the lights pointed at them as he maneuvered the car past another and up the ramp leading to the freeway.

"Where they at, nigga?" Doom tried to peek out the rear windshield until it shattered.

"They on our ass, nigga! Shoot that motherfucker, man!" Stacy weaved in and out of cars and trucks—the Mustang easily surpassing the traffic and going as fast as 100 miles per hour.

Once the sounds of the rapid gunfire faded, Doom raised up. He reached under his seat and grabbed the Mack-11 from there. "I think I hit one of them niggas, Stacy."

"And how in the hell would you know that?" Stacy checked his rearview mirror for the umpteenth time and began to slow down, seeing they'd passed most of the cars on the freeway and had a huge gap between them and the rest of the drivers.

"You see them hoes ain't still chasing us."

Stacy slammed his hands on the steering wheel. He closed his eyes and cursed. "Fuck!"

"What's up, bro?"

"Them hoes most likely hit up the spot," he told Doom.

"Bitch! I did notice that the window was knocked out," Doom confirmed.

"Them niggas probably just walked up and opened fire into the motherfucker." Stacy's mind was racing.

"Naw, they ain't going to sit in the parking lot after doing some shit like that. Them niggas was waiting for us."

Stacy slowly nodded. "They must've not known what we were in. That's the reason they waited before gunning us."

"You think that was Peanut and them?" Doom looked over at his boy.

"I know for a fact it was that nigga. Either him or them damn Mexican motherfuckers."

Doom looked behind them, both the Mack-11 and the FN at the ready. "What we going to do now?"

"We got to get us some bread, homie. We get at this Peanut nigga and head for Atlanta. That's what we do now," he told him.

Stacy cursed himself for leaving so much in the motel room. There was part of him telling him that everything was gone, then there was part of him saying that there was a possibility that they didn't even go into the room. The latter voice convinced him that the sooner they could get back and see for themselves, the better the chances the money and dope was still there.

"I knew I should've gotten at that nigga when he was sitting in that driveway." Doom checked the clips on both the guns and set the Mac-11 in his lap. "Let's go find that nigga, Stacy."

"Yeah, but first let's circle back and see if we can check the room. They might not even have went in that motherfucker, and you already know that crackhead motherfuckers gonna be trying to take all kinds of shit out of that room. I left my jewelry and everything in that bitch."

Stacy exited, seeing the Illinois exit coming up. They'd circle back around, see if there was anything left of their amassed fortune, and go from there.

"Some pussy saved a nigga's life, bro. If we wouldn't have been fucking with them hoes, whoever that was waiting on us would've caught us up in that motel room," Doom told him.

"Ain't that some shit?"

Stacy thought about just that. He was glad and thankful at the same time. They owed Reniya and Coffee their lives. The money they'd given them was the best money they'd ever spent.

Chapter Twenty-Three

Two days had passed since the lick on Stacy and Doom, and Chris was still feeling a type of way when it came to how Marcus was handling things. Not only that, but he was ordered to return to work at the Sonic eatery, after walking out just weeks ago. Luckily, his supervisor still hadn't filled his spot and was in need of an experienced worker.

Chris had stopped by early this morning to see if he could talk Casci into doing something different, when it came to allowing Marcus to play the leading role.

Coffee and Reniya were sitting at the dining room table, eating breakfast, and Casci was still under the huge comforter on the couch, when he stopped by with his Sonic uniform on. They'd already made plans for the day and couldn't wait to hit the Galleria and the surrounding boutiques. Ariel had already left early for work, and the conversation they were now having could be conducted without filter.

"I'm serious, Casci. That nigga gonna do the same shit he did way back when." Chris was standing next to the arm of the couch she was sleeping on, constantly pulling at the comforter.

"Can we talk about this shit later, Chris? A bitch still trying to get some sleep." Casci peeked at him from under the comforter's edge.

"I don't like this shit. Y'all got this nigga thinking he running the show and shit." Chris spun to face Coffee and Reniya and said, "I'm the one who thought about hitting them niggas."

Coffee and Reniya looked at each other before saying in unison, "Motherfucker, *we* thought of that shit."

"Y'all know what I'm talking about. It was *me* who was going to do the shit before he was even thought about," Chris explained.

"Chris, please take your ass to work. We'll fuck with that shit later, man." Casci sighed, threw the comforter back over her head, and turned toward the couch's backrest.

"And how long am I supposed to wait on this nigga before I can make my money? For all we know, that nigga selling our shit so he can pay them damn Mexicans without using his own money."

Casci ignored him.

"Just last week, y'all wanted to kill the nigga. Now y'all acting like the shit is all good. Fuck that!"

Casci snatched the covers from her head and faced him. "Look, nigga. If Marcus has a better play than the ones we coming up with, then

177

that's what we're going to run. I'm not worried about that nigga fucking over us right now."

"Why? Why is he making plans for us in the first place? Y'all told me it was all about us."

"And it is, Chris. That's what you need to understand. We're going to be alright. You just sit back and ride."

"Fuck riding and being that nigga's bitch. Y'all just give me my shit and let me do my thing."

Reniya snapped her fingers from where she sat. "Hey, hey, hey! Check that shit, nigga. If that nigga wants to safe house that shit, then let him. That's just one more thing you don't have to worry about. And if the nigga do sell the shit, that's a plus for you. All we're saying is that you don't need to be under nobody's scope right now, when it comes to that dope."

"But I didn't get shit. No money or no dope. I was just as much a part of that lick as anybody else," Chris told them.

Coffee forked some eggs into her mouth. She told him, "Hell, you ain't going to do nothing but let them niggas jack you for the shit anyway."

Reniya fired up what was left of the blunt they'd been smoking before breakfast and held it out for him. "Here, nigga. Hit this and calm your ass down. You in here tripping on nothing."

"I don't need that nigga babysitting me. I'm a grown ass man." Chris took what was left of the blunt and shook his head.

Coffee waved her fork at him and said, "I'll let you hold a couple dollars until you get on your feet, my nigga."

"See, y'all sitting on money. The only motherfuckers who didn't get paid was me and Casci," Chris told her. "That's fucked up."

***

For the past couple of days, Stacy and Doom had been staying in separate rooms at the Ranch Motel, which was located across town from the Southern. By the time they made it back to the Southern Motel, the cops were everywhere. It wasn't until the next day that they actually got a chance to go check the room.

As figured, the money and drugs were gone, his jewelry was missing, and most of the clothes they kept there were scattered throughout the parking lot. Doom found a pair of his denim jeans, and Stacy found one of the Jordan shoes he had there. All they had now was the cash they had in their pockets, and the clothes they had on their backs.

Stacy had called Ariel over earlier that morning, hoping he caught her before she left for work. He knew she had some money put up, and he was needing that right now. He also wanted some sex.

"So what are you going to do now?" Ariel asked, after hearing that they'd been hit for everything.

"Thinking about going to Atlanta still, but I need to get my pockets right first."

"I still have that money you gave me a while back. You can have that."

Stacy lowered his head. "I'm going to need more than that, babe. I might need you to hit up Casci and see if she and that nigga will give you a loan. I'm going to pay it back once I make a couple of moves."

"Oh, now you want me to ask the nigga for something? *After* you done jacked him for his money?" Ariel watched him, hoping he was able to make sense out of what he was asking her.

"They don't have to know it's for me." Stacy stood, walked over to the dresser, and put his back to it. He faced her.

"Nigga, they gonna know it ain't for me. How much it is that you need anyway?" Ariel opened her purse.

"At least twenty-five thousand."

Ariel looked at him with a perplexed expression.

"Either that, or tell 'em to front you a couple of them bricks Marcus gave her." Stacy's expression softened.

Ariel closed her bag and sighed. "I'll see what I can do, but they going to know it ain't for me, nigga."

"Just tell them you're going to pay it back." Stacy rubbed his stomach and headed for the bathroom. "Hold up right quick."

Once Stacy had disappeared into the bathroom, Ariel stood and walked over to the window. She still hadn't told her girls that there was talk about her and Stacy moving to Atlanta. It was a topic that came up every so often, but she never really put too much thought into it. Now that her man was having to make a desperate move, it was something she really had to think about. Just as she was about to pull the curtain back, Stacy's phone began vibrating. She looked from the partially lit phone to the partially opened bathroom door. It vibrated a second time.

"I might not be able to get a couple bricks from Casci, but..." she told him, in attempt to drown out the sounds of his iPhone.

She picked it up, saw that it was a text from some other woman, asking if he was still coming by. She hurried to scroll through his contacts and stopped when seeing Reniya's number as one of the most recent texts. Knowing the history they had, she read the most recent text between the both of them.

She frowned when seeing the one from just days ago. It was the same night he'd called her begging for some pussy. It was the same night the girls didn't come home until early the next morning. Ariel read where Reniya questioned about his whereabouts, and the one saying that she was at the hotel waiting. Ariel couldn't believe her eyes.

She pressed the button at the bottom of the phone when hearing the toilet flush and placed his phone face down where he'd left it. She walked back to the window.

"If nothing else, let's see if that nigga Marcus will let a nigga hold something," Stacy told her, re-entering the room.

Ariel was silent—her mind taking her from the motel where she was standing to the arguments and fights she had with both Reniya and Coffee in the past. Let them tell it, he was always the one pursuing them, but from what she'd just read, Reniya was the one waiting at some hotel room on him.

"You hear me, babe?"

Ariel was snatched from her thoughts when he wrapped his arms around her shoulders. He kissed her cheek.

"What—what were you saying?"

"I said this shit is all fucked up right now. Atlanta seems like the best option for me and Doom."

"You and Doom? I thought me and you were going to Atlanta?" Ariel turned to face him, as she folded her arms.

"Yeah, we are. But right now, me and Doom need to make a few moves. I'll come get you once we get things situated down there."

Ariel saw his lips moving, but her mind was elsewhere. She asked him, "So what happened the other night?"

"What night?"

"The night y'all got robbed, nigga. Where was y'all at while them niggas was hitting ya spot?"

Ariel watched him for any and every sign that he was lying, and she found them as soon as he opened his mouth.

"Aw, um. Me and that nigga, Doom, was in the streets. I think we were on the Northside or something. All I know is that I'm glad we wasn't in the room."

"The Northside?" she asked, trying to remember if there was a Deluxe Hotel in that area.

"Hell yeah." Stacy leaned down and began kissing her neck and lips.

Ariel pushed his face away. "Stop, nigga. You know I have somewhere to be."

"Babe, you tripping," he told her, immediately picking up on the shift in her mood, after hearing that she wasn't going to Atlanta right now. "Once me and Doom get things set up, I'm coming to get you."

"You told me—"

Stacy cut her off with a kiss. He asked her, "Are you going to give me some of this pussy, or am I going to have to take it?"

"Move, Stacy. I'm not playing with you."

Stacy straightened himself, saw that she was really in her feelings, and held her at arm's length. "You serious?"

"You got me fucked up, nigga. You call me over here talking about asking another motherfucker for some money and dope for you, and you got other plans. You out here fucking with those snake ass bitches and think I'm the bitch to call when you need something. Nigga—"

Stacy backed away from her. He was already dealing with too much. He told her, "I don't have time for this shit, Ariel. I really don't. Me and my nigga just lost everything, and you standing here, talking about me fucking with some bitch. Come on, babe."

By the time Ariel made it to her car, she was beyond pissed. Here she was being faithful to a nigga, who didn't know what the word meant, and loyal to a bitch, who would fuck any and everybody for money. Her first mind was to go home and chew Reniya up, but it would be like all the times before. She'd swear he was the one trying to get at her and that she was actually the one who didn't want shit to do with him. They always spoke down on Stacy when it came to their relationship, and now she knew why.

Reniya had been wanting him for herself. There was no other explanation for her texting him in the middle of the night if it wasn't so she could hook up with him. There was nothing her girl could say to justify what she'd just read in Stacy's phone. Then there was the fact that Reniya had damn near half a pound of the very Kush Stacy was known to have sold. It was all coming together now.

***

Casci was sitting on the couch, trying to get Chris to understand the moves they were about to make, and the need for him to chill out. She'd continually promised him that things would work out sooner than later, and that he'd be able to move without being moved on, but he wasn't trying to hear it.

"I don't know why you still explaining the shit to him, Casci. You see the nigga on some more shit right now," Reniya told her from where she and Coffee sat, smoking the Kush-filled blunt she'd just rolled.

"Dizzy ass bitch, what about me? I shouldn't have to borrow from nobody, and y'all know it."

Chris thought about the past week or so, when he and Casci were riding around, sitting in the parking lot of the Gardens, talking about the moves they were going to make. Now she was letting another nigga run the plays. Not only that, but they weren't even bending corners like they used to. Casci was now with Detrick more than with him, and now that Marcus was back in the picture, it was all about him.

"Chris, just trust me, nigga. I got you," Casci told him, before answering her phone. She looked from Chris to Reniya and Coffee, when hearing the familiar voice. "I'll be right down," she spoke into the phone, and ended the call.

"Who was that?" Coffee asked from the kitchen table.

"Detrick. He's downstairs." Casci pushed past Chris and made her way out the door. She'd been waiting on him for two days now.

"I know your pussy ain't that good, bitch," Coffee told her, before walking over to the window and looking down on scene below them.

Reniya walked over to join her. They watched Casci climb into Detrick's truck. "I don't know about that, sis. She ain't fucking like you be fucking, so her shit might be a little tighter than yours." Reniya laughed.

"Look." Coffee pointed. "She getting back out."

"He gave her a backpack." Reniya frowned. Every other time he came through, he gave her a shit load of bags.

"Maybe it's some work for Chris." Coffee looked back at him.

Chris walked over to where they stood and looked down himself. He thought of just that, but knew better. Marcus wasn't the type of nigga to switch the play, but then, too, he was the same nigga who fucked over Casci.

They watched Casci walk through the door with the backpack.

"What you get this time, bitch?" Coffee walked over and lifted the pack from her shoulder.

"Damn, bitch," Casci told the both of them. She walked back to the couch and flopped down. She already knew what was inside.

"Ain't shit in here but money," Reniya told her, while pulling out stack after stack of bills. "How much is this, Casci?"

Coffee pulled out several stacks also.

Casci pulled her legs under her. She told them, "That should be fifty thousand."

"Oh." Reniya placed the money on the table and went back to smoking the blunt she and Coffee had.

"Oh? Why ain't nobody bringing me no money like that?" Chris went off.

Coffee scoffed. "This is Ariel's cut, nigga. Damn, stop crying."

"Big booty ass girl, I'm not crying. I'm broke. There's a huge ass difference right there."

Instead of correcting Coffee, Casci let it go. She still hadn't told them she cashed in on the bounty and split it with Detrick. There was no way Chris would understand that.

"Y'all bitches fucking me, man. All you motherfuckers shoving ya dicks in my ass." Chris was serious.

"Take this dick, bitch," Coffee joked. She then walked over to him and began twerking her ass. She threw her ass on him until he stepped back. "Take this dick, nigga."

Reniya stood, took a stack of the bills, and began making it rain on Coffee. She yelled, "Beat a bitch's ass, suck a little dick, make a lot of money, we lit!"

She and Coffee danced and twerked under hundred-dollar bills.

"Beat a bitch's ass, suck a little dick, make a lot of money. We lit!" They sang in unison.

Casci sat back and smiled. Her girls having a good time made it all worthwhile. She picked up on Chris's sullen mood, despite the half-naked ass being thrown on him and the money in the air. Chris was in his feelings, and she knew it.

She watched him head for the door.

"Where you going, nigga?"

"Work. I can't sit up and shake my ass all morning. I work at Sonic, remember?" Chris walked out and closed the door behind him.

Reniya shook her head. "That weak ass nigga in his feelings, Casci."

"Fuck, Chris. We've been taking care of that nigga for the longest. If he's gonna trip on this small shit, he can take his ass on," Coffee told them, while picking up some of the bills.

Casci shrugged. There were things Chris wasn't trying to hear, but she knew the importance of patience. Him not having the drugs at the moment was for the best. She did understand his frustration, and at the same time, he had to understand that the moves she made were about her and her girls. And all he had to do was sit back and ride.

"All that nigga got to do is sit back and ride. You know how many niggas would love to be in his position?"

Reniya and Coffee laughed. They yelled, "Stacy!"

Chapter Twenty-Four
Two Weeks Later

Casci was sitting on the couch, talking with Reniya and Coffee, when Ariel walked into the room and headed for the kitchen. She'd been noticing Ariel's distance for the past couple weeks and wanted to know what was up with her.

"Hey, Ariel. Come here right quick." Casci patted the couch beside her.

Ariel sighed, looked upward, and went to sit beside her friend.

"What's up with you? Lately, you've been walking around here, looking like shit, and acting real funny toward a bitch."

Ariel folded her arms and scoffed. She looked over at Reniya, rolled her eyes, and said, "Some shit been on my mind, is all."

Coffee blew a thick stream of smoke in the air, and said, "The bitch probably pregnant."

"Pregnant? I thought you were taking your pills?" Casci regarded her with concern.

"That's fucked up," Reniya told them.

Ariel once again looked skyward, before rolling her eyes. "It ain't got shit to do with a bitch being pregnant. Thank you."

"Umph." Coffee handed Casci the blunt and crossed one leg over the other. "Well, spill it."

Ariel inhaled deeply, looked straight at Reniya, and asked the girls, "Did y'all know Reniya been fucking Stacy behind my back?" She then looked over at Casci, then Coffee.

Coffee stood and walked toward the back room. She said, "Here we go."

Reniya reached for the blunt Casci held out. She matched Ariel's stare, and asked, "You sure you ready to do this? You ready to defend that nigga, again?"

Ariel frowned. "What the fuck you mean?"

Casci placed her hand on Ariel's, seeing her about to stand. "Ariel."

"Oh, so everybody know but me, huh?" Ariel scoffed again. She couldn't believe what she was witnessing.

Reniya reached for her phone. She tsked, shook her head, and asked, "Is that what he told you?"

"Nah, bitch. I saw ya little text with my own eyes. And just so happen, it was the night y'all didn't come home until early in the motherfucking morning."

Reniya set her phone down on the table in front of them. She leaned back, crossed her arms, and looked off. There was nothing to talk about.

Before Ariel could question her actions, Stacy's voice spoke from the phone.

"I'll tell you what, Reniya. I'll pay you. I'll give you what you want. You know how bad I've been wanting to fuck with you?"

Ariel leaned forward, looking at Reniya's phone with a confused expression. She listened on.

"The only reason I started fucking with Ariel was because you wasn't trying to give a nigga the time of day."

Hearing that, Ariel closed her eyes and began shaking her head.

"Nigga, you tried to fuck me and Coffee. Remember that?" she heard Reniya ask in the audio.

"Okay, I was tripping back then. I just wanted a bad bitch on my team."

Ariel grabbed the phone and turned it on its face, ending the conversation they were all listening to.

"Oh, it's more on there," Reniya told her.

Ariel smiled, looked over at her friend, and bit her bottom lip. She turned to face Coffee, when she reentered the room and dropped a backpack onto her lap.

Coffee shrugged. "We all fucked that nigga, Ariel. You too."

Ariel looked down at the pack and frowned. She slowly opened it.

"Them niggas out here killing kids, Ariel. It's only a matter of time before someone get at they ass," Casci explained.

"So we jumped first," Reniya added.

"And that's your cut. We've been holding it for you." Coffee bent over and kissed Ariel on the forehead.

Ariel thumbed through the bills in silence. She looked toward Reniya and said, "I—"

"Buy a bitch a pair of shoes and a bag, and we cool," Reniya stated, cutting her off.

"You bitches can't be serious?"

"Fifty-thousand dollars serious," Coffee told her.

"And here I was debating whether or not to ask Marcus for a front for his punk ass." Ariel lost herself in thought. She then told them, "I'm going to cut—"

Casci handed her the blunt Reniya passed over and told her, "No. You're going to stay the hell away from his ass. Some of everybody trying to get at them niggas behind what they did to them kids. But fuck all that. You good now?"

Ariel inhaled and exhaled as deeply as she could. Her heart was broken, but she wasn't about to trip, not after what she'd just heard and seen. "Yeah, I'm good."

"Now let's go spend some of this money."

Coffee was the first to run to the shower because she'd been dying to spend a little change. Calls to Marcus were daily because of his promise to help her buy her first car, and she was going to hold him to it.

Reniya stood, walked over to her friend, and pulled her up from where she was sitting. She embraced her in a tight hug before kissing her cheek. "My loyalty is here, Ariel. Fuck everybody else. You hear me?"

Ariel nodded, lowered her head, and looked at the floor.

"Look at me." Reniya grabbed her chin and picked it up. She told her, "This is about us."

"I know, I know. A bitch just got slapped with the dick too many times, I guess." Ariel laughed.

Reniya held her at arm's length and told her, "I had to show that nigga my pussy that night. He didn't fuck, but I did let the nigga lick my shit a couple of times."

Ariel shrugged. "I ain't tripping. Fuck that nigga. He should've known not to fuck with my best friends anyway."

"Yeah, he should've," Casci agreed.

***

Chris was on his way to work when he noticed Marcus' 550 Benz enter the parking lot and head in his direction. He and Marcus hadn't spoken since the night of the lick, and he was sure Marcus was coming through to see Casci and the girls.

The beef between them was obvious, and as long as Casci allowed Marcus to call and run the plays, he was going to do his own thing. He was still sitting on some work from the time Casci gave him the four kilos, and was looking forward to a couple of sales later that same day.

He kept his head low, while crossing the parking lot. He refused to be the first to acknowledge him.

"Look out, Chris."

Chris' heart began beating faster. He was slipping, and the memory of what could've happened the last time came to mind. He'd heard about the way Marcus used to be, and getting blasted was something he knew could very well be about to happen. He slowly turned to face him.

"Hey, you got a minute?"

Chris heard the passenger's door unlock.

"Jump in for a minute," Marcus told him.

Chris swallowed, reached for the handle, and climbed in. He immediately noticed the Ruger sitting on Marcus' lap.

Marcus pulled up a ways and backed into a vacant parking space. He threw the car in park.

"Look, Chris. I'm not here to fight you, homie." Marcus pointed toward the ashtray where two blunts sat.

"Naw, I'm good."

"If I could take it all back, I would, Chris. I'm talking about this lifestyle." Marcus reached for the blunt and fired it up himself. He told him, "I used to want this shit more than anything, but that was before I knew what it meant. I fucked up, homie. I was standing right where you standing right now."

Chris looked over at him. He could hear the sincerity in his voice.

"This shit ain't what you think it is, Chris. Casci probably painted you some embellished picture of the game, and the outcome of it, but that's bullshit. I did the same with her, and it turned out the complete opposite, man. This shit ends one of two ways. A nigga get killed or a nigga end up in prison with linemen numbers."

Chris adjusted himself in the butter-soft leathers of the Benz. He asked, "And yet, you're still fucking around out here. Why's that?"

"Because I fucked up. I did what you think you're wanting to do right now. All that's left for me is to ride this shit out and see where it goes. I pray I end up in prison instead of getting slumped in one of my cars or caught slipping coming out of my home. Once you jump in this lane, ain't no crossing back over, nigga. You ready for that? You really think you ready for this shit?"

Chris remained silent.

"I know that's your girl, but you really think Casci got your back? You don't think she'll cash your ass in for herself or one of them girls?

Well, guess again, nigga. If push comes to shove, she'd be the one to slide a blade across your throat or put a bullet in your chest. Don't let that pretty girl shit fool you, Chris. Casci's thought long and hard about this shit."

Marcus paused, before continuing. "The more you think about it, the darker your thoughts have to get, and to actually act on the shit, ya heart got to be black as hell, homie." Marcus patted his chest. "I taught her that, and I hate it. The ones you least expect be the ones to dig your grave."

Marcus held out the blunt until Chris grabbed it. He continued, "I'm not telling you this because I want you to stop fucking with her. I'm telling you this so you'll be careful. As soon as you start slipping, she's going to throw you to the wolves. It's called self-preservation."

Marcus reached behind the passenger's seat and pulled out a small duffle. He handed it to Chris. "That's five kilos." He then handed Chris a phone. "When it ring, you answer. Get at me when you finish with these, bro."

Chris climbed out of the car and stood there. He watched as Marcus' sedan turned and disappeared from sight. His thoughts were on Casci. Marcus' words made him think about something Casci said not too long ago.

"Gotta play this shit nigga."

He then thought about the day he and Ariel had words, and how Casci only looked on when Reniya and Coffee threatened him. If it was one thing he did know, it was that Casci would do anything for her girls.

Chris sighed deeply, looked down at the duffle he was holding, and made his way to his car. There was no turning back now. At least that was what Casci had told him.

***

Doom and Stacy's patience had finally paid off. They were down to their last $10,000 and were desperate. Ariel still hadn't come through, and there was no one else he could trust when it came to his whereabouts or his money.

He and Doom were making rounds on the north side, following a tip they'd gotten, when they saw Peanut walk into the Benny's Eatery. A few seconds later, another familiar face appeared.

Doom pointed. "Ain't that the bitch who shot J-Rod?"

"Damn sure is. What the fuck she doing here?" Stacy asked himself. "You think—"

Those words were answered the minute they saw her walk up to Peanut, and greet him with a hug. They sat by the window, facing the lot, and Stacy and Doom could literally see what was ordered.

"I knew that bitch was playing us, homie. I told you we should've smoked that bitch," Doom went off.

Stacy looked around the area at all the passersby. He even noticed a patrol car at the other end of the area. His first thoughts were to run up on Peanut the minute he walked out of the Restaurant, but there were just too many people around. Then, there was the fact that he and Doom were now broke, and Peanut had to have been sitting on some of their money and drugs. Either way, it was in their best interest to follow and see where he led them.

"Let's hit this nigga and be done with it, Stacy." Doom checked the lever on his gun and set it in his lap.

"Nah, we got to get some of our shit back, bro." Stacy sat back in the driver's seat of the SUV they'd rented and kept his eyes on Peanut and the girl.

"So what happened with that issue Ariel was supposed to handle?" Doom asked, before also making himself comfortable.

"Man, fuck Ariel. She ain't trying to do nothing for a nigga but run hoes off. I'm tired of her shit anyway."

Doom had heard the same line many times before, especially when it was something Stacy wanted her to do and she didn't. He only looked in the opposite direction.

"I need a bitch that's gon' get out there and get it, when I can't," Stacy told him. His thoughts went to Reniya. He could definitely use a bitch like her on his team.

"Yo, Stacy. Look." Doom pointed.

Stacy sat upright, lowered the cap he was wearing over his eyes, and put the SUV in gear.

"I know that nigga ain't leaving already, is he?" Doom asked.

They watched him climb into the Ford F-150 that pulled into J-Rod's driveway.

"As soon as we bleed this nigga, we getting out of here, homie," Stacy told him.

Chapter Twenty-Five

While Reniya, Coffee, and Ariel talked about the boutiques, other high end stores, and fashion, Casci thought about all it would take to get one up and running. Where many of the boutiques she liked sold over-priced merchandise, she was wanting to make things reasonably affordable. And where many of the stores employed sale reps and the likes, she was wanting it to be a place for her and the girls.

Casci stopped at the entrance of the high fashion boutique, envisioning the grand opening of her own. "Casci's Garden," she whispered it to herself and smiled. It seemed like a life time ago that she dreamed of having a place she could call her own. It was that long ago a dream so small was snatched away from her, and it was in that time that she vowed to take it back. Only this time, nothing would keep her from it.

"Casci! Come on. Reniya in her tripping," Coffee told her from the boutique's entrance.

Casci's first thoughts were that Reniya had gotten jammed up by the security, but remembered that each had over $10,000 to spend. It was the amount Marcus approved for them. She rushed to where Reniya and two of the saleswomen stood. She looked from one to the next, before her eyes landed on Reniya. "What's up, Ren?"

"These hoes standing over a bitch, like I'm going to steal they shit or something. Don't nobody want to steal nothing from this weak ass store," Reniya went off.

"Steal?" Casci frowned. She started to turn around and see where Coffee and Ariel were. But they'd used this very ploy before, and she didn't want to mess the play up, if they were running it. There was a time when she was the one causing the disturbance in the stores and Reniya and Coffee wee stuffing their shopping bags and purses with all kinds of things.

One of the saleswomen stepped forward. "My apologies, but lately we've had some major losses, and now we're having to police the store and its patrons a bit more. And when customers request so many items, we have to take precautions," she explained.

Casci then noticed the six boxes of shoes on the floor and the ottoman. There were Gucci boots, Louis Vuitton heels, several designer tennis shoes, and even a handbag that she knew Reniya didn't own.

"And these bitches acting like they don't have my size, so they don't have to bring out more shit." Reniya added.

Casci smiled, she understood both sides of the argument. For the very first time, them having the money to cover an expense wasn't an issue. The wigs, the oversize shades, and the outfits, they weren't just disguises used to stake out new stores, or discarded when trying to evade arrest. For the first time in forever, Casci didn't have to worry about coming up with the money needed to post a bond, to help Ariel buy supplies for work after she'd given her money to her boyfriend, or even rent, and it felt damn good.

With the show of a little money, Reniya walked out of the high fashion boutiques with two bags filled with shoes, boots, and heels. It wasn't until they were entering a second store that Casci questioned her about the Prada handbag hanging from her shoulder, and the gold and silver bangle bracelets on her wrist.

"Bitch, I know you didn't walk out of that store with that bag and the bracelets. Not after all of that?" Casci looked over at a smiling Ariel.

Reniya smirked and said, "You know them hoes can't fuck with me, Casci." She then opened the Prada handbag and pulled out two pair of signature channel shades and a rose gold watch. "You gotta play this shit, sis. And I play to win."

***

Later that same night, when all the girls were there, Casci stood nervously at the window overlooking the parking lot. She'd texted Chris twice already and was really wanting him to be there when she made her announcement. He was now a part of their team, and she wanted him to know as much.

"You waiting on somebody?" Reniya asked, walking over to where Casci stood. It was evident that Casci's mind was elsewhere.

"Yeah, I was waiting for Chris to get here, but—"

"That nigga had some runs to make when he got off work. I forgot to tell you," Reniya told her.

After they were all standing and sitting around the small living room, Coffee asked the crew, "When are we going to Houston?"

"Yeah, let's go break some of the baller niggas," Ariel suggested.

Casci stood, walked in front of the huge flat screen they had, and nodded. That was in order.

"Me and Reniya still got that nigga hook up that pulled up on us after the club that night,"

Ariel handed Reniya the blunt and reached for her phone.

Reniya stood, walked to where Casci stood, and frowned. She handed her the blunt. "What's on your mind, Casci? You over here all quiet and shit."

Casci turned towards them and half smiled. "I got something to tell y'all."

"Bitch, I know you ain't pregnant." Coffee walked over and raised the front of Casci's shirt.

"No, I'm not pregnant. That's some shit you bitches need to worry about." Casci sighed, looked from Coffee to Ariel, and said, "I'm moving out."

"You're what?" Reniya took a step back and looked her over with raised brows.

To Be Continued...
Pretty Girls Do Nasty Things 2
Coming Soon

Lock Down Publications and Ca$h Presents assisted publishing packages.

BASIC PACKAGE $499
Editing
Cover Design
Formatting

UPGRADED PACKAGE $800
Typing
Editing
Cover Design
Formatting

ADVANCE PACKAGE $1,200
Typing
Editing
Cover Design
Formatting
Copyright registration
Proofreading
Upload book to Amazon

LDP SUPREME PACKAGE $1,500
Typing
Editing
Cover Design
Formatting
Copyright registration
Proofreading
Set up Amazon account
Upload book to Amazon
Advertise on LDP Amazon and Facebook page

***Other services available upon request. Additional charges may apply
Lock Down Publications
P.O. Box 944
Stockbridge, GA 30281-9998
Phone # 470 303-9761

Submission Guideline

Submit the first three chapters of your completed manuscript to ldpsubmissions@gmail.com, subject line: Your book's title. The manuscript must be in a .doc file and sent as an attachment. Document should be in Times New Roman, double spaced and in size 12 font. Also, provide your synopsis and full contact information. If sending multiple submissions, they must each be in a separate email.

Have a story but no way to send it electronically? You can still submit to LDP/Ca$h Presents. Send in the first three chapters, written or typed, of your completed manuscript to:

LDP: Submissions Dept
Po Box 944
Stockbridge, Ga 30281

DO NOT send original manuscript. Must be a duplicate.

Provide your synopsis and a cover letter containing your full contact information.

Thanks for considering LDP and Ca$h Presents.

<u>NEW RELEASES</u>

FOR THE LOVE OF BLOOD by JAMEL MITCHELL
CONCRETE KILLA 3 by KINGPEN
RAN OFF ON DA PLUG by PAPER BOI RARI
THE BRICK MAN 4 by KING RIO
HOOD CONSIGLIERE by KEESE
PRETTY GIRLS DO NASTY THINGS by NICOLE GOOSBY

PAID IN BLOOD III

CARTEL KILLAZ IV

DOPE GODS III

Hood Rich

SINS OF A HUSTLA II

ASAD

RICH $AVAGE II

By Martell Troublesome Bolden

YAYO V

Bred In The Game 2

S. Allen

CREAM III

THE STREETS WILL TALK II

By Yolanda Moore

SON OF A DOPE FIEND III

HEAVEN GOT A GHETTO II

By Renta

LOYALTY AIN'T PROMISED III

By Keith Williams

I'M NOTHING WITHOUT HIS LOVE II

SINS OF A THUG II

TO THE THUG I LOVED BEFORE II

IN A HUSTLER I TRUST II

By Monet Dragun

QUIET MONEY IV

EXTENDED CLIP III

THUG LIFE IV

By **Trai'Quan**

THE STREETS MADE ME IV

By **Larry D. Wright**

IF YOU CROSS ME ONCE II

By **Anthony Fields**

THE STREETS WILL NEVER CLOSE IV

By K'ajji

HARD AND RUTHLESS III

KILLA KOUNTY III

By Khufu

MONEY GAME III

By Smoove Dolla

JACK BOYS VS DOPE BOYS II

A GANGSTA'S QUR'AN V

COKE GIRLZ II

By Romell Tukes

MURDA WAS THE CASE II

Elijah R. Freeman

THE STREETS NEVER LET GO II

By Robert Baptiste

AN UNFORESEEN LOVE III

By **Meesha**

KING OF THE TRENCHES III

by **GHOST & TRANAY ADAMS**

MONEY MAFIA II

LOYAL TO THE SOIL III

By **Jibril Williams**

QUEEN OF THE ZOO II

By **Black Migo**

VICIOUS LOYALTY III

By Kingpen

A GANGSTA'S PAIN III

By J-Blunt

CONFESSIONS OF A JACKBOY III

By Nicholas Lock

GRIMEY WAYS II

By Ray Vinci

KING KILLA II

By Vincent "Vitto" Holloway

BETRAYAL OF A THUG II

By Fre$h

THE MURDER QUEENS II

By Michael Gallon

THE BIRTH OF A GANGSTER II

By Delmont Player

TREAL LOVE II

By Le'Monica Jackson

FOR THE LOVE OF BLOOD II

By Jamel Mitchell

RAN OFF ON DA PLUG II

By Paper Boi Rari

HOOD CONSIGLIERE II

By Keese

PRETTY GIRLS DO NASTY THINGS II

By Nicole Goosby

Available Now

RESTRAINING ORDER **I & II**

By **CA$H & Coffee**

LOVE KNOWS NO BOUNDARIES **I II & III**

By **Coffee**

RAISED AS A GOON I, II, III & IV

BRED BY THE SLUMS I, II, III

BLAST FOR ME I & II

ROTTEN TO THE CORE I II III

Pretty Girls Do Nasty Things

A BRONX TALE I, II, III

DUFFLE BAG CARTEL I II III IV V VI

HEARTLESS GOON I II III IV V

A SAVAGE DOPEBOY I II

DRUG LORDS I II III

CUTTHROAT MAFIA I II

KING OF THE TRENCHES

By **Ghost**

LAY IT DOWN **I & II**

LAST OF A DYING BREED I II

BLOOD STAINS OF A SHOTTA I & II III

By **Jamaica**

LOYAL TO THE GAME I II III

LIFE OF SIN I, II III

By **TJ & Jelissa**

BLOODY COMMAS I & II

SKI MASK CARTEL I II & III

KING OF NEW YORK I II,III IV V

RISE TO POWER I II III

COKE KINGS I II III IV V

BORN HEARTLESS I II III IV

KING OF THE TRAP I II

By **T.J. Edwards**

IF LOVING HIM IS WRONG…I & II

LOVE ME EVEN WHEN IT HURTS I II III

By **Jelissa**

WHEN THE STREETS CLAP BACK I & II III

THE HEART OF A SAVAGE I II III

MONEY MAFIA

LOYAL TO THE SOIL I II

By **Jibril Williams**

A DISTINGUISHED THUG STOLE MY HEART I II & III

LOVE SHOULDN'T HURT I II III IV

RENEGADE BOYS I II III IV

PAID IN KARMA I II III

SAVAGE STORMS I II III

AN UNFORESEEN LOVE I II

By **Meesha**

A GANGSTER'S CODE I &, II III

A GANGSTER'S SYN I II III

THE SAVAGE LIFE I II III

CHAINED TO THE STREETS I II III

BLOOD ON THE MONEY I II III

A GANGSTA'S PAIN I II

By J-Blunt

PUSH IT TO THE LIMIT

By **Bre' Hayes**

BLOOD OF A BOSS **I, II, III, IV, V**

SHADOWS OF THE GAME

TRAP BASTARD

By **Askari**

THE STREETS BLEED MURDER **I, II & III**

THE HEART OF A GANGSTA I II& III

By **Jerry Jackson**

CUM FOR ME I II III IV V VI VII VIII

An **LDP Erotica Collaboration**

BRIDE OF A HUSTLA **I II & II**

THE FETTI GIRLS **I, II& III**

CORRUPTED BY A GANGSTA I, II III, IV

BLINDED BY HIS LOVE

THE PRICE YOU PAY FOR LOVE I, II ,III

DOPE GIRL MAGIC I II III

By **Destiny Skai**

WHEN A GOOD GIRL GOES BAD

By **Adrienne**

THE COST OF LOYALTY I II III

By Kweli

A GANGSTER'S REVENGE **I II III & IV**

THE BOSS MAN'S DAUGHTERS I II III IV V

A SAVAGE LOVE **I & II**

BAE BELONGS TO ME I II

A HUSTLER'S DECEIT I, II, III

WHAT BAD BITCHES DO I, II, III

SOUL OF A MONSTER I II III

KILL ZONE

A DOPE BOY'S QUEEN I II III

By **Aryanna**

A KINGPIN'S AMBITON

A KINGPIN'S AMBITION **II**

I MURDER FOR THE DOUGH

By **Ambitious**

TRUE SAVAGE I II III IV V VI VII

DOPE BOY MAGIC I, II, III

MIDNIGHT CARTEL I II III

CITY OF KINGZ I II

NIGHTMARE ON SILENT AVE

THE PLUG OF LIL MEXICO II

By **Chris Green**

A DOPEBOY'S PRAYER

By **Eddie "Wolf" Lee**

THE KING CARTEL **I, II & III**

By **Frank Gresham**

THESE NIGGAS AIN'T LOYAL **I, II & III**

By **Nikki Tee**

GANGSTA SHYT **I II &III**

By **CATO**

THE ULTIMATE BETRAYAL

By **Phoenix**

BOSS'N UP **I , II & III**

By **Royal Nicole**

I LOVE YOU TO DEATH

By **Destiny J**

I RIDE FOR MY HITTA

I STILL RIDE FOR MY HITTA

By **Misty Holt**

LOVE & CHASIN' PAPER

By **Qay Crockett**

TO DIE IN VAIN

SINS OF A HUSTLA

By **ASAD**

BROOKLYN HUSTLAZ

By **Boogsy Morina**

BROOKLYN ON LOCK I & II

By **Sonovia**

GANGSTA CITY

By **Teddy Duke**

A DRUG KING AND HIS DIAMOND I & II III

A DOPEMAN'S RICHES

HER MAN, MINE'S TOO I, II

CASH MONEY HO'S

THE WIFEY I USED TO BE I II

PRETTY GIRLS DO NASTY THINGS

By Nicole Goosby

TRAPHOUSE KING **I II & III**

KINGPIN KILLAZ I II III

STREET KINGS I II

PAID IN BLOOD **I II**

CARTEL KILLAZ I II III

DOPE GODS I II

By **Hood Rich**

LIPSTICK KILLAH **I, II, III**

CRIME OF PASSION I II & III

FRIEND OR FOE I II III

By **Mimi**

STEADY MOBBN' **I, II, III**

THE STREETS STAINED MY SOUL I II III

By **Marcellus Allen**

WHO SHOT YA **I, II, III**

SON OF A DOPE FIEND I II

HEAVEN GOT A GHETTO

Renta

GORILLAZ IN THE BAY **I II III IV**

TEARS OF A GANGSTA I II

3X KRAZY I II

STRAIGHT BEAST MODE

DE'KARI

TRIGGADALE I II III

MURDAROBER WAS THE CASE

Elijah R. Freeman

GOD BLESS THE TRAPPERS I, II, III

THESE SCANDALOUS STREETS I, II, III

FEAR MY GANGSTA I, II, III IV, V

THESE STREETS DON'T LOVE NOBODY I, II

BURY ME A G I, II, III, IV, V

A GANGSTA'S EMPIRE I, II, III, IV

THE DOPEMAN'S BODYGAURD I II

THE REALEST KILLAZ I II III

THE LAST OF THE OGS I II III

Tranay Adams

Nicole Goosby

THE STREETS ARE CALLING
Duquie Wilson
MARRIED TO A BOSS I II III
By Destiny Skai & Chris Green
KINGZ OF THE GAME I II III IV V VI
Playa Ray
SLAUGHTER GANG I II III
RUTHLESS HEART I II III
By Willie Slaughter
FUK SHYT
By Blakk Diamond
DON'T F#CK WITH MY HEART I II
By Linnea
ADDICTED TO THE DRAMA I II III
IN THE ARM OF HIS BOSS II
By Jamila
YAYO I II III IV
A SHOOTER'S AMBITION I II
BRED IN THE GAME
By S. Allen
TRAP GOD I II III
RICH $AVAGE
MONEY IN THE GRAVE I II III
By Martell Troublesome Bolden
FOREVER GANGSTA
GLOCKS ON SATIN SHEETS I II
By Adrian Dulan
TOE TAGZ I II III IV
LEVELS TO THIS SHYT I II
By Ah'Million
KINGPIN DREAMS I II III
RAN OFF ON DA PLUG

By Paper Boi Rari
CONFESSIONS OF A GANGSTA I II III IV
CONFESSIONS OF A JACKBOY I II
By Nicholas Lock
I'M NOTHING WITHOUT HIS LOVE
SINS OF A THUG
TO THE THUG I LOVED BEFORE
A GANGSTA SAVED XMAS
IN A HUSTLER I TRUST
By Monet Dragun
CAUGHT UP IN THE LIFE I II III
THE STREETS NEVER LET GO
By Robert Baptiste
NEW TO THE GAME I II III
MONEY, MURDER & MEMORIES I II III
By **Malik D. Rice**
LIFE OF A SAVAGE I II III
A GANGSTA'S QUR'AN I II III IV
MURDA SEASON I II III
GANGLAND CARTEL I II III
CHI'RAQ GANGSTAS I II III
KILLERS ON ELM STREET I II III
JACK BOYZ N DA BRONX I II III
A DOPEBOY'S DREAM I II III
JACK BOYS VS DOPE BOYS
COKE GIRLZ
By Romell Tukes
LOYALTY AIN'T PROMISED I II
By Keith Williams
QUIET MONEY I II III
THUG LIFE I II III
EXTENDED CLIP I II

By **Trai'Quan**
THE STREETS MADE ME I II III
By **Larry D. Wright**
THE ULTIMATE SACRIFICE I, II, III, IV, V, VI
KHADIFI
IF YOU CROSS ME ONCE
ANGEL I II
IN THE BLINK OF AN EYE
By **Anthony Fields**
THE LIFE OF A HOOD STAR
By **Ca$h & Rashia Wilson**
THE STREETS WILL NEVER CLOSE I II III
By **K'ajji**
CREAM I II
THE STREETS WILL TALK
By **Yolanda Moore**
NIGHTMARES OF A HUSTLA I II III
By **King Dream**
CONCRETE KILLA I II III
VICIOUS LOYALTY I II
By **Kingpen**
HARD AND RUTHLESS I II
MOB TOWN 251
THE BILLIONAIRE BENTLEYS I II III
By **Von Diesel**
GHOST MOB
Stilloan Robinson
MOB TIES I II III IV V VI
By **SayNoMore**
BODYMORE MURDERLAND I II III
THE BIRTH OF A GANGSTER
By **Delmont Player**

FOR THE LOVE OF A BOSS
By C. D. Blue
MOBBED UP I II III IV
THE BRICK MAN I II III IV
THE COCAINE PRINCESS I II III IV V
By King Rio
KILLA KOUNTY I II III
By Khufu
MONEY GAME I II
By Smoove Dolla
A GANGSTA'S KARMA I II
By FLAME
KING OF THE TRENCHES I II
by **GHOST & TRANAY ADAMS**
QUEEN OF THE ZOO
By **Black Migo**
GRIMEY WAYS
By Ray Vinci
XMAS WITH AN ATL SHOOTER
By Ca$h & Destiny Skai
KING KILLA
By Vincent "Vitto" Holloway
BETRAYAL OF A THUG
By Fre$h
THE MURDER QUEENS
By Michael Gallon
TREAL LOVE
By Le'Monica Jackson
FOR THE LOVE OF BLOOD
By Jamel Mitchell
HOOD CONSIGLIERE
By Keese

<u>BOOKS BY LDP'S CEO, CA$H</u>

TRUST IN NO MAN

TRUST IN NO MAN 2

TRUST IN NO MAN 3

BONDED BY BLOOD

SHORTY GOT A THUG

THUGS CRY

THUGS CRY 2

THUGS CRY 3

TRUST NO BITCH

TRUST NO BITCH 2

TRUST NO BITCH 3

TIL MY CASKET DROPS

RESTRAINING ORDER

RESTRAINING ORDER 2

IN LOVE WITH A CONVICT

LIFE OF A HOOD STAR

XMAS WITH AN ATL SHOOTER

Pretty Girls Do Nasty Things

CPSIA information can be obtained
at www.ICGtesting.com
Printed in the USA
LVHW042034220822
726558LV00007B/42

9 781958 111122